He Ain't Heavy

A story of addiction, resilience and unbreakable bonds.

Jodie Barnard

EAST ANGLIAN PUBLISHERS

Prologue

I pressed harder on the accelerator staring at the lines on the road stretching endlessly ahead of me like the problems I was trying to outrun.

The landscape was rushing past indistinct and meaningless. No matter how much my speed increased the feelings were still there, clinging to me like angry waves crashing in, overwhelming and powerful. The tension built with every mile, the adrenaline masking my anxiety but never erasing it.

I was trying to use the sound of the engine to drown out my inner turmoil..... the shouting, the bruises, the cloud of smoke constantly lingering in the air, the screaming, the laugh of the child that was never mine, the pinching, the smashing, shouting again, so much shouting! Years of memories repeatedly stabbing me in the stomach and the heart as I continued my drive.

Last time I felt this overwhelmed I tamed it, I calmed down and returned to the house where the chaos had broken out, composed and well-rehearsed, ready to apologise and take the blame for everything that wasn't my fault just to restore peace.

But this time felt different. This time the waves were too powerful, and I was drowning.

The speedometer lit up in front of me 87, 90, 93, ... A surge of power rushed through my veins as I pushed the limits of my Skoda Octavia even further, but it was fleeting, like trying to hold water in your hands. The road, once a refuge suddenly became a cage, its endlessness a reminder of the inescapability of my thoughts.

Suddenly something changed. My focus narrowed to a concrete outline in the distance gracefully arching its way over a crossroads and thoughts occurred to me, coupled with a momentary thrill...

Its dark. Nobody is here.
I can finish this now.
I am alone on the road.
Nobody else can get hurt.
Yes, I like that no more hurt.
I must make it stop,
Calm the tide once and for all.

I blinked allowing my tears to drop to my chest and clear my vision a little. Still no headlights appeared on the other side of the road or any side of the road for that matter. Just me in the darkness and the haze of the lampposts shooting past drawing fuzzy lines in the air then disappearing.

In my madness, I made a deal with the devil. *If nothing comes the other way by the time I get to the bridge I will do it. I will stop the madness, stop the chaos in my head.*

My exhilaration increased and I instantly felt happier, already a fleeting sense of freedom rushing through me just before a new surge of emotions hit again and the drowning feeling started to repeat itself. I rolled my eyes up to heaven "it's in your hands now."

My eyes widened, straining for a clearer view of the bridge, sobering myself I sat straighter and adjusted myself in the seat. The enormity of the concrete giant in front of me became more evident with every second that passed. The eery emptiness continued across the dual carriageway, it was my sign...

I tried to shake off the images of my children reaching out to me. All rational thought left my mind with the tide of emotions as words echoed angrily in my head.

'You are disgusting. You are useless. You are nothing. You have nothing!' My tears spilled once more.

"I'm sorry. I love you!" I sobbed as I homed in on the image of their beautiful faces, my god I really did love them. My children were the only reason I had made it this far, but at that moment it was all too much. They would be better off without me.

The speedometer continued to flash angrily in front of me ... 97, 99... The speed didn't bring the relief I was looking for. It only amplified the emptiness as the echoes of shouting returned again - the sound of smashing of crockery against the wall, the sound of my neck cracking every time I was pushed, the pain of the pinching, the wince of every sudden movement... the constant sound of my heart pounding in my ears and that same thumping roused me back to the road...

Still there is no sign of headlights around me! It was 11:37pm, The bridge now seconds away and for a fleeting moment I reconsidered.

I can't!

You can!

I cant do it. I was taunting myself.

Do it, do iiiitt!

No.

I'm so sorry! I took a deep breath.

Its so close.

You can do this!

As I reconsidered once more feeling the pull of my love for my children I saw him in my head again overpowering any rational thoughts;

You are nothing... You'll never have the guts to leave!.. and the laughter. The cold callous laughing sound mocking me as he threw his head back towering over me. I winced again at the memory.

At that moment I lost all rational thoughts and control. My hands yanked the steering wheel to the left locking it as hard as I could, sending my car screeching towards the barriers and shattering them like glass.

I could see the road ahead of me as I span and for a fraction of a second time stopped. I was floating, trying to make sense of everything. Waiting for that flip book of memories to hit me in slow motion like you see in Hollywood films as somebody nears the end of their life – A montage playing to "Here Comes the sun" by the Beatles making my last minutes warmer, but the images I longed for didn't come, it was all happening too fast.

I was desperately searching for something to cling on to, something good to take with me, something to make my blood warm and fuzzy one last time as my car lifted through the air and I was upside down. I felt genuinely cheated out of my last moments. Here I was on the edge of the world expecting my life to end with visions of rainbows and unicorns, but nothing! There had been a million good times in my 30 years on earth, I knew there had. Where were they now? Why didn't they come to me?

Then I saw my children again, clearer now, they were the warmth in my heart. I clung onto that image smiling and in-haled deeply like I could smell them. They dissolved into the dusty cloud around me and all I could see was concrete, lots of concrete, the blurry green haze of the land either side of me, the white painted lines in the centre of the road like a run way, the end of my world flying towards me at lightning speed in the mist and darkness and ... shit - HEADLIGHTS flying towards me! I gasped.... Darkness.

Chapter 1

"Jack! Let me in!!! Just let me in! Please Jack please!" My desperate cries went from stern and angry to whiny and pleading. I didn't let up pounding my fist on the hollow, wooden door, whilst at the same time frantically rattling the handle nearly loosening it from its hinges.

I could hear him in there, the faint clinking of metal, the shuffling of feet, the eerie silence in between. My heart pounded in my chest, matching the rhythm of my fists as I continued desperately banging on the door.

"Jack let me in!" I screamed, panic lacing every word. I knew what he was doing. It wasn't the first time, and it wouldn't be the last. My brother, once so full of life and light, was slipping away in the tiny downstairs toilet at my mums end of terrace house. The house where we would smile and greet our neighbours, happy, vibrant, and glowing like the immaculate flower garden out the front, offering the world an image of a well-presented, working-class family.

"Please, open the door Jack PLEASE!" I yelled again, my voice cracking.

For what felt like hours, there was no response. Just the sound of my shallow breaths and the ticking of the clock on the wall. My hands trembled as I pressed my forehead against the cold wood slowly admitting defeat. I didn't know what to do. At fourteen years old how was I meant to fix this? How do you get your brother back when he's already halfway gone?

I stopped banging as my arm began to ache and my pleas were left unanswered. I spread my fingers out wide and pushed the palm of my hand flat against the door as if reaching out to him. I stared my fingernails - jagged, uneven, and torn to match the skin around them. I pulled a face at the sight, screwed my hand up and sighed twisting my forehead downwards to find myself looking at the thick grey carpet of our hallway and started following the lines in the pattern with my eyes.

I remained there losing time for what was only seconds yet felt like an eternity. Suddenly I heard the click and the handle turn, it made me jump and I stepped back quickly my first thought being if he flings the door open at speed it would plough into my forehead leaving me with a blue lump the size of the moon for all the world to see.

The door opened and time stopped. It felt like Deja vous except deja vous is fleeting, you get a glimpse of the past and can't quite pin down where it's from. This was real. Like reading the same page of a book over and over again until you knew every inch, every word, every colour and crinkle of the page so well you could recreate it with your eyes closed. This image of my brother was something I was extremely familiar with but could never ever get used to or prepare myself for. I glanced at the discarded needle on the avocado sink. The brown hand towel had fallen to the floor onto a pink carpet. Nothing matched in my mother's house, but it didn't matter, it was hers, she loved it and she worked hard for it.

I took in the figure that was standing in front of me attempting to unsuccessfully tuck a black strap into his jeans pocket. The eyes that met mine were no longer my brothers. He had disappeared inside himself again, a hollow empty shell until it wears off. It wears off quicker nowadays. Now he does it so frequently the highs and lows for him have merged together and he is just an empty shell, existing, blocking out time, spending his days doing anything and everything to find new wings that may lift him a little further off the ground.

This was not the brother I grew up with, not the one who would kick a football with me (or at me) or sneak sweets into my room after bedtime. Jack's eyes were glazed, distant, like he was looking at the world through fog. Sighing once more, my internal robot kicked in. I ran to the kitchen and grabbed a cup that was sat upside down drying next to the sink, filled it with water and returned to Jack thrusting the cup toward him, my voice small now, unsure. "Here, drink this. It will make you feel better." Even at fourteen years of age I knew already there wasn't a hope in hell that a cup of tap water was going to make him feel better, but that's what we do isn't it. Try to fix what we can with what little we have. I stared at him intently my arm starting to ache as I held the cup mid air waiting for him to respond.

If I could hold his gaze maybe I could keep him strong. Maybe he would see inside me and know and feel how unbelievable loved he was. Maybe he would see the sadness and hurt we feel for him and want to stop and help himself. My eyes bore into him telling him a thousand things without speaking. I wanted him to know I was there - I would always be there! I would be his strength for as long as he needed.

No matter how much I tried his eyes could not meet mine. His pupils were the size of Saturn and his once beautiful blue eyes sank back into a pale white face surrounded by a dark brown matt of hair.

"Please come back to me Jack! You are ok. Its ok you've got this." My words were a soft whisper as my smile pleaded with him to come round.

I continued talking to him, reassuring him he was ok, and he was safe. I tried to wake up good times inside him. Hoping a memory would stir him, make him smile and bring him back to me again. I craved him laughing with me, I craved him bullying me, anything would suffice I just needed him to come back to the land of the living.

Jack swayed on the spot like the smallest breeze would send him flying. My arm was starting to get pins and needles as I stayed stretched out willing him to take the water. Just as anger began to rise in me and I was fighting off the urge to lose my temper and slap him, a limp, pale hand reached out to take the cup. My heart sank as my eyes landed on the skin on his wrist which displayed a thousand tiny holes. I followed the purple and blue bruises up to his forearm until they disappeared underneath the sleeve of his polo shirt.

Unable to grasp the handle of the cup properly, its contents poured all over the carpet followed by the cup itself. At that point as I watched it hit the floor time seemed to stop. I don't remember him falling. Everything happened in such slow motion and a heaviness was now compressing my chest as I had fallen awkwardly, and he passed out on top of me. My head was fixed at a right angle against the side of the armchair forcing my chin to my chest making it twice as difficult to breathe.

Jack, eight years my senior only weighed an unhealthy 9 stone for his height but having him as a dead weight on top of me now was fast cutting off my air supply.

I could have moved. I should have moved, but I didn't. I was frozen, paralyzed with fear, lying there with my brother draped over me, his body heavy and lifeless. His chest wasn't rising, his breath wasn't there. My mind raced, spiralling into dark places I wasn't ready to go. I started to panic.

What if he was dead?
What if this was it?
What would I do with his body?

How would I tell Mum? The thought of her face, the way it would crumble, made my chest tighten even more.

The more I thought about it the more annoyed I was getting. Why couldn't he faint sideways like a normal person instead of using me like a gymnastics mat! I mean what do you even do with dead people?

The silence was deafening. I could hear the faint ticking as the living room clock passed seconds and minutes, stopping for no one. I listened to the distant hum of cars passing outside with people going about their business unsuspecting of what was happening in our beautiful house at the end of Chestnut Grove. The musty smell was making me feel sick and I was beginning to feel extremely dizzy. With the dead weight of him on top of me I could only take small hollow breaths at a time, I felt completely numb.

The clock on the wall clicked again, louder this time, each second stretching out into eternity. I stared at the ceiling, feeling his weight on me thinking of all the times he'd been there to protect me and my mum. I rolled my eyes toward the glass door that led out of the hallway, still wide open where Jack had staggered through it, followed by me only minutes earlier. I saw the image of my mum being pushed through it, remembering the sound of the glass like it was physical. I remembered Jack rushing to her aid with more than a measly cup of water like I'd just offered him. He was always so strong. Now I couldn't help him. My heart pounded, my body trembled beneath him as my blood ran cold. In the silence all I could do was lay there and wonder if I'd ever get my brother back or if this time it really was it, and we'd lost him for good.

Come on Luce Move! Roll him off you! I tried to give myself a pep talk, my brain testing nerve endings in the rest of my body, willing myself to kick and thrash around, to throw him off me, get up, get help, ring somebody, the police? Ambulance? Who do you ring for dead people? I needed to do something, anything.

If my arms were not buried under my brother id have slapped myself there and then. Then I realised one of my arms was in fact entirely free, in fact I think it just moved.

I widened my eyes like I was having some sort of out of body experience watching myself, fascinated, waiting to see what I would do next. I moved again.

I don't think that was me though? A breath and a twitch on my chest –

Nope that definitely wasn't me.

The movements were small, almost imperceptible at first, but then his body twitched, and his breath came in a ragged gasp. Relief flooded through me.

Jack shifted his weight off me looking around the room like a man waking from a nightmare, dazed, and confused. He creased his forehead, and I could see his brain trying to put the pieces of this messed up jigsaw puzzle together.

He pushed himself slowly to his knees and pulled himself up to standing using the bannisters to balance. He looked at me turning his nose up like there was a bad smell in the air and I was instantly offended and wanted to defend myself. I wanted to tell him the smell was him and not me. I wanted to yell at him for being such an idiot and scaring the living daylights out of me. But I was still on the floor unable to move or speak. I was grateful for the release on my chest and being able to inhale properly. I followed his gaze until it fixed on the wet carpet.

Oh god the water, I must clear that up!

Rooted to the ground motionless trying to gather my thoughts, still paralysed from the afternoon's events I focused on regulating my breathing. Jack looked at me. Looked me directly in the eyes, his pupils now returned to their normal size thank God.

As my body began to relax the enormity of the situation hit me, my eyes filled up with water. I thought he would reach out to me, offer me a hand, help me up and hug me. Apologise for being such an idiot and promise he would never do it again but instead, without a word, WITHOUT A SINGLE FUCKING WORD he turned and walked out of the house.

Chapter 2

I walked into the school gates of Bellview High School, my oversized backpack bouncing awkwardly on my back. Even after 3 years I still hadn't gotten used to senior school. Every time I returned after the 6 weeks holidays it felt bigger, louder, and far more intimidating than ever. Now fourteen and going into year 10 I had expected to feel older, more mature, maybe even a little cooler. Instead, I felt smaller than ever.

As I approached my classroom, I spotted the usual crowd hanging by the door. Kacey Western, the self-proclaimed Queen of Year 10, leaned against the wall, surrounded by a few of her adoring fans. I had avoided their gaze for weeks, always managing to slip past unnoticed, but not today.

"Oi, Lawson!" Kacey called, using my last name. "What's in the bag? Half your house or something?" I forced a smile and shrugged, feeling my face heat up. Without any guidance at home, I had packed everything I might possibly need - notebooks, snacks in the form of a sandwich, a packet of Tesco's own brand crisps and even an extra jacket you know, just in case the world freezes over while I'm at school or something. I carried out the same routine everyday, as if being over-prepared would somehow protect me from the jungle that was Bellview High.

"Nothing much," I mumbled, quickly heading for the classroom door. I could hear the sniggers behind me but chose to ignore them. It wasn't worth it. I wished I could be one of them. Although bullies never targeted me, I wasn't cool either. I felt like a nobody in between worlds.

My first class was English with Mr. Jarvis, one of the few teachers I actually liked. Jarvis was young, with a sharp sense of humour and he didn't talk down to the students like most of the teachers did. The majority of them were clipboard police that seemingly hated their lives. Why on earth anyone would choose to work in a senior school was beyond me. A zoo would be easier surely?! And definitely more rewarding! That day in English, we were working on creative writing, something I was good at but never admitted to. It wasn't exactly the kind of thing that earned you any cool points in Year 10.

"Alright, everyone," Mr. Jarvis announced, "today's prompt is about turning points. A moment that changes everything. I want you to really think about it. It could be something small, something big, something unexpected."

I stared at the blank page in front of me, the tip of my pen hovering above it. A turning point? My mind wandered back to my first day at Bellview, walking through those thick black gates, the weight of expectations and nerves crashing down all at once. Nothing had been the same since, but there was nothing dramatic or life-changing in that. No sudden epiphany or big event, just... change. My mind kept drifting to Jacks son Liam. My adoring nephew that at 3 had already become such a huge part of my life. I was looking after him more and more in recent months. The heavier my brother's drug addiction became, the deeper his wife sank into depression and denial and the more Liam was handed over to me. "Just for a few hours Luce, overnight Luce, for the weekend Luce, can you pick him up from nursery Luce..." The list went on. I didn't mind really, I loved that little pickle more than anything...

Someone sneezed in the class and brought me back to the task in front of me. Was Jack and Liam my something big? My thoughts returned to my blank page. I couldn't write about that, none of it. I wasn't about to share my deepest secrets with anyone or taint my family in any way. My mum was already wearing herself out working 2 jobs and her mental health was hanging on by a thread trying to keep us above water. I couldn't and wouldn't burden her further by broadcasting our home life to the school, opening a whole new can of worms for us to deal with.

While the rest of the class scribbled away, I remained stuck, frustrated by the blankness of my page. Then the door creaked open and someone entered the room. Late. It was Jimmy, the new boy. He had started new to our school at the beginning of year 10, quiet and distant, with an air of mystery that intrigued some and scared others. He walked in barely glancing at the class and took the empty seat at the back near me.

"Sorry I'm late," he mumbled to Mr. Jarvis, who nodded him in. Jimmy caught my eye for a moment then looked away. Something about that brief connection made my heart race, though I didn't understand why. I turned back to my blank page. But now suddenly, my mind buzzed with a story.

The moment I started writing, my thoughts flowed. The story was about a child, not unlike myself, feeling lost in a place that seemed too big, too fast. But then, something, or someone, came along and changed everything. I wrote about courage, about stepping out of the shadows, about making a stand, however small. I guess I was writing about my hopes and fears. We all want to be our own superhero, don't we?

When the bell rang, I was the last to leave, still lost in my pages scribbling words as the rest of the class shoved books into bags and raced to the door. Just as I gathered my things, a voice broke through my thoughts.

"That was good," Jimmy said quietly.

I blinked, surprised to see him standing over me, his bag slung over one shoulder.

"Huh?" I mumbled, caught off guard.

"What you wrote," he clarified, his voice barely above a whisper. "I could see it from here. It looked... good." *See it from here* I echoed in my head slightly panicked at what he had read. Words had spilled out onto my page at such speed I didn't even know what I'd written, it was a proverbial brain dump. I hoped he hadn't seen anything! I stared at him, unsure how to respond. Jimmy wasn't like anyone else in the school. He was direct but soft-spoken, confident yet shy in his own way.

"Thanks," I managed to say awkwardly.

He shook his head, then gave me a half-smile, the kind that hinted at secrets untold. I wondered if his secrets were anything near mine. I smiled at him my mind drifting back to my family again and how on the surface we looked perfectly normal but underneath it all was a car crash. My mum was working tirelessly yet was halfway through a nervous breakdown. Abused by the men she surrounded herself with and torn apart with worry over my brother's heroin addiction. I bet Jimmy's mum was softly spoken. I pictured her wearing an apron when cooking him a nice meal every evening humming to herself. I imagined her to look like Mrs Clause I have no idea why. I bet he had siblings that played jovially in the living room without a care in the world...

"Not really. I'm more of a PE person." Jimmy interrupted my thoughts bringing the focus back to school and snapped me out of yet another daze. I nodded, not knowing what to say. The hallways were emptying fast, and soon it would just be the two of us. I cleared my throat awkwardly.

"Well... if you ever need help with English or anything, I can, you know, help you out or whatever." What was that? I was thinking. Surely there was something better I could have come out with - twat!

"Maybe," he said, eyes twinkling with something I couldn't place. "I might take you up on that." I smiled. As Jimmy walked out, I stood frozen for a moment. It was a small exchange, nothing grand or life-altering, but it felt like a shift. Maybe senior school wasn't just about getting by, about avoiding trouble and blending in. Maybe it was about moments like this, finding connections in unexpected places.

That night, as I lay in bed, staring at the ceiling, I thought about turning points again. Maybe, I realized, it wasn't about big, dramatic events. Maybe a turning point was something small, like meeting someone who saw you when no one else did.

I didn't know if I'd see Jimmy again the following day or if we'd actually ever become friends, but for the first time since starting Year 10, I didn't feel so invisible.

And that, I decided, was enough for now.

It was becoming a regular thing, making excuses to get out of class early so I could pick up my nephew Liam from nursery. Jack had to 'work late,' a lot recently and somehow, it was left to me to make sure Liam wasn't stranded. The problem was, Liam finished nursery five minutes before I finished school, and his nursery was a 20-minute walk away. The maths just didn't work, but Jack being Jack didn't notice or care about this problem. So the onus was on me to fix and I had limited choices; I could ask mum for help - That was never going to happen. I didn't do asking for help at the best of times and mum was on a downward spiral herself, like a rubber band being pulled to its limits ready to snap any minute. No, that was not an option, it has to be me. This narrowed it down to two alternatives - Either escape last period or at least half of it and leg it out the school gates after feigning illness, or being late to collect Liam which raised its own set of problems in the form of questions and nobody needed teachers asking questions, especially when the answers would summon Social Services quicker than I could say my prayers.

I loved Liam. He was a ball of energy, with his blonde curly hair and cheeky grin, but picking him up from nursery after a full day of classes, that was another story and could feel a little exhausting at times. I was already stressed about my exams and trying to juggle my own life. I was monitoring Jack and inadvertently becoming his little side kick, accompanying him on far too many mis endeavours and never being able to say no to him, coupled with mum's outbursts that were becoming more frequent. It felt like a lot.

At first, it wasn't so bad getting out of class. I could make the odd excuse here and there, and no one really thought any-thing of it. But lately, as it had become a regular necessity, I was running out of things to say. I'd already used up the usu-als, headaches, stomach aches, doctor's appointments, dentist appointments I even faked fainting once which was an epic fail because suddenly all eyes were on me and instead of being able to make a run for it, I had two fellow students eager for any reason to escape class, escort me to the first aid room. That episode made me an hour late to collect Liam, teachers far from impressed had been calling his house number to no avail. It was disastrous and a near miss for anyone to get involved in our 'situation' so fainting was quickly struck off the list of excuses and I decided to stick to the trusty old stomach cramps in future.

I was getting more and more nervous that the teachers were starting to catch on. Worse, I kept worrying they'd call my mum, and she'd find out what was really going on. So far, I'd managed to dodge that bullet, but it felt like I was always only one step away from everything coming out.

Sat in Geography class nerves were getting the better of me and I was barely paying attention. It wasn't like I'd miss much escaping this lesson, it wasn't exactly my favourite subject. My eyes kept darting to the clock as the minutes crawled by and I was thinking about which excuse I could use today.

At ten to three, I couldn't wait any longer. I raised my hand, trying to keep my face neutral even though my mind was racing. "Sir, may I be excused?"

Mr Bennett Looked at me over his glasses with that great big unibrow edged further towards his nose (B.O Bennett, we called him because although always smartly dressed, those long-sleeved shirts were never short of sweat patches.) I stared him out. Why do this generation of people look at you over their glasses? Surely the point of having glasses is that you can see better through the lenses not above them?!

I paused, tensed for an argument, ready to protest my case if my early absconding was denied. Lucky for me he just huffed out of his nose and nodded re-adjusting his glasses, his unibrow returning to a perfectly straight line across his forehead and continued his monotone lecture on metamorphic rocks.

Phew! I grabbed my bag and made a swift exit out the class feeling proud that my masterplan had worked once more. Except it hadn't. Unfortunately for me Mr Parson was patrolling the front gate and made a beeline for me the second I came into sight.

"Miss Lawson Leaving early?" I'm not sure if it was a question or a statement. He looked at his clipboard, I'm not entirely sure what for as I'm pretty convinced he didn't have an escapee list on that piece of paper of his. I crossed my arms over my stomach and turned on my best self-pity expression

"I have the worst stomach cramps. Mr Bennett said I could go home."

"Uh huh" he said slowly still searching his clipboard. I stepped sideways trying to look at his clipboard myself. I mean seriously there is a thousand kids in this school. I'd bet my last penny there's no names on it. "On you go then" he said after what felt like five actual years of waiting. The anticipation made me need a wee.

I hurried down the street, fake stomach-ache forgotten. My long, brown hair whipping behind me as I checked my phone for the time again - 3:15 PM. I was late for the second time this week. I muttered to myself in frustration, weaving between pedestrians, my school bag bouncing on my shoulder. I thought about the amount of times Jack was 'working late.' I of course knew this wasn't true. I knew whatever high he was currently chasing would have by far taken precedence over his family. But he was my brother and convincing myself he was in fact working late made it an easier pill to swallow.

As I rounded the last corner, the bright red sign of the nursery came into view: Merrylands Daycare. I sped up my pace, feeling the guilt sink in. I hated the idea of Liam waiting, sitting by himself while the other kids were already gone. Mind you I equally hate my wait in the playground with the eyes of other parents boring into me with their opinions. I'm sure they thought I was a teenage mum. I'd heard Chinese whispers about our family as the other parents tried to fill in the missing pieces with their own assumptions. Waiting outside with them was always a painful experience I would smile a nervous smile and fidget on the spot pretending to examine my fingernails so as not to make eye contact. At least I wouldn't have to endure that today but equally I seriously hated being late.

I reached the front gate, slightly out of breath, and rang the buzzer. After a brief moment, the familiar click of the gate unlocking came through, and I pushed my way in. Inside, the nursery was a warm chaos of tiny chairs, colourful toys, and the faint smell of paint and crayons. Ms. Harrigan, the nursery teacher, stood near the door with a tired but understanding smile. She was used to me being late now.

"Hi, Lucy," Ms. Harrigan greeted. "Liam's just finishing up his snack."

"Sorry I'm late," I apologized, feeling the familiar wave of embarrassment. "Crazy day." I said bolstering my shoulders out and standing a little taller trying to sound like an adult.

Ms. Harrigan waved it off. "Don't worry, he's been fine. We've been drawing dinosaurs."

I smiled as I spotted Liam at the small table, his legs swinging under his chair, happily munching on an apple slice. His face lit up when he saw me.

"LUCY!" he shouted, jumping off his chair and running toward me with his arms open wide. I knelt down just in time to catch him as he crashed into me, wrapping his tiny arms around my neck. His giggle, light and infectious, immediately made the stress of the day melt away.

"Hey, little man," I said, ruffling his curls. "Sorry I'm late."

"S'okay," Liam replied, his speech still adorably toddler-like. "I drew a T-Rex! Wanna see?"

"Of course, I do!" I stood up, still holding him on my hip as he showed me the scribbled, green and brown mass on the paper. It didn't exactly look like a T-Rex, it more resembled someone using a fly swat to splat some paint around the paper, but I wasn't about to tell him that.

"Wow, that's amazing! It's so big and scary!" I said, exaggerating my reaction.

Liam beamed, clearly pleased with the praise.

"It's the biggest dinosaur ever!"

"It sure is!" I held his coat open ready for him to push his arms into. We said our goodbyes to Ms. Harrigan, and I walked out of the nursery, balancing Liam on one hip and carrying his backpack in my free hand. He was getting heavier, but I didn't mind I'd let him walk once we'd escaped the nursery gates.

As we walked down the street, Liam babbled on about his day; the new toy he played with, how another boy had shared his sandwich with him, and how he had built the 'bestest tower' in the world. I half-listened, smiling at his excitement, but my mind kept drifting back to the growing list of things I had to do for school, and how things had slowly developed between me and Jimmy. How we had recently spent time engaging in long conversations, enjoying break times together and his numerous invitations to for me to hang out with him after school that I constantly blew out with weak excuses. It's amazing he even bothers still trying.

"Lucy," Liam suddenly interrupted my thoughts, looking at me with his big, curious eyes. "Are you tired?" I blinked, caught off guard by the question. I didn't expect a three-year-old to notice.

"A little," I admitted, forcing a smile as I thought about the question. "Why?"

"You work a lot, like Daddy," he said simply, resting his head against my hip.

My heart clenched a little. It was true. Jack was absent a lot from Liam 'supposedly at work' leaving Liams mum Scarlet to cope mostly on her own. I had stepped in more than I ever thought I would so Scarlet could continue her work, cleaning in a hospital, trying to keep their little family going. I was babysitting, running errands, and of course, these regular nursery pickups. Sometimes, it felt like the weight of responsibility came crashing down too hard and too fast and absolutely yes, I was tired, was the true answer to his question. I sighed as I thought about our circumstances and wondered where Jack was at this precise moment and whether he was even giving his son a second thought. I looked down at Liam, small and innocent, looking at me with wide eyes. He had seen so much in his little 3 years. I'm sure he's been in this world before, he has such wise eyes for such a tiny person.

"Yeah, I guess I do," I replied softly. "But it's okay. I love spending time with you."

Liam nodded, his little arm wrapping round the top of my leg as we continued to walk. "I love you Lucy, you're the bestest."

I felt my chest tighten with a mix of emotions. I wasn't sure if I deserved the title of 'the bestest,' but to Liam it seemed simple. I was there, I showed up and maybe right then that was all he needed. As we approached our street, I shifted hands with Liam so we could cross the main road. He was still chatting, now talking about the clouds and how they looked like animals, his imagination running wild. I listened (genuinely this time) and enjoyed the simplicity of his little world.

As we arrived at my mum's house, I put the heating on to warm the house through and made us both beans on toast. Liam had a scoop of his favourite bubble-gum ice cream for dessert. I gave him a bath and we sat on the sofa to watch Hercules (our favourite animated film) with him nestling into me.

The weight of the day, of school, exams, and responsibilities still loomed in the background, but in that moment, it didn't feel so overwhelming. Liams world was uncomplicated, filled with wonder and joy and just for now I wanted to borrow a bit of that. We enjoyed the film together until the doorbell rang and I handed Jack a very tired, worn out, very nearly asleep little man. It was ten to nine in the evening. I didn't bother asking why he was so late, I'm used to it.

Chapter 3

It was a cold, damp evening when my brother had popped round asking for £20 for some 'Reebok Classics' he'd managed to get hold of that were conveniently in my size.

Another favourite past time of his - selling me clothes and trainers that I would discover didn't actually exist after parting with the cash.

"I don't have £20 Jack".

"You can find it you know you can. I won't have them for long and you'll never buy

them this cheap anywhere!" Sold.

At fifteen and wanting to fit in with the cool kids at school one hundred percent I wanted a crisp white pair of Reebok Classics and £20 was a steal, and maybe just maybe this time he'd actually turn up with the goods. After much debating I messaged my mum at work my heart sinking as we were taking from her again. I asked her to transfer me £20 for new mandatory school items that I 'forgot I needed' and needed to buy now. Not entirely a lie, right? I'd wear them for PE - it totally counts!

"I'll need to draw it out Jack. Let me grab my coat."

Jack walked with me to the cash machine and said he'd walk me home after, but we needed to pit stop on the way back. The thought instantly sat uneasy with me, but I bowled along with an air of false confidence wanting to fit in with my big bro. I didn't want to go. I never did. However at fifteen, saying no to my older brother was never really an option. I wanted his approval, to be a part of something even if I didn't understand what that 'something' was.

The flat we arrived at was buried deep in a block of about two hundred, towering above the shops in Lowcroft Centre. The walls outside were streaked with grime, graffiti scrawled across them in angry bursts of colour. A faint, acrid smell hit me before we even stepped through the front door.

He stopped at number 39 and knocked gently. Inside, it was worse. The air was thick, filled with a haze of smoke that clung to my clothes the second we walked in. The windows were covered with makeshift curtains, thick, stained blankets nailed to the walls, blocking out what little light the evening had left to offer. The floor was littered with coke cans, fast food wrappers, and crushed cigarettes and the only furniture in the living room was an old, tattered brown sofa pushed against one wall, sagging in the middle like it was dying under its own weight.

We were met with two further people inside. One of them, a man in his twenties I guessed although he looked like he just stepped off the set of Beetlejuice, sat slouched on the couch, a cigarette dangling between his thin lips. He had dark, greasy hair that hung in limp strands over his eyes, his skin pale and sunken in like he hadn't slept in days or maybe even weeks. His clothes were loose, hanging off him like he'd lost too much weight, and his hands trembled as he held the cigarette to his mouth.

Next to him, on the floor, was a woman. She couldn't have been much older than my brother, but her face was worn, with deep lines etched into her skin, a ghost of whatever she'd once been. She sat cross legged, methodically heating the end of a spoon with a lighter. Her fingers were thin and skeletal, her nails chipped and dirty, but her eyes, hooded as they were, were focused. There was something almost robotic about the way she worked, like it was a ritual she had done too many times to count.

I stood frozen by the door, watching them as the room closed in around me. My brother walked in like it was nothing, giving a nod to the man on the couch before sitting beside him. The man's eyes flicked up at me, dull, barely registering my presence, before he returned to the cigarette.

"You brung your sister?" his voice was thick, like his throat was coated in smoke and dust.

"Yeah," my brother muttered, not looking at me. "She's cool." Cool? Yes! That's what I wanted to be. I wanted to be like my brother, wanted to be a part of whatever world he had slipped into over the past few years. But standing in that flat, my stomach twisted with something ugly and unfamiliar. The woman on the floor looked up at me, her eyes half lidded but sharp, like she could see right through me. She held up the spoon, now bubbling with a thick, amber liquid, and offered me a lazy smile.

"Wanna try?" she asked, her voice smooth, almost inviting. "Won't hurt...."

My heart pounded in my chest, and for a second, I thought I might say yes. I wanted to. I wanted to be like them, to show my brother I wasn't afraid. But something about the flat, the darkness, the filth, the way their bodies sagged like they were too heavy for them to carry, made me pause. I looked at the spoon, the way the liquid shimmered in the dim light, and felt the weight of my brother's gaze on me. He wasn't saying anything, but I could feel the expectation. He let out a shallow laugh at my expense. He wanted me to join in, to cross that invisible line between us and become part of whatever it was that he had become.

But I couldn't. My hands were shaking, I shoved them into my pockets stepping back until I felt the cold surface of the door behind me. I mumbled something, an excuse, I think, something about needing fresh air, and without waiting for a response, I turned and pushed my way out of the flat.

The air outside was sharp, biting at my skin, and I sucked in deep breaths like I'd been suffocating inside. I didn't feel cool. I didn't feel brave. All I felt was relief that I hadn't given in. That I hadn't followed them into that place where the smoke hung like a ghost and the people inside seemed more like shadows than anything real.

I waited outside, hands stuffed in my pockets, trembling. Now fifteen, confused, and afraid, I stood there in the cold as my brother stayed inside, part of a world I couldn't, wouldn't ever understand. I composed myself and took one last deep breath and was about to re-enter the flat when sirens blared in the distance, getting closer. Too close. At that point, my brother and his shadows appeared next to me ushering me to start running - Wait. What??

My heart pounded in my chest, adrenaline surging through my veins as I followed them, my mind trying to piece everything together. I don't know if it was nerves but for a second, I wanted to laugh. What the hell was happening? Were we running from the sirens? Why, what did he do? What did I have to do with it, he's the one that brought me here?! The sirens were now loud and close, fear set in, and adrenaline took over. The road was wet from the rain, glistening under the dim streetlights as evening had started to settle in, and my breath fogged the cool air in frantic bursts. I could hear the crackle of police radios, and the unmistakable sound of footsteps pounding against the pavement after the vehicle skidded to an unmistakable halt. They were after us, well they were after Jack, but I was with him AGAIN!

Struggling to keep up I turned a corner, my shoes splashing in a puddle, and skidded to a halt. Dead end that way. A brick wall loomed in front of me too high to climb. Panic surged through me as I glanced back the way I'd come. I didn't have much time, there was nowhere to go. And then I saw it, a skip.

"Get in" Jack said appearing by my side.

"I'm sorry what? NO!"

"Get in you idiot and DONT move or make a sound until I come back for you got it!" I stared at him. "LUCE GOT IT?!"

I didn't have time to 'get it' He pushed me into the skip, flipping my legs behind me. It was overflowing and the stench of rotting rubbish hit me immediately, but right now, it was my only option.

I scrambled in the rubbish trying to keep my head upright and looked pleadingly at Jack "Duck down for fuck's sake! And Remember DON'T MOVE!" Jack said quietly but sternly as he pulled cardboard and rubbish over the top of me. Then everything stopped moving and I listened to his footsteps sprint into the distance.

The smell was unbearable, a mix of decaying food, wet cardboard, and something else I didn't want to identify. I shuffled myself around trying to remain as hidden as possible and curled into a foetal position as quietly as I could.

Darkness enveloped me and I felt possibly the smallest and most worthless I had ever felt in my life. I tried to calm my breathing, but the fear was too strong, every breath shallow and shaky. The sounds of the streets were muffled, but the sirens were still there, louder than ever, and I could hear the echo of voices, as the officers called out to each other as they continued their search.

I pressed myself against the side of the skip, my back wedged uncomfortably against a pile of damp newspapers and pulled even more cardboard over the top of me allowing myself a gap at the side to breathe. The smell was thick and sour, but I fought the urge to gag. If they found me here, it was game over. The footsteps came closer, echoing off the brick walls. I squeezed my eyes shut, willing myself to disappear, to become invisible. Sweat trickled down my forehead, mixing with the rain that still clung to my clothes and skin. I tried to shake off images of being arrested.

What if I went to prison? Can I go to prison at fifteen? I didn't do anything wrong.

They would want to know where Jack was and I genuinely don't know. What if they think I'm part of it all? I hate Jack. I can't believe he brought me here with him!

My thoughts tormented me over and over again with 'what if's' as my heart pounded in my chest, echoing in my ears and I fought off the urge to cry.

"Check down here!" one of the voices called out, closer now. Much closer.

I held my breath. The skip rattled slightly as someone brushed past it, and I could hear their boots on the pavement, inches away from where I hid. My heart was pounding so hard I was sure they'd hear it, the rhythm of fear loud in the suffocating darkness. For what felt like an eternity, I waited, every second dragging by like hours. The voices outside seemed to linger, their words indistinct through the metal walls of my hiding place, and I imagined them circling the skip, their torches cutting through the rain as they scanned every nook and cranny.

"Anything?" a voice asked.

"Nothing here," another replied.

The footsteps started to fade, moving back away from the street. I didn't move. Not yet. I couldn't be sure they were gone.

I crouched there, breathing through my mouth to avoid the stench, ears straining for any sign that they were coming back. The rain continued to patter on the skip, and the faint hum of people going about their daily lives filled the silence. I wanted to believe I was in the clear, but I knew better than to trust my luck. They could come back. They could be waiting, and Jack told me not to move. I think it was about then that I completely zoned out. The coldness of the rain, the fear of being found and the unfairness of it all weighed in on me and I seemed to shut off. I focused on some flies going about their business and tried to watch carefully every move they made. I wondered if they ever fell out with their siblings or said no to each other? *Do flies even talk?* The thought made me laugh quietly.

Then without warning a sick lump formed in my throat as I landed back into reality. The smell and stress had gotten to me forcing me to gag, bringing me out of my crazy thoughts of insects talking to each other. I tried to breathe slowly and stop the retching, but I could not escape it. The enormity was too much.

It was now extremely dark, and I couldn't contemplate how long I had been there for? After a few more agonizing minutes, when I accepted that Jack was never going to return for me, I dared to lift my head a fraction, just enough to peek out. The road ahead of me was empty. The flashing lights had disappeared, and the sound of the sirens was now a distant wail. Slowly, cautiously, and suddenly feeling extremely weak I climbed out, wincing as my legs cramped from crouching for so long. I was covered in filth, the smell clinging to my clothes. I headed up the road towards home praying that I would make it before mum got home from her evening job. I had no idea of the time but was always supposed to be home by dark and this would take some serious explaining if she was in.

I looked around, scanning for any last-minute sign of Jack. Nothing.

Walking towards home squinting at every shadow, my heart seizing in my chest, the smell still clinging to me like a constant reminder of the evening's events. I dragged my feet urging myself to move quicker and tried to escape the overwhelming loneliness. My nose was running, I couldn't allow myself to cry, If I did the tears would never stop.

I approached my house, and relief ran through me when I saw the Silver Honda was not yet parked on the driveway. I let myself in and ran to the backdoor stripping off completely. I stuffed my clothes into a carrier bag angrily like I could discard everything that had happened that evening by throwing it away. I tied a knot so tight locking up the shadow of my brother's face, locking up the stench of the rubbish and the metal and the cardboard and locking up the hurt that he didn't come back for me.

I left the bag in the garden with a plan to discard it in a bin on the way to school the next day, then hot footed it upstairs to have a hot bath. I sank back into the warm bubbles and tried to absorb the sweet lavender smell. I scrubbed my skin until it was sore and repeatedly held my breath, dunking myself under water trying to let the warm sooth me. But it was having an adverse effect, and I was drowning in the memories. I enjoyed holding myself under water, allowing the heat to engulf me. I wanted to pass out in that warm. I stayed under water until I really struggled. My lungs were bursting, my chest tightening until my reflexes took over forcing me to sit up sharply. The heaviness of it all became too much. Tears filled my eyes and poured down my face and I allowed myself to sob, really sob.

I had taken myself to bed by the time mum came home. I heard the creak of my bedroom door opening ajar as she stuck her head round to look in on me. I remained still with my back to where she was standing careful to keep my breathing light and not move a muscle. She closed the door gently behind her and I allowed more silent tears to roll down my cheeks.

I had no idea where Jack had run to or if he had been caught. I had no idea if he was currently in a cold cell or sat on another filthy sofa losing himself in the comfort of his heroin. Had he returned home and taken up his role as husband and dad acting like nothing had happened? I guess id find out soon enough. Thinking about him being at home brought my thoughts to Liam and Scarlet and what they would do if Jack had been caught. Someone had to be strong for that little boy. 'Strong like Hercules' as Liam would say regularly showing off his non-existent little toddler muscles when we watched the film on repeat. I took deep breaths trying to calm the storm circling inside me. I was safe, for now, but I knew this wasn't over. Not by a long shot. Tomorrow was another day. I fell into a restless sleep.

Chapter 4

The night had finally arrived - A Friday sleepover at my friend's house, free from the clutches of homework and the endless pressures of school. We were fifteen, at that magical age where the world felt thrilling, and nothing mattered more than these moments together. My friend's dad, trying to be the 'cool' parent, had bought us a couple of bottles of Lambrini, bubbly and sweet enough for us to pretend we were sophisticated, but still just innocent fun. Alongside the pizzas that had been ordered, we had everything we needed.

It started out with the usual chatter, the kind that filled the room the moment me and my other friends walked through the front door at Jessica's house. Me, Maddy, and Gemma had all brought our duvets, and we'd set up camp in the living room. Blankets spread out across the floor, fairy lights casting a soft, warm glow, it felt like our own little world, far away from anything real. The second we arrived we were instantly talking over each other and laughing about school gossip. Jess's Dad was in his usual weekend mode, which meant he was sprawled out on the sofa half-watching a documentary about birds, half reading a newspaper. He gave us the same greeting he always did:

"Hey, girls! Pizzas been ordered. Have fun, don't burn the house down."

"Did you see what Ellie was wearing today?" Jess started; her face full of exaggerated horror.

"Honestly, what was that skirt?" Maddy added, eyes wide as she took a sip of Lambrini, already feeling the slight buzz from the fizz.

We all erupted in giggles, the kind that start deep in your belly and just can't be stopped. That was how it was with us. Everything was funnier, lighter. The stresses of school, boys, friendships that sometimes felt like battles, they all melted away when we were together. Especially on nights like this.

The pizza arrived just as we were discussing the latest drama at school. I grabbed the largest slice and felt a warm, gooey comfort in every bite. Between mouthfuls of pizza and sips of our drinks, we gossiped about the boys in our class, who was cute, who was definitely not, who we secretly hoped would ask us out.

"Okay, let's play a game," Maddy suggested, her eyes twinkling mischievously. "Truth or dare?"

The room went silent for a moment, the air thick with anticipation. Truth or dare was always dangerous with this group, no one played it safe.

"Jess, you first," Maddy said, the corners of her mouth curling into a grin. "Truth or dare?" Jess thought for a moment before picking,

"Dare."

"Ok I dare you to text Jimmy and task him out," Maddy said, her smile widening. Jess's face flushed immediately. I choked on my Lambrini!

"What?! No way!" I managed through splutters. I didn't want Jess anywhere near Jimmy "Noooo" I heard myself saying just in case the first choking message didn't get across. The others looked at me and there was a stunned silence. "I mean that's no fun" I recovered "Message Billy instead!"

"Yeeeeeesssss" The others said in unison. Phew the relief as I could fill the colour returning to my face!

"No way"

"You have to!" we all chorused, urging her on. It was all in good fun, and deep down, we all knew she liked him secretly. Reluctantly, Jess grabbed her phone and, with trembling hands, typed out the message. As soon as she pressed send, we all burst out laughing, her face a mixture of horror and excitement.

For the rest of the night, we did silly dares, running around the garden in pyjamas, calling random numbers, and making up ridiculous stories. There was no judgment, no embarrassment. Just pure, unfiltered joy. Every laugh was real, every smile came from the heart.

After we stuffed ourselves with pizza and finished off the bottles of Lambrini Jess announced the next game of the night;

"Let's play Who's Line Is It Anyway? but, like, we'll film it with your dad's camcorder." I loved that camcorder. It was this old bulky thing, we always used it to make the silliest videos when we got together. The fact that it was grainy and out of focus just made everything we did seem more ridiculous, in the best way possible.

The first scene we did was a classic the 'Questions Only' game. Gemma took it way too seriously, throwing out ridiculous things like,

"Why is there a giraffe in the bathroom?" Jess countered with,

"Are you saying you didn't invite him?" We all broke character and laughed so hard we almost cried. Of course, we didn't stop there. Next, we played 'Scenes from a Hat,' but instead of hats, we pulled ideas out of an old cereal box.

The scenarios we came up with were ridiculous, like 'What aliens think humans do at parties' and 'Things you shouldn't say to your schoolteacher.' It was stupid, but it was our kind of stupid. For a few hours, all we cared about was making each other laugh until our stomachs hurt.

As the night wound down, we decided to play Look Through the Keyhole. We'd take turns videoing and walking room from room mimicking the voice of Lloyd Grosman saying.

"And who lives in a house like this?!..." We filmed all of it, zooming in dramatically on each other's faces like we were in some kind of reality show. None of us could keep a straight face, so most of the footage was just us laughing hysterically.

By the time we were done, the camcorder battery was almost dead, and we were all sprawled across the living room floor, completely exhausted but feeling so good. I glanced over at Jess's dad, who had fallen asleep on the leather sofa with his repeat episodes of Red Dwarf still playing and wondered what my own dad was doing right now. He never bothered with us. I shook off the sting and brought myself back to the present.

At some point, the conversation shifted to things that really mattered. Life, dreams, the future. Jess talked about wanting to travel the world; Gemma admitted she was terrified of growing up and having to figure out what she wanted to do. Maddy, the most confident of us all, talked about how much pressure she felt from her parents to be perfect. I felt that deeply as I thought about my dad before he left for Canada, his drink induced sleep, a bottle of malt whiskey by his side. His insistence of me going to university and making something of myself were constantly in the back of my mind.

As the night wore on, we forgot all the things that made being a teenager so hard. The cliques, the tests, the feeling of never quite fitting in, they seemed so far away. It was just us, and in that little bubble of warmth, it felt like we could conquer the world. We didn't need to be anything other than ourselves.

The Lambrini bottles had run dry, and the pizza had long since disappeared, but the laughter never stopped. We were sprawled out on the floor, half-asleep, still giggling over something stupid that had happened hours before.

It was in those quiet moments, when the laughter had died down and we were just lying there, side by side, that I realized how special this night was. The kind of night you remember forever. No drama, no stress. Just us, being silly and free.

We fell asleep in a tangle of duvets and pillows, our heads buzzing from the fizzy drinks and our hearts full of the friendship. Outside, the world continued its relentless march, but in here in our little weekend slice of heaven, everything was perfect.

Chapter 5

I couldn't believe I was finally doing this. Walking home with Jimmy (Like actual Jimmy eeeekk.) The boy I'd been quietly crushing on for as long as I could remember. He'd asked me to come over to his house a number of times before, and I'd always made excuses. But today I have no nursery pick up to do... today, I said yes.

We walked side by side home from school, the late afternoon sun dipping below the trees, casting long shadows on the pavement. He talked about football, making me laugh, just like he always did. I tried to act like this was no big deal, but inside, my heart was doing somersaults. I couldn't believe I was actually going to his house.

Meeting Jimmy mum for the first time felt like a big moment. When we reached his place, a neat little house with a small picket fence out the front, I felt my nerves spike. I wasn't sure what to expect, but when his mum, Sharon, opened the door, all my tension eased. She greeted me with the warmest smile, like I'd been there a thousand times before. She did not look like the

Mrs Clause that I'd conjured up in my head but she was equally warm and gave off a soft loving energy.

As soon as I walked into the house, the smell hit me, a rich, mouth-watering scent of home cooked lasagne filled the air. It was comforting, like stepping into the heart of a warm family home. I immediately hoped I'd like it because the thought of politely forcing down food I didn't enjoy was terrifying.

"Hello, love! Come on in," she said, ushering me into their cozy living room. "I've heard so much about you."

I blushed but felt a slight panic creep in that I tried to brush off. "Oh, really?"

"All good things," she teased, then winked at Jimmy, who rolled his eyes in that easy, comfortable way boys do when they're embarrassed by their mums.

I liked her immediately. She made me feel at ease, like I didn't have to be anything other than myself here. But that's the thing, I wasn't really myself. I had to be the girl everyone thought they knew, the one who was always smiling, always making people laugh. That's who they expected, and that's who I needed to be.

"So, tell me about your family," Sharon asked as we sat down in the kitchen, I thankfully had nothing in my mouth to choke on. "Jimmy says you're really close with your brother."

I nodded, sliding into my well-rehearsed version of my life. "Yeah, my brother's great. He's got a little boy, my nephew, he's 4 now and I'm really close to him. We're one big, happy family."

That part wasn't entirely a lie. I loved my nephew, and my brother... well, when he wasn't caught up in the whirlwind of drama, but I didn't mention any of that. The drama was private they didn't need to know. I didn't want them to know.

"Are your mum and dad together?" Now I wanted to something to choke on, I could feel my eyes grow wide.

"No" I said smiling politely wondering if I actually did like Sharon after all. How nosey is she!

"Do you see them both?"

"MUM!" Jimmy thankfully interrupted, annoyed.

"No, it's ok honestly" I said thinking how absolutely not ok the questions were and I started to get fidgety. "Yes, I live with my mum and my dad has moved to Canada for work (I missed out the part where he beat my mum senseless in front of us). They're workaholics, but we're all very close." I continued to smile and took a mouthful of drink to brace for any more questions.

Sharon smiled warmly. "That's so lovely, Family's important." (I instantly liked her again.)

"Yeah," I agreed, my voice steady, even though my insides were churning. I couldn't help but think about my real life, the one where my mum was barely keeping it together these days, where arguments and tension were the norm, and where I had to play peacemaker just to keep things from falling apart. My dad busy in his own world of work, alcohol and escapism bragging to strangers that I would be his star one day when I got my degree. He didn't even know me. All he cared about was status which was hilarious since he'd nearly killed my beautiful mum with his bare hands! What did he know about status?!

But none of that mattered right now. Not here, in Jimmy's kitchen, where everything felt so... normal. So, calm.

We sat at the table, chatting easily, and I found myself laughing more than I had in a long time. It was easy to pretend here. To slip into the role of the carefree, happy, laughing girl everyone thought I was. Thankfully, the lasagne was delicious, and my worries melted away with each bite.

After eating, we moved into the living room, where I played with Jimmy little sister Emily. She was the cutest little thing, full of energy, bouncing around while Dora the Explorer played on repeat in the background. There was something about the way the family interacted, the way they all seemed to glow with affection. You could feel the love radiating off them, it wasn't just the food or the laughter, but the warmth they shared with each other. It was a real, genuine family atmosphere, and I couldn't help but feel welcomed into their world.

After spending time talking to his family, we headed up to Jimmy's room. My heart raced as we climbed the stairs, my mind buzzing with the realization of where I was, alone, in Jimmy's room. He was the kindest boy I'd ever known, and being around him felt like a warm blanket, something comforting and safe.

We sat on his bed exchanging stories and watching Friends on his small TV, laughing at the same jokes, and quoting lines we'd both heard a thousand times. It was easy, comfortable.

Everything felt natural. We were surrounded by the quiet hum of his room, away from the world, just talking about life. Conversations flowed from one topic to another, school, the future, random memories that didn't seem all that important until we started laughing about them. We shared stories about teachers, tests we both dreaded, and the little dramas that happened every day at school. Then we'd veer off into deeper topics, like what we really wanted out of life, who we were becoming, and what scared us. It was one of those rare moments when you felt you could say anything (well almost anything) and not be judged.

There was something comforting about being in that space, where nothing had to be perfect, and time seemed to slow down.

Then, somewhere between a joke about Chandler and a scene where Rachel stormed out of Central Perk, Jimmy turned to me, his eyes soft and warm. He leaned in, and before I knew it, his lips brushed against mine. It was gentle, sweet. My stomach flipped, butterflies erupting inside me. I kissed him back, my mind spinning, wondering how I could've gone so long wanting this, and now it was actually happening. When we pulled apart, he smiled that handsome, crooked smile of his, and my heart melted a little more.

Every time after that when I went to Jimmy's house, it felt like stepping into a different world. A world where things were simple, where families laughed together over dinner and the air didn't feel so heavy with unspoken words. His mum was always there to greet me with a smile, her warmth wrapping around me like a soft blanket. It felt so good to hear the sound of plates clinking and soft laughter filling the room. Sharon would cook meals that tasted like home-cooked comfort, spaghetti Bolognese one-night, roast chicken another. Nothing fancy, just good, hearty food. The kind that made you feel full, not just in your stomach, but somewhere deeper. Sharon had this way of pulling everyone into conversation, making me feel like I was part of something. Part of their family, even if only for a few hours at a time. It was the kind of family I imagined existed in movies or in other people's lives, heartwarming meals, kindness, and the easy rhythm of people who genuinely liked being to-gether.

We'd laugh about silly things, school, Jimmy's attempts at cooking (which were always a bit of a disaster), and the little things in life that in their house, didn't seem so complicated. It was the kind of laughter that filled up the space, making it easy to forget about everything else.

Jimmy was always there beside me, so comfortable in his own skin, so relaxed in his little world. We'd sit on the couch after dinner, his hand brushing mine, making me feel like I was in a bubble that could never burst. In those moments, it was easy to believe that life was as simple and carefree as it felt inside these walls.

At school and at Jimmy's house, I was the girl who laughed the loudest, who always had something funny to say. That's what people saw when they looked at me, the happy, go-lucky girl who never seemed to have a bad day. I liked it that way. It was a role I'd mastered, one that kept people at arm's length. I didn't want anyone looking too closely, peeling back the layers to see what was really there. I wasn't about to share my secrets with anyone. They didn't need to know about the chaos that waited for me at home, the fights, the mess. That wasn't part of the image I'd created, and I intended to keep it that way.

Being with Jimmy was different. He never pried, never asked about the things I didn't want to talk about. He just let me be. We'd spend hours in his room, lying on his bed watching Friends or talking about the future about all the things we wanted to do when we finally grew up. He'd talk about traveling, about seeing the world, and I'd nod along, pretending that I wasn't terrified of how different my life might turn out.

The truth was, I liked living in his world, even if it was just borrowed time. I liked pretending that I had the kind of life where I could invite him over to my house, where we'd sit around my family's dinner table and laugh the same way we did at his. But I couldn't do that. I could never take him into my world. It was too messy, too complicated, and I didn't want to shatter the version of me he saw; the smiling, carefree girl.

I kept the two worlds separate. At school, I was the girl everyone knew. The one who was always making jokes, the one who never seemed to have a care in the world. I enjoyed people thinking I was that girl because it was easier that way. If they thought I was happy all the time, no one would ever ask the tough questions. No one would look beyond the surface. And with Jimmy, I could let my guard down a little. Not enough to show him everything, but enough to enjoy his company, to lose myself in his kindness and his steady presence. He was the kindest boy I'd ever met, and when I was with him, I felt like I could almost believe in the version of myself that everyone else saw. The version that had it all together.

So, I laughed, I smiled, and I stayed in that world with him for as long as I could, knowing that eventually, I'd have to go back to my real life. But for those few hours at a time, when I was sitting at his family's table or lying in his room with his hand in mine, I allowed myself to pretend that everything was as easy as it seemed, and that was enough. For now.

Chapter 6

The drive to the airport was silent. The three of us, me, Mum, and Jack, lost in our own thoughts. Mum clutched her steering wheel like a lifeline, her knuckles white, eyes darting between Jack in the back seat and the road ahead. Jack's eyes, though open, seemed vacant, staring out of the window but seeing nothing. I wanted to speak, but words felt meaningless now. What could I say that hadn't already been said a hundred times before?

This wasn't the first time we'd driven Jack somewhere, hoping it would be the last. The other rehabs had been shorter stays, local places where the pull of heroin and the people he owed money to still lingered close by. He'd walk out, high before the sun set, and we'd be back at square one. But this time was different. This rehab was in Ireland, far away from anyone who could get to him. We were desperate, clutching at the idea that distance might save him this time.

We arrived at Stansted, and the reality of it all hit me like a wall. Thousands of people swarmed the airport, preparing for holidays, business trips, adventures. Jack, though, was here to save his life, or at least we hoped. As we reached the check-in desk, Jack disappeared, mumbling something about needing the toilet. Mum looked at me, her eyes wide with panic, but I tried to stay calm. "It's fine, he's just nervous," I reassured her, though my stomach churned with doubt.

Minutes passed. Mum started pacing, her anxiety building. "Where is he? He needs to get on that plane!" Her voice was rising, drawing the attention of people around us. I glanced at the men's toilets, hoping he hadn't slipped out a back way. Jack had begged me not to let Mum send him. He had begged to stop the whole thing, but we couldn't back down now. Not after everything.

"I'll go and find him, Mum. Just sit tight." I gently pushed her down into a chair, rubbing her shoulders to calm her. "He's fine. He just needs a minute."

But I wasn't sure at all.

I made my way to the men's toilets, feeling sick, my heart pounding in my chest. As men came in and out, I watched for any sign of Jack, but no one seemed to have seen him. I finally asked one guy, "Is it empty in there?"

"Yeah, think so," he shrugged.

I swallowed hard and walked in, hoping beyond hope that he hadn't passed out or worse. As I entered, I saw one cubicle door closed. Relief washed over me, though it was short-lived.

"Jack?" No answer. I hesitated. Should I look under the door? If anyone walked in and saw me kneeling on the floor of the men's toilets, it wouldn't end well but I couldn't leave him in there. There was a seed of doubt that it might not be him either. God knows what vision might sting my eyes if I stuck my head under the cubicle and it wasn't him. I decided not to look. "Jack?" I knocked gently. "Open the door or I'll have to climb over and make a scene."

Finally, the lock clicked. Grateful it clearly was him and that he hadn't managed to abscond from the airport, I pushed the door open slowly. There he was, slumped on the toilet, fully clothed thankfully but defeated, his head in his hands. I didn't need to ask; I knew he had used. The glaze in his eyes, the hollow look on his face it was heroin's signature. It had numbed him, but not enough. Not anymore. It didn't give him wings anymore, didn't lift him like it used to. Now it just kept him trapped, sinking deeper.

"Jack, you have to do this," I said softly, crouching down beside him. "You're killing yourself, and it's killing everyone around you. This can't go on."

His eyes were lost, swimming in whatever place the drug had taken him. He didn't respond. I squeezed his hand, trying to reach him, trying to pull him back from wherever he was sinking.

An announcement came over the Tannoy, calling for all passengers to board the flight to Ireland. Time was running out.

"What's it going to be, Jack?" I asked, my voice trembling. "I need you to do this. Mum needs you. Liam needs you. How do you see this ending if you don't try?"

For a moment, I thought I'd lost him completely. His gaze drifted, unfocused. But then, slowly, he nodded. I stood up, firmer now. "Come on, Jack. Let's do this. I'll call you every day. We'll talk, or we won't, whatever you need. But you have to try."

He stood up, slowly, like the weight of the world was on his shoulders. Together, we walked out of the toilet, hand in hand, trying to look normal. I nodded at the men coming in like I was passing them on the street not in the men's toilets at Stanstead airport.

Mum saw us, and the second she did, she started to crack. "Where were you? What's going on? We don't have time for this!"

"Mum, stop!" I said sharply, stepping between her and Jack. "He's here. It's fine. Just breathe." But I could see the toll it had taken on her. She looked as dead as he did.

We walked Jack to the gate, watching as he handed over his ticket and shuffled toward the plane. He didn't turn back to look at us. He just walked, head down, shoulders hunched, a shadow of the man he used to be.

As the airplane doors closed behind him, Mum broke. She crumpled to the floor, sobbing, and I knelt beside her. I held her while the rest of the airport went on around us, oblivious. People came over, offering help, but I waved them away. We just stayed there on the cold floor, my arms wrapped around her, her head nestled into my neck as her wracking sobs continued, waiting for a relief that never came.

Chapter 7

It was my sixteenth birthday, and I was standing in front of the hallway mirror at Mum's, putting the finishing touches on my makeup. Tonight, I was going to the cinema with Jimmy, and I could barely contain the excitement bubbling up inside me. Sixteen felt like a milestone. It felt important. And spending it with Jimmy made it even more special.

I was halfway through applying mascara when the doorbell went. I didn't have to look to know who it was. Jack, here on cue every night to have his methadone that mum weirdly kept in our alcohol cupboard. He'd come home from rehab only a few weeks previous. He came in and out of our lives like a gust of wind, sometimes warm and comforting, but mostly unpredictable and chaotic.

I heard him shuffle into the living room, his movements slow, deliberate. A knot tightened in my stomach as I wondered what he wanted this time. But when I stepped out to see him, something in his eyes was different. He was holding something small in his hand, and for a second, I froze, wondering if it was drugs or something he'd try to pawn or if this time he had genuinely made that change.

He extended his hand toward me offering me the little pale blue box with a bow on it. I looked at him in surprise as I opened the gift revealing a gold Claddagh ring, it was beautiful, there were two hands holding a heart, my throat tightened.

"Happy birthday, sis," he said, his voice rough but soft, like he was afraid I wouldn't believe him. I stared at the ring for a second, my mind whirling. He remembered. For once, he wasn't here to take something from me, but to give me something. I didn't know what to say. My eyes welled up with tears, and I bit my lip hard, trying to hold them back.

"You remembered," I whispered, my voice cracking.

"Course I did," he said, avoiding my eyes. "Sixteen's a big deal."

I took the ring from his hand and slipped it onto my finger. It was beautiful, delicate, and felt like it belonged. But, in the back of my mind, darker thoughts crept in. I couldn't stop wondering where he'd gotten it, whose it had been before. Had he stolen it? I flashed back to the gold necklace Mum had been looking for, for months, the one that vanished without a trace or an explanation for its disappearance. I couldn't remember Jack going upstairs, and mum kept her jewellery in her bedroom so it may not have been him but deep down it wouldn't have been the first time and wouldn't be the last.

Maybe it wasn't stolen, maybe, just this once, he'd actually done something right. He definitely had the money to buy it if he wanted to, I should know I was hiding it for him. I'd never seen so much cash before and nearly died the day he handed it over to me in a Christmas card box and told me I needed to 'look after it.' I couldn't leave it anywhere easy to get to - Mum was a frantic cleaner. Especially when she had one of her 'episodes' when she discovered something missing and decided to ransack her own house rather than accept the inevitable. This ransacking literally involved everything in every room going flying, it wasn't pretty and wasn't easy to clean up. Consequently, I had to hide Jacks money somewhere that would take some serious effort to get to. I had buried it in a hole at the back of my wardrobe near the floor. I thought about the money in the box as I stared at Jack. He didn't know where it was either so would have needed to ask me to access it.

I wanted to believe he had genuinely bought this ring for me but that but the dark place inside of me told me something different. I squashed the thought down quickly, refusing to let it ruin this rare moment. Regardless of where it had come from I was its new owner and I'd never know the truth. All I could do was pray it came with a receipt and accept the gift graciously.

"Thank you," I said, wrapping my arms around him and pulling him into a hug. He smelled like cigarettes and stagnant water, but I didn't care. I loved him so much, despite everything. I wished, more than anything, that I could save him from the world he was drowning in. I kissed his cheek, lingering for a second, before pulling away.

"I've got to finish getting ready," I said, giving him a small smile.

He nodded, shoving his hands into his pockets. "Yeah, yeah. I'll leave you to it" he said opening to cupboard ready to pour his daily methadone. I was proud of the steps he was taking, it was a big change for him but hopefully this time rehab really had worked.

As he left, I stood there staring at the ring, still feeling uncertainty in my chest. I didn't want to ruin the night by thinking too much about where it came from. It was my birthday, and for once, Jack had remembered. That was what I needed to focus on.

I finished applying my make up and a car beeped outside. I headed out the door, where Jimmy was waiting for me on the step. His smile, as always, was the kind that could calm any storm inside me. He was so handsome too. My stomach always did summersaults when I saw him. His mum greeted me with a warm smile and drove us to the cinema. We bought popcorn, sat in the dark and lost ourselves in the film, laughing together and sharing inside jokes. For a while, everything felt perfect. Just me and him, the way I wanted my life to be all the time.

When the film ended and we stepped out into the cool evening air, I checked my phone, and there it was, a voicemail from Mum. My stomach twisted as I stared at the notification. I hit play, my heart pounding.

"Lucy... have you seen my crystal glasses? The ones in the cabinet? They're missing. Did you move them?"

I felt my heart drop, even though I knew the answer already. Of course I didn't have them! I hardly pinched two crystal glasses to fill up with an Ice blast and sip in the cinema to celebrate the release of 'Titanic' did I?! We both knew that, but now it was clear who had taken them, and my stomach churned with guilt. How had I been so careless? I should have kept an eye on him, watched him closer when he was there earlier. I heard him open the cupboard but that's where we kept his methadone, so I thought he was just having some of that. I shuddered knowing the state the house would already be in before she'd decided to call me. I knew I would walk back in and find a scene looking like a tornado had just blasted through every room ripping drawers out, throwing its contents across the floor. But it was my birthday I wanted to allow myself this night. I didn't want to rush back to clean up after whatever destruction had occurred in my absence.

I forced myself to take a breath and slipped my phone back into my pocket. Jimmy was looking at me with concern, his hand reaching for mine.

"What's wrong?" he asked, his voice soft and full of care.

I shook my head quickly, forcing a smile. "Oh, nothing. Mum just lost something. It's no big deal."

I squeezed his hand and leaned into him, willing the guilt away. I couldn't let this ruin my night. I couldn't let Jack, or the chaos of my home life, bleed into this part of my world. I smiled at him, bright and carefree, like nothing in the world could touch me.

"Come on," I said, changing the subject. "Let's go get ice cream or something."

And just like that, the moment passed. I kept smiling, holding onto the image of the girl everyone thought I was. The girl who was always happy, always laughing, and never let anything get her down, but as we walked away, the ring on my finger felt heavier.

At sixteen, I was used to the chaos of my life. I had been for a while now. It wasn't like I planned on being the one responsible for my four-year-old nephew, but here I was again blowing my friends out for a night to babysit Liam. I was trying to figure out how to get him to eat his dinner without spilling it all over the floor.

Liam was sitting at the kitchen table, fidgeting with his fork, pushing peas around his plate. His big brown eyes, just like his dad's, stared up at me, a mixture of innocence and stubbornness. "I don't want peas," he mumbled, dropping his fork with a clatter. I sighed, leaning against the table resting my chin on the palm of my hand, my phone buzzing with texts from friends about a party happening that night. But I couldn't think about that.

"Come on, buddy," I said softly, trying to stay patient. "Just a few more bites, okay? You like chicken nuggets, right?"

Liam looked at the chicken nuggets, then back at me, suspicion in his eyes. "Not these ones," he muttered, crossing his little arms over his chest. I bit my lip, glancing at the clock. It was almost 7 p.m. I was in the middle of my GCSE's, I had homework to finish, an essay due, my room was still a mess, and I had exchanged an invite to an epic party for some burnt chicken nuggets and a demon four-year-old. I huffed trying to shake off my frustration. I made every effort to remind myself that none of that mattered right now. What mattered was making sure Liam ate, had his bath, and was ready for bed before 9pm on the off chance my brother might actually turn up for him.

"Please, Little man" I tried again, a little firmer this time. "Just a few bites, and then you can have some bubble-gum ice cream. Deal?"

That got his attention. His eyes lit up, and after a long pause, he reluctantly picked up his fork again. I watched him take a few bites, feeling a small sense of relief.

This wasn't supposed to be my life. I should have been going to parties, worrying about exams, and texting my friends about stupid teenage stuff. But instead, my world revolved around Liam, getting him to School, picking him up, making sure he had dinner, reading him bedtime stories. Jack was never around anymore, after seven failed rehabs he would no doubt either be out with his friends or locked away in his world of heroine, chasing his next fix or passed out on the sofa in some stranger's house, oblivious to the world moving on around him.

I resented him for it. For dumping all the responsibility on me, for never stepping up. But I couldn't say anything. Every time I thought about confronting him or asking for help, my mum's tired face flashed through my mind, and the words died in my throat.

Mum was barely home as it was. She was trying, really trying to keep everything together. Jack had been a mess ever since he was teenager. He had watched our own father lose himself to drink and throw himself at my mum time and time again. He would slap her, punch her, torment her emotionally and all she could do was love him and kill herself trying to 'be better'. If his dinner wasn't what he wanted, it would be tossed in the air, the plate smashed and he would grab her. If he wanted to go out and she questioned him he would grab her. If the house wasn't his definition of clean enough... you get the picture. Jack had jumped into many a fight as a young boy trying to save his mother as we watched her sink further and further into herself. Eventually the day came and dad went too far. That day we don't discuss but it broke all of us. It was that heartbreak had made Jack retreat into himself, but that wasn't an excuse for his behaviour now. Not anymore.

Liam deserved better.

"Lucy, can I have ice cream now please?" Liam asked, pulling me out of my thoughts.

I nodded, put some ice cream in a bowl and put it in front of him. He grinned, his previous frustration forgotten, and I couldn't help but smile a little. He was sweet, even when he was stubborn. I loved him more than anything.

"After ice cream, it's bath time," I reminded him, already bracing myself for the inevitable protest.

"Noooo!" Liam groaned, pushing his bowl away. "I don't want a bath." I shook my head, giving him a look. "Bath time, then PJs, then a story. That's the deal."

He pouted but didn't argue, knowing I wasn't going to budge. I quickly cleared the dishes, then led him upstairs to the bathroom. As I filled the bath, Liam played with his toy cars on the floor, making engine noises and narrating a high-speed chase between two brightly coloured trucks.

Once the bath was ready, I helped him undress and plopped him into the warm water. He immediately started splashing, sending droplets everywhere, and I couldn't help but laugh despite myself.

By the time I got him washed, dried, and dressed in his dinosaur pyjamas, it was close to 8:30. Liam curled up on the sofa with his favourite blanket while I found the film he loved so much - The Infamous Hercules. How he wasn't bored of it by now was beyond me. At only four he could recite it word for word and so could I for that matter. I sat beside him, exhaustion creeping into my bones, but there was a small sense of contentment, too. In moments like this, it was easy to forget everything else, the stress, the frustration, the unfairness of it all.

Liam leaned against me, his head resting on my arm, his little body warm and soft. "I love you, Lucy," he murmured, his voice sleepy.

My heart squeezed. "I love you too, buddy." I ran my fingers through his messy curls as the film played in the background, the bright colours flashing on the screen. Slowly, Liam's breathing evened out, and soon enough, he was fast asleep, his small hand still clutching the edge of his blanket.

I carefully slipped out from under him, covering him with the blanket before turning off the TV. I glanced at the clock on the wall. I could hear the low hum of our next-door neighbour's music playing and other than that the house was still and silent. I wondered about Jack and where he was, and the familiar weight of anger settled in my chest.

When the feeble knock at the door came, I opened it, greeted by Jack with his eyes glued to his phone, barely acknowledging my presence.

"Jack," my voice was low but firm. He looked up, his expression tired and uninterested. "What?"

"It's, ten to ten" I said, struggling to keep my voice steady. "I can't keep doing this."

Jack sighed, running a hand through his hair.

"I know, alright? I know. I'm just... trying to figure things out." I clenched my fists, trying to hold back the wave of frustration.

"Well sorry to interrupt your busy schedule but your son needs you now, not when you've 'figured things out' Now! Seriously Jack get your shit together!"

Jack stared at me for a moment, his face blank, and for a second, I thought he might actually listen, but then he just sighed again and looked away. I really wanted to push him off the doorstep and launch his phone into a bush.

"I'll do better," he mumbled, but the words felt empty, like he'd said them a hundred times before.

I stood there for a long moment, my anger slowly fading into disappointment. I wanted to scream at him, shake him, make him understand what he was missing. But I knew it wouldn't change anything. Without another word, I turned and walked back into the living room whilst he followed closely behind me. I stroked Liams head and carefully picked him up trying not to disturb him and handed him over to my brother. As I closed the door behind them, I felt the weight of responsibility pressing down on my shoulders, heavier than ever.

If this is how adults feel I don't want to be one! But no matter how tired I was, no matter how unfair it felt, I knew one thing for sure, I wasn't going to let Liam down. Not like his dad had. Not ever.

Chapter 8

The remainder of that year was a whirlwind, a rollercoaster of roles I didn't ask for but somehow carried. I was everything to everyone, playing mum to Liam, while his real mum was absent, lost in her own world of grief, financial burden and work, a relationship with a heroin addict that was killing her slowly. I was big sister to Jack when he stumbled home out of his face, needed someone to cry to, some cash, if Scarlet had thrown him out for the umpteenth time or if someone he owed money to was after him. Mum's mental health was spiralling, she was getting clumsy and kept forgetting everything. She looked like a zombie and I didn't know how to help her. Her outbursts were regular and unpredictable and could start over the slightest inconvenience. She would trash the house, pulling drawers out of their sockets, and tossing everything she could get her hands on, clothes, ornaments, cutlery she wasn't selective, if it wasn't bolted down it would go for a flying lesson. This would carry on until she had exhausted herself when she would succumb to her own grief and collapse in a heap on the floor crying into a tea towel. Other nights she would stand out the front of the house and cry loud wailing sobs into the night like an injured wolf calling for help from her pack. I'd have to calm her down and coax her back into the house. That scared me more than her rage. In those moments she seemed invisible, just another ghost in our family and it took an eternity to settle her into a restless sleep.

I had become popular at school and met with crowds of girls at break but constantly had to turn down any after school meet ups. Then there was Jimmy I was still trying to be a girlfriend. Trying to be Jimmy's girl, even though I knew deep down I wasn't from his world and actually he knew absolutely nothing about mine.

At first, Jimmy had been my escape. His kindness, his laughter, his family dinners, they all felt like a safe place, a glimpse into a life that wasn't weighed down by chaos. But the kinder he was, the more I shut myself off from him. It wasn't fair to let him in, not when he started asking all the questions I couldn't answer. He wanted to understand why I had to rush home to babysit Liam all the time, why the police were sometimes outside our door, why my mum cried more than she smiled. Why my mum worked so many hours. He wanted to help, to save me, but I couldn't let him. The closer he got, the more I panicked and knew I had no choice but to back away.

I couldn't let my mess bleed into his life. I loved him, and he melted my insides in the most incredible way, but my world wasn't for him, it was full of babysitting and drugs, of trying to keep Jack out of trouble, of playing the adult when no one else could. And the worst part was, I didn't know if my chaos would ever end.

I made the hardest decision I'd had to make to date and I separated myself from Jimmy. I let him go. It broke my heart in ways I didn't know possible, but I had to free him from the storm that was my life before his parents started asking too many uncomfortable questions and before they got themselves involved. I couldn't risk it. Liam had become my priority. I had to protect him, even if it meant losing the one person who was truly kind to me. I thought about Jimmy for a long time afterwards, trying to let go of the what ifs, wondering what my life might've been like if things had been different. But they wasn't different, so I made my choice.

Despite it all, I passed my GCSEs with good grades, surprising even myself. It should have felt like an achievement, but I didn't have the time or energy to celebrate properly.

I got accepted into a Performing Arts college that summer that felt like a small glimmer of hope, like maybe I could find a way out. I loved being on the stage and pretending to be somebody else. But after three months, the weight of everything outside of college was too much, and I had no choice but to quit. I couldn't focus on acting and dance when I needed to earn money to be independent. I felt like I couldn't breathe in my own life anymore. I needed to escape, to isolate myself from everyone and everything. I got a job almost instantly. Not just for survival but for freedom.

I spent my seventeenth birthday getting wasted with friends. It was one of the few times I managed to get out. I let go, letting the alcohol wash over me, feeling giddy and carefree for a night. It was rare for me to let my guard down like that, but I loved it. For just a few hours, I wasn't responsible for anyone but myself. I was shocked at how many people turned up to share it with me, I didn't realise I had that many friends and felt extremely humbled.

I was determined to pass my driving test and bought myself a car, a small, old Vauxhall Nova that would at least take me away from all of it when I needed to run. I passed my driving test after 3 months of unstoppable practice (This was shocking news after a small incident with a cat and a debate about whether or not I should have stopped for it, but we resigned that the cat had a narrow escape and I didn't put us in danger.) It was thrilling that little piece of paper offering me a new sense of freedom.

After much deliberation I made the decision to move out of Mum's house. It was as much to protect her as well as me. Too many people knew my association with Jack and would come knocking expecting me to bail him out. I should have been flattered, that's what I wanted wasn't it? To be a face in his world but I wasn't flattered, I was young, stupid and terrified and had no idea how deep Jack was in it when I accompanied him to multiple destinations to be his 'look out' while he disappeared for what was only minutes, but felt like hours. I wasn't entirely sure where they thought I could pluck their demands from when they arrived on our doorstep but patience was not on their radar and they would not have hesitated to make me physically pay if jack didn't come up trumps with the goods he owed them. The straw that broke the camels back came when I was offered twenty four hours to pay up or lose my limbs. It sounds laughable saying it out loud - like a scene from a gangster film, opening the front door, just a crack, to be faced with two men standing on my door step in black trench coats, housing a gun that they were not afraid to display, spitting threats at me. Most people would sit back detached from these kinds of films and enjoy the scene over a bowl of popcorn, but this was real. This was happening daily in my brother's underworld that I didn't understand and I knew beyond reasonable doubt from past experiences, that they meant every word, and would indeed return the following day for their severance pay.

In desperation I called the police for the first time in my life. I swallowed the lump in my throat and braced myself to find the strength to speak up and give the police an entrance into the drugs ring that was breeding more ghosts than the plague. I tapped my foot anxiously, blood draining from me as I prepared myself to give a statement. Now willing to do anything to protect me and mine. However, the phone call and cry for help was short lived when they told me to call back if anything actually happened to me! I hung up baffled and deflated that the only people that could truly help me would not do so until they found my lifeless body on the side of a road somewhere, at which point no doubt they would suddenly have enough interested staff to investigate. I needed to find another way to fix this and as a last resort I called my dad. I told him mum was suffering and lied that we needed four hundred pounds as we were behind on the payments for the house. I was ready to fight him on it and shamelessly remind him of 'that nights events' should the need arise. It didn't. Dad came up trumps for the first time in his life and transferred me the money. I paid the shadows the next day when they arrived on cue then told them to fuck off and leave us alone. "Next time shoot Jack, I'm really past caring!" And I was. Jack had gone awol of late, obviously in hiding leaving me to sweep up his shit as always.

It was now dangerous for mum me living here, so I packed my bags and did the unthinkable. I reported her to Arundel mental hospital. I didn't do it with malice, I just fell short on an answer for everything that was unravelling. I knew once on their radar she would receive the medical help she needed. As it turned out, in addition to sedatives and untold amounts of medication, the doctor that she had seen referred her to a specialist group for families of addicts, and there she met her new partner David. They met on common ground, both rock bottom in their grief, finding solace and comfort in each other, it was magic. She seemed happy for the first time in a long time even if it was fleeting between Jack dramas and psychotic outbursts. I promised I would visit her daily. I was so relieved that she had found a new shoulder to cry on, somebody on her level to talk to and sympathise with, somebody to make her smile and offer her some good in life. I'd carried her for so long that it felt good to share that load with somebody else and to know the doctors were keeping close to her because I was all out of ideas.

Although walking away from her made me feel uneasy, it was time. The day I left she was on good form, I gave her the biggest squeeze and told her I loved her more than anything in the world. Randomly she handed me a single roll of toilet paper. I laughed, not thinking much of it. But when I opened the front door to my new home, I realised it was the best parting gift I could have ever received. It was practical, something you don't think about until you're stuck without it. That was Mum in a nutshell - doing the best she could with what little she had. It wasn't much, but it made me smile, and somehow, it was the perfect goodbye.

I loved the freedom of driving and living alone. It wasn't much, but it was mine, and for the first time in years, I felt like I had a little bit of control over my life. I'd left behind the chaos of home, but I carried the emotional weight of it with me wherever I went. There was no escaping it completely. But here I was making a fresh start with a new address that Jack didn't have. I still spent time with Liam more often than not, which was easier now I had a car. It meant we could go to the park further away and I could take him home with me for weekends and watch Hercules of course coupled with a bowl of bubble-gum ice cream. The little pleasures I had long come to appreciate. I checked in with Scarlet every time I collected him, she was silently withering away but I couldn't take responsibility for her. I would ask after Jack curious to know he was ok but not curious enough to want to see him. I visited mum daily as promised but as night fell and I sat wrapped in a blanket on my sofa watching nothing and everything on my small television I felt truly content. Life was good.

Chapter 9

I never thought I'd end up working in a factory. It wasn't part of the plan but plans change, especially when money gets tight. College and living at mums felt far away, almost like a dream that belonged to someone else. My mum was unable to help, I refused to ask my dad and the bills kept piling up. So when I saw a sign in a shop window that a factory down the road was hiring with a salary that paid more than my retail job, I went for it. Beggars can't be choosers as they say.

The first thing that hit me when I walked through the door was the noise. Machines hummed, clanked, and buzzed all at once, like a mechanical orchestra that never stopped. I could barely hear myself think which was actually a welcome change. The air smelled of oil and metal, a mix that made my head swim at first. But everyone seemed to move through it like they didn't notice. People were used to it, I guessed.

The foreman, Mr. Hargrove, was waiting for me near the front. He was a big guy, probably in his 50s, with a thick moustache and a no-nonsense look about him. His hands were calloused, and he wore the kind of tired expression that comes from doing the same job for decades.

"You're the new kid?" he asked, squinting at me like I wasn't what he expected.

"Yeah," I nodded, trying not to sound nervous. "I'm Lucy." He grunted, then pointed across the floor.

"You'll be working on the assembly line. Pretty straightforward stuff. Keep your head down, do your work, and we'll get along fine."

I didn't know what else to say, so I just nodded again and smiled that was my answer to everything "smile and wave!" He gave me a brief tour of the factory, but it was hard to focus with all the noise. There were conveyor belts running all over, carrying metal parts that looked identical to me, but apparently, each piece had its own place in the process. Machines hissed and clattered, and workers moved between them like clockwork, fitting parts together or inspecting products before they were packed.

Finally, Mr. Hargrove led me to my station, a long metal table beside a conveyor belt. My job was simple, at least in theory: take each plastic part that came down the line, attach a small rubber seal to it, then send it along. Over and over again.

"You'll get the hang of it," he said, then walked off, leaving me standing there with nothing but a pair of gloves and a few curious glances from the other workers.

I started the shift awkwardly, fumbling with the seals as I tried to keep up with the steady pace of the belt. The pieces moved faster than I expected, and after the first few minutes, I was already falling behind. My hands felt clumsy, and I could feel my face getting hot, embarrassed that everyone around me seemed to have their routine down to a science.

By lunch, I was exhausted. My back ached from standing for hours, and my fingers were stiff from the repetitive motions. I grabbed my lunch, just a sandwich and a bottle of water and sat outside by myself, trying to block out the hum of the factory that still buzzed in my ears. It wasn't the life I'd imagined, but it was work. And that's what I needed.

Marcus found me halfway through my sandwich and plopped down next to me. He had been working at the factory for almost a year and looked like he belonged, with his worn-out work boots and grease-stained hands.

"How's the first day treating you?" he asked, grinning like he already knew the answer.

"Honestly? It's rough," I admitted, taking a sip of water. "How do you do this every day?" He shrugged.

"You get used to it. At first, it sucks. But after a while, your body just... deals with it, I guess."

I wasn't sure I believed him, but I didn't have much choice. This job was important, even if it was just temporary. I needed the money to survive on my own.

The second half of the day was a blur. I focused on getting into a rhythm, trying not to let the conveyor belt get ahead of me. It wasn't easy, but I started to catch on. After hours of sealing metal parts, my hands moved without thinking, and I found myself keeping pace. The minutes crawled by, but eventually, the bell rang, signalling the end of the shift.

My feet ached as I walked toward the time clock, and my whole body felt heavy. But as I punched out, I couldn't help feeling a small sense of accomplishment. It wasn't glamorous, but I'd made it through my first day.

On my way out, I ran into Mr. Hargrove again. He was talking to a couple of the older guys but paused when he saw me. "Not bad for your first day, kid," he said with a nod.

"Thanks," I replied, surprised by the compliment. "I'll get better." He gave me a look that was hard to read, but there was something almost approving in his eyes.

"You keep showing up, and that's half the battle."

That stuck with me as I headed home. The job wasn't fun, and it wasn't easy, but I could see why people did it. The routine, the steady pay, there was something dependable about it, something solid. It wasn't a dream job, but it was a job.

That night when I got home, I collapsed onto the sofa, completely drained. I thought about the day's events, I thought about the lives of others around me and how my mum had fought hard to survive on her own. I smiled to myself. My little two-bedroom home wasn't anything glamorous. It was tiny and the walls were plain, but it was my space where I could escape. My home that I would make lovely. I thought about the things I wanted to buy once I had enough money. I had taken my bed and Tv with me from mums house. The house had a lovely little kitchen with a space for a table and chairs once I had the money. I was excited about buying pictures and making it cosy. I was still smiling, a new sense of happiness that I had allowed to wash over me. My space I thought as I sipped a mug of tea and watched out the window at nothing.

It was one of those grey, rainy afternoons when everything feels heavy, like the world itself is tired. I sat at my kitchen table, sipping lemonade that had basically lost its 'ade' and was just flat lemon. Staring out the window I watched the steady patter of rain on the glass, it was comforting, a soundtrack to my solitude.

A knock at the door broke the silence, sharp and unexpected. I wasn't expecting anyone. For a moment, I thought about ignoring it. Maybe it was just a delivery, maybe it would go away. But the knock came again, more urgent this time.

Sighing, I pushed back from the table and went to the door, my mind running through possibilities. As I opened it, I felt my stomach drop. Standing in front of me was Jack.

I hadn't seen him for a while I thought he'd gone awol. The last time, he'd tried to tell me he was clean or at least, trying to be (again.) I still hadn't forgiven him for the visit from 'the shad-ows' and wondered if he even knew about it. His face was gaunt, skin stretched thin over his sharp cheekbones, eyes hollow and bloodshot like the 'ghosts' I met with him in number 39 that day. His clothes hung loose on his frame, soaked from the rain. His hands shook slightly, betraying his nerves. I was instantly annoyed that mum had obviously given him my address as no one else had it. I made a mental note that 'in case of emergency is not Jack randomly asking for it!'

"Hey," he mumbled, his voice barely louder than the rain. "Can I come in?"

For a moment, I hesitated. Part of me wanted to slam the door in his face, shut him out, pretend I didn't see the ruin in front of me. But this was Jack, my brother I'd grown up with, someone who for a while had been my friend before he got lost in this world of highs and lows. I stepped aside, and he shuffled past me into the hallway, dripping water onto the floor. I closed the door and followed him to the kitchen, the weight of his presence already making the room feel smaller.

He didn't sit down. He just stood there, his arms crossed tightly, like he was trying to hold himself together. I noticed the way his eyes darted around the room, taking everything in, but not really seeing it.

"You want coffee?" I asked, unsure of what else to say.

He shook his head. "No, man. I just... I didn't know where else to go." I nodded slowly, leaning against the door frame, keeping my distance.

"What's going on, Jack?"

He rubbed a hand over his face, sighing deeply. "I messed up, Luce. I... I've been using again. For a while now. I thought I had it under control, but... it got bad. Worse than before."

I stayed quiet, my heart sinking as he spoke. I had hoped, after the last time, that he would actually get clean. That the rehab, the therapy, the support from his family, something would stick. But heroin had its claws in him deeper than anyone could have imagined.

"I can't go back to home," he continued, his voice cracking. "She doesn't want me there anymore. Says I've burned too many bridges. And I don't blame her. I just... I don't know where to go. I thought maybe..."

He didn't finish the sentence, but I knew what he was asking. He wanted to stay, at least for a while. Maybe longer. He needed a place to crash, someone to help him get back on his feet AGAIN.

But I'd been down this road before when he'd asked to stay at mums. The late night calls, the desperate texts, the broken promises to get clean. Every time, I told myself it was the last time I'd let him back into my life. And every time, I caved, because this was Jack. But this time, it felt different. He looked worse than I'd ever seen him, like there was almost nothing left of the person I used to know.

"Jack..." I started, but the words stuck in my throat. How do you tell someone you care about that you can't save them?

He must have seen it in my face because he looked down at the floor, his jaw tightening. "I get it," he muttered. "You don't have to say it. I know."

Silence filled the room, thick and suffocating. I could hear the rain picking up outside, the wind rattling the windows. For a long moment, neither of us spoke.

"I'm not mad at you," I finally said, my voice soft. "But I can't do this again. I can't keep watching you destroy yourself and pull everyone else down with you."

He nodded slowly, still staring at the floor. "Yeah. I know." I took a deep breath, trying to find the right words, knowing there wasn't any.

"You need help, Jack. Real help. A place that can actually get you clean and stay clean."

"I've tried," he whispered, his voice barely audible. "But I keep failing. I don't think I can do it anymore."

Hearing him say that broke something inside me. I wanted to grab him by the shoulders, shake him, tell him that he could, that he had to keep trying. But I knew that wouldn't change anything. Not really.

"I can't let you stay here," I said, forcing the words out. "I'm sorry. But I can drive you to a clinic. We can find somewhere that'll take you in. Mum has found so many places for you Jack what about one of those?"

Jack didn't respond for a while. He just stood there, his whole body trembling now. I thought he might explode, scream, cry, something. But when he finally looked up, his eyes were empty, like he'd already given up.

"I'll figure it out," he mumbled, turning toward the door. "I shouldn't have come."

"Wait," I said, reaching out as he started to leave. "Let me help you. Just not like this. Let me drive you somewhere. It took every ounce of my being not to retract what I had said and to make it better and let him stay with me. But this was my little home, my safe haven in the town of Rudford where the police didn't know us, where People wouldn't knock because Jack owed them money. I wanted to be away from that. I couldn't live that life anymore.

He shook his head, already halfway out the door. "No. You don't have to do that. I'll be fine."

I watched as he walked out into the rain, his silhouette fading into the grey mist. For a moment, I stood there, frozen, part of me wanting to run after him, drag him back inside, and fix everything. But I knew I couldn't. Not this time.

As I closed the door, the house felt emptier than before. I leaned against the wall, feeling the weight of guilt and helplessness settle over me. I'd done what I could. But it didn't feel like enough.

It never does.

That night I sat at my new table, the familiar heaviness consuming me and I wrote to him. A poem, it seemed somehow less painful than a letter,

Years ago when you were just sixteen, given envy and friendship and grace,

For reasons I cannot see behind, you let something so lethal take your life's place.

Was it just a game to start with? Something you thought you would try.

Was it a cry out for help? Something you knew would help you to die?

In two seconds you swallowed, waiting 8 for it to sink in,

Your head started rushing, you were feeling so ill, Dear brother what were you thinking?

Did you do it because you wanted to? Or was it all just for a dare?

Your problem started at that time, and it didn't stop there.

You have continued to take it again and again, now you no longer have self-control,

Nothing seems to be enough, as you are digging yourself into a deeper hole.

For many years I have watched you grow from a boy into a man,

Now you have no clue what's going on around you, because of your drug diet plan.

You have so many people that care about you, you have no reason to stay in this hell,

You have offers of help every day of your life, yet it's in this pain and misery you are choosing to dwell.

It is hurting the people around you to see that a drug is now what you rely on to live,

I feel so empty and worthless for all the pointless help I have tried to give.

Now I can no longer help you my brother, you are lost inside your own head,

I am helplessly watching you hurt yourself more, knowing that you'll soon be dead.

Please remember for me this fact of your life, that it was your decision to close your own door,

Unlike lots of others you have had the choice, of whether to live or to sleep evermore.

No matter where life takes you, I want you to know that my love never dies,

But I now have to shut you off Jack, as I can no longer cope with the hurt in your eyes.

As tears dripped onto the envelope. I closed it and would post it first thing in the morning. With that I took myself to bed. Feeling heavy but freer than ever.

Chapter 10

The factory was loud, like always. Machines clanked and roared, drowning out any chance of real conversation. The air was heavy with the smell of oil and hot metal, mixing with the sweat of people who had been there for hours, maybe even years. I was still new, just a few months in, but the routine had already become familiar. Days blurred together, one shift after the next.

I worked at a station assembling parts for some kind of engine. I didn't know much about what I was doing beyond the steps I'd memorized: attach, screw, pass it down the line. Repeat, repeat, repeat. Eight hours of that, with the occasional whistle blow for a lunch break. It was mindless, but it paid well enough to keep me going.

That's when I met Wes.

He worked on the line a couple of stations down, doing the same monotonous task. At first, we didn't talk much just a quick nod or he'd mutter "What's up" during breaks. But after a while, we started sitting together in the break room. He was older, probably in his mid-20s, and had a laid back attitude about everything, like nothing ever fazed him.

"You ever get sick of this place?" he asked one day as we sat outside, leaning against the back of the factory wall. He lit a cigarette and offered me one, which I waved off.

"Yeah, pretty much every day," I laughed, though there wasn't much humour behind it. "But it's a job, right?"

Wes smirked, taking a long drag. "Sure. But there's more to life than just this grind, you know?" I didn't answer. What was I supposed to say? I was still only seventeen, just busy trying to save up some money and figure out what the hell I was going to do with my life. College hadn't worked out the way I thought it would, and the idea of being stuck in this factory for years was already weighing on me. The hours worked for school pick-ups though 6am until 2pm gave me the rest of the day so I could always be there for Liam if and when ever required. I smiled at the thought of the bedroom in my perfect little house that I had decorated for Liam. This job had allowed me another puzzle piece in my life that offered me freedom with the money it paid and that was priceless. I didn't have another plan. This was it for now.

One night after a shift, Wes asked if I wanted to hang out for a bit. I didn't have anywhere else to be, so I agreed. We ended up in his clapped out Fiesta with a sound speaker practically the same size as the car itself, driving around town with the windows down, music blaring. It was nice to feel the breeze on my face after being stuck in the stuffy factory all day.

Eventually, we pulled up to an empty car park behind some old warehouse. Wes turned off the engine and leaned back in his seat, pulling something out of his pocket. A small bag with white powder inside.

I froze. I'd heard about crack before, of course. It was the drug people took to stay awake, to work harder, party longer, whatever. I knew it was bad news. I knew I shouldn't even be there in that moment, watching him casually pour a little bit onto a piece of foil, like it was no big deal but it wasn't heroine was it.

"You ever tried it?" Wes asked, noticing the look on my face. I shook my head.

"Nah, I don't mess with that stuff."

He shrugged, lighting a flame beneath the foil and inhaling. He exhaled slowly, his eyes glazing over just a little. "It's not as bad as everyone makes it out to be. Just a little pick-me-up. Makes the long shifts easier, you know?"

I didn't know what to say. Part of me was screaming to get out of the car, to walk away from this. But the other part, the part that was tired of feeling tired, that was sick of the grind, of the monotony, was curious. What would it feel like to just... escape for a bit? To not care about anything for once?

Wes must have sensed the hesitation because he grinned, holding the foil out toward me. "Look, if you don't want to, no pressure. But if you do... I promise, it'll make you feel like you can take on the world."

My heart was pounding. I knew it was wrong. I knew there were a million reasons why I shouldn't. But in that moment, I was so tired. Tired of feeling like I was going nowhere. Tired of being stuck.

So, I took it.

The first hit wasn't what I expected. There was a burn in my throat, and for a second, I thought I'd cough it all up. But then it hit, slowly at first, then faster. My heart raced, but instead of fear, I felt... alive. My body buzzed with energy, like I could run a marathon or stay awake for days. The world around me sharpened, every detail suddenly clearer.

Wes looked over at me, nodding. "Feels good, right?"

I nodded, unable to find the words. Everything felt good. The factory, the endless shifts, the uncertainty about my future, it all faded into the background. None of it mattered anymore. All that existed was this moment, this rush of energy coursing through me.

For the first time in months, I didn't feel stuck. I didn't feel trapped. I felt free. But deep down, even as the euphoria took over, I knew I'd made a mistake. I knew this wasn't the answer to my problems. It wasn't going to fix anything. It was just a distraction, a temporary escape.

That night, when I finally made it back to my house, I couldn't sleep. My mind raced, my body still buzzing with energy hours after the high had worn off. I lay in bed, staring at the ceiling, my thoughts spiralling. What had I just done?

I couldn't shake the guilt. I couldn't shake the fear that this was the start of something I wouldn't be able to control. The factory, the job, the life I was trying to build, it was all still there, looming over me, and no amount of speed was going to make it go away.

The next morning, I dragged myself into work, feeling the weight of my decision hanging over me. Wes was there, same as always, nodding at me like nothing had changed. But for me, everything had. I'd crossed a line and id liked it, and now I had to figure out how to make sure I didn't cross it again.

In many ways life was good, it really was. I had Liam, with his infectious laugh and his wide-eyed excitement about the world. Watching him grow was a constant source of joy, his smile a reminder that innocence still existed. Today was no different. We spent hours at the park, his high-pitched voice breaking into song as I pushed him on the swings. His little hands grasped the chains tightly, eyes closed, as if he could soar above all of us if only he believed enough.

I chased him around the park, our laughter filling the open air. He was so fast for a kid about to turn five, and it always surprised me. But I could see the pure joy radiating from him, his happiness so uncomplicated. It was moments like this that kept me grounded, that helped me remember what mattered.

As we sat on the bench with our bubble-gum ice cream, still Liam's favourite, I watched the sky change colour. The sun was dipping low, casting a warm orange glow over the park, and I took a deep breath, feeling content. Liam smeared bright blue ice cream across his face and grinned up at me, his toothy smile melting my heart like always.

"You got a bit there," I teased, pointing to his sticky cheek. He giggled, licking the ice cream off with the dedication of someone who believed it was the greatest treat in the world. And maybe, for him, it was.

For me? Life's sweetness had a different flavour once. A darker one. One that I tried not to think about too often, though it crept into my thoughts, especially when things got too quiet. It wasn't that long ago when I'd found a different kind of escape, a sharper, more dangerous one. Drugs had been an answer to—an easy one. And for a time, I'd loved it. Maybe too much.

Wes was good company. He never asked for much, but he'd been around when things were harder, when I couldn't stand the silence in my head or the weight on my chest. I hadn't seen him as much recently, though. He wanted to see me more, and honestly, I missed the calm he brought with him, the ease in which he moved through life. But I wasn't sure I could trust myself around him. Not with what we shared, not with the pull I still felt.

I hadn't told him I was trying to forget. How much I'd enjoyed it, the high, the feeling of invincibility. And that was the hardest part. It wasn't just the drugs. It was the version of me that didn't care about the consequences, that liked not caring.

But I wasn't that person. Not with Liam needing me, not with his mum working long hours at the hospital, her shifts swallowing up her time. I didn't see Jack anymore, not since I sent him that poem. I wasn't sure what he thought about it, if he even read it. He had his own life. We were both moving in different directions, even if part of me still ached at his absence no matter what chaos it brought.

As I sipped my tea later that evening, once I had dropped Liam home, I felt the familiar stir of restlessness beneath my skin. Tea. The answer to everything when you were an adult, or so I told myself. It wasn't bubble-gum ice cream, but it would have to do.

I busied myself with the mundane, washing dishes, wiping down the kitchen sides. Keeping my hands moving so my mind wouldn't wander. But even so, the memories crept in, uninvited. The late nights, the way my heart raced in my chest, not with excitement but with the sheer adrenaline of it all. It was intoxicating in a way I didn't want to admit out loud. But I secretly craved that escape. Maybe I could just take a little my eyes kept glancing at the phone. It wouldn't hurt anyone would it. I opened a can of beans to put on my toast and stared at the sharp edge of the tin. Without hesitation or thought of any kind I dragged my finger across it. The cut was deep and bled for England. I don't know what I was thinking. Why did I just do that? The pain was a release. I enjoyed the distraction of that sting. I wrapped the cut in tissue and threw the beans away shaking my head to try and makes sense of what I'd just done.

I thought about calling Wes. He never judged me but I didn't trust myself to be around him without slipping, without remembering how good it felt when nothing mattered in the midst of our high.

But I couldn't. Life wasn't about that. I had a job, good friends, a home. A life that, on the surface, was solid. I had responsibilities. Liam needed me, and I wasn't about to let him down. Not him, not his mum, not my mum. I had to be a person they could count on.

As the days blurred into each other, I kept myself busy accidentally on purpose cutting myself regularly on any sharp objects I came across. Then I would sit in my own quiet for a minute letting the pain envelope me, hoping that eventually, I would forget my other cravings. That the pull would lessen, that I wouldn't have to fight so hard to stay on this side of the line. Because life was good. It was enough. I had to believe that. Even on the nights when the memories of Jack and the events we suffered together felt closer than they should. I reminded myself of what I had now.

Tomorrow, I'd take Liam back to the park, and we'd chase each other around again. We'd sing songs, eat more ice cream, and for a while, I'd forget again. Just for a while.

Chapter 11

I was enjoying work in the factory. During a quality audit I suggested that our procedures were out of date and offered to rewrite them myself. I was organised and self-motivated which led me to being moved away from the machines and picking up administration work. I was given a desk in the huge office that overlooked the factory floor. I enjoyed banter with my colleagues that I now considered my friends. As I sat looking through our monthly report my mobile phone rang, cutting through the steady hum of the machinery just outside the window. I glanced at the caller ID - Mum. A chill ran down my spine. She never called during work hours unless something was wrong and if it was Dave telling me she was having another one of her fits he'd have to get help elsewhere I couldn't keep leaving work early. I answered, my voice low.

"Mum?" She was sobbing. My stomach turned.

"It's Jack..." My blood ran cold. "they've arrested him." My blood returned. Relief, I think.

I felt like the floor dropped out from under me. I had been waiting for this call. For months, maybe even years, I had dreaded that something would happen to my brother, that one day I'd hear he was dead, found in some alley, or overdosed in some dingy flat. But this... this was almost a relief. At least he was alive. Arrested, but alive.

"They raided the house," Mum continued, her voice cracking, "Luce... oh God, they turned the house upside down, Scarlet is in bits..."

I swallowed hard, a wave of nausea rising up. I pictured it, the police tearing through the house, their shouts filling the small space while Liam watched, confused, terrified. My chest tightened as Mum's sobs echoed in my ear.

"Mum. Where's Liam? Mum?" She continued to sob, and a deep voice cut in the other end. The wailing started "Luce its David." "OK hi. Where's Liam?" Mums partner was gently spoken with a deep voice. "Your mum is struggling Luce." No shit sherlock! "She's extremely upset and worried about what's going to happen to Jack." Jack? Fuck Jack! I thought but thankfully kept my thoughts to myself.

"Ok give her a big squeeze and tell her I love her more than anything. I'll come and see her soon." I hung up knowing David would take good care of her. Already standing up from my desk, I looked at my boss "I've got to go." He didn't try to stop me or ask for an explanation as I grabbed my bag and hurried out of work.

My thoughts were racing, my hands shaking as I rummaged in my bag for my car keys. The drive to Jack's house felt endless. Every red light, every slow-moving car in front of me stretched those twenty minutes into an eternity. I kept thinking about Liam. His sweet little face, the way he looked up at me with so much trust. How could he possibly make sense of any of this?

When I finally arrived, the front door was wide open. I hesitated for a second before stepping inside, my heart pounding in my chest. The house looked like it had been ransacked, everything tipped over or scattered across the floor. The lid of the toilet basin was off, drawers yanked from their places, contents spilled everywhere. Perhaps they could give my mum a job!

Scarlet was sitting on the sofa, smoking, her face streaked with silent tears. She stared ahead, glassy-eyed, completely motionless except for the occasional tremble of her hands. But Liam, where was Liam?

I scanned the room, stepping through the mess, trying to ignore the knot tightening in my stomach. Then I saw it, a small leg sticking out from the gap between the sofa and the wall. I rushed over and crouched down, my heart breaking as I saw that little body curled up, his hands still clamped over his ears, his face flushed red from crying. He had hidden himself away from the chaos, trying to block out the terror of it all I'm sure and yet somehow, managed to fall asleep.

I reached for him gently, lifting him into my arms. His little body nestled against me, his breath hiccupping with soft, broken sobs as he stirred. He clung to me, his fingers gripping my shirt, and I could feel the deep, lingering tremor of fear running through him.

"It's okay, I've got you," I whispered, rocking him slightly as I stood. "You're safe now."

I moved to his bedroom, or what was left of it. The drawers had been pulled out, clothes and toys tossed across the floor like nothing in that house mattered. I grabbed some of his things, throwing them into a small bag, trying to ignore the hollow ache in my chest.

Back in the living room, Scarlet hadn't moved. She just stared into the distance, the cigarette between her fingers burning down, unnoticed. I stood in front of her for a moment, Liam heavy in my arms.

"Why don't I take him for a couple of days to give you some time to get sorted?" Silence. "Do you want me to call anybody?" I continued softly, not wanting to startle her. She didn't respond at first, but I knew she heard me. Her eyes flickered briefly in my direction, then back to the floor. I didn't know what the best thing to do was. I wanted to get out of there I knew that much. I'd like to have taken her with me as well as Liam. There's an idea they can both stay in my spare room together. "Scarlet do you want to come back with me? It will give you a break away from this?" Still nothing. The cigarette was nearly touching her fingers as she blinked away tears and continued staring in front of her.

"Ok well, how about I take Liam today and give you some time then we can talk tomorrow?" Another blink, another tear but still silence. "I can help you clean up when I come back," I added, more for my own guilt than anything else. I didn't want to leave her alone, but Liam came first. I just needed to get him out of there, away from the chaos and the wreckage.

Before I left, I made her a cup of tea. It was the only thing I could think to do, something small in the face of everything, but maybe it would help. I set it down next to her, then leaned in and kissed her forehead, feeling the coolness of her skin. Scarlet was petite she has green eyes once so bright and full of life and thick black hair that fell down her back. She looked lost in her oversized jeans and a baggy t shirt. I felt so sad for her. She was lost in her own torment, but I couldn't help her. I didn't know how. She didn't say anything, didn't even look up, but a further single tear slid down her cheek.

"I'll be back," I promised. I wasn't sure if I believed it, but I needed to say it. I needed to believe that somehow, I could fix at least some part of this mess.

With Liam still clinging to me, I walked out of the house and didn't look back, his soft hiccups the only sound breaking the silence. As I buckled him into the car, his eyes fluttered open for a moment, still glazed with exhaustion and fear.

"Can we go home?" he whispered; his voice so small it almost broke me.

I brushed a strand of hair off his forehead and nodded. "Yeah, buddy. You're coming home with me."

As I pulled away from the house, my mind raced with thoughts of Jack, of the raid, of how everything had come to this. I knew he'd chosen his path, made his decisions, but it was hard not to feel the weight of it all crashing down on everyone else. On Mum, on Scarlet, on me and now on Liam, too. I would have to ring David and see if mum was ok, but for now, I had to focus on the little boy in the backseat. The rest of it would have to wait.

Chapter 12

I had only been living on my own for a short while, barely getting the hang of it when my world turned upside down and I took Liam to stay with me. The thought itself was surreal. I had turned up to Scarlets house the following day as promised to find her still sat in the same spot, wearing the same clothes. Not crying, not speaking just fixated on the wall. I couldn't get a response out of her so cleaned what I could of the wreckage whilst Liam played with his toys making no attempt to engage with his mother. I made her tea with five sugars in to attempt to kickstart her again but she remained frozen and would not take the cup from me. When all else failed and I had tidied up the house I called 999. I had no contact numbers for scarlets family and could not hack the password to get into her phone. I didn't know what else to do and she was scaring me. Maybe the ambulance could get her to drink something. Im not sure why tea is my answer to everything? I felt so useless. I needed help and that help arrived quickly in the form of an ambulance. I watched them wrap scarlet in a foil blanket and attempt to move her. She would not respond to anybody at all. Shock they said. Break down they said. They took her away that day. The house was tidy when I left, it hid a thousand truths of the last few days events. In the space of just two days Liam had watched his parents marched out of the house, at least the latter exit was more gentle. I had no choice but to return home with Liam in tow and prepare for a few weeks of him staying with me whilst Scarlet received the help she needed.

Liam had been through a lot. Too much, for someone his age. His world had been ripped apart, and I was terrified of what that meant for both of us. I knew how much he loved his dad and seeing him hurt like this broke my heart, but in the midst of all the chaos, Liam knew me. He trusted me. Somehow, that made me feel like I had to be strong.

The first few nights he stayed with me, he slept in my bed with me "Do you want a bedtime story?" I asked, hoping to make him feel at ease. His wide eyes stared at me, tired but trusting.

"Okay," he whispered.

I picked out 'Guess how much I love you,' that I'd bought for him the previous year. I read it over and over again until he fell asleep, curled up like a little ball. For a second, I let myself feel proud when I had managed the first couple of nights. However, the real challenges began the next day.

Taking Liam to school was a new reality that would have to be part of my daily routine. I had to figure out how to work my shifts around his schedule, pack lunches, and drop him off in the mornings. That morning, I sent him with a packed lunch that I quickly threw together hoping it would be approved.

I arrived in the car park to drop him off at School, and the look on his face nearly broke me. He clung to my leg, his small hand gripping me like I was his lifeline. I knelt down to his level, feeling panic rise in my chest as I tried to figure out how to reassure him. "You'll be okay, buddy. I'll pick you up right after school, I promise," I said, hoping that sounded convincing.

His big eyes, filled with uncertainty, searched mine for a moment. Then he nodded. The teacher took his hand and led him into the classroom as he looked back at me with solemn eyes.

At work, I couldn't focus. My mind kept drifting back to him, wondering if he was scared or confused or missing me. We hadn't discussed what had happened with Jack and the arrest and I wasn't quite sure how, when or whether to approach it. I decided against talking to the school about it for now, the Authorities had intervened enough already and I was unsure how long our new arrangement would last. I clocked out from work as early as I could, racing back to the school. When I saw him standing there waiting for me with a smile on his face. The relief was overwhelming.

But as the days went on, things got harder. Meal planning, which I had never been great at even for myself, became a guessing game. Liam was picky. He liked chicken nuggets, chocolate cereal, and snacks, definitely not the kind of stuff I should be feeding him every day. Nuggets was fine for babysitting him and for myself I lived on ready meals, but now he was staying with me I felt a new responsibility that he would need vitamins and fruit or something to keep him growing. I needed to be his strong which meant strong healthy food. I spent nights scouring the internet for easy, healthy meals that I could actually afford on my tight budget. I knew nothing of the benefit system and even if I had been aware, I wouldn't have been brave enough to ask for help for fear of losing Liam as well as Jack.

In the coming weeks I learned how to make pasta with vegetables, homemade smoothies, and even a child-friendly stir fry so I counted that as a win.

Liam had boundless energy I could barely keep up with. After work and school, he'd want to run, play, and pretend he was a superhero saving the world. Meanwhile, I was exhausted, crashing on the couch as he zoomed around the house in his make-believe world.

The hardest part was the worry. The constant knot in my stomach. Was I doing enough for him? Was he okay? I'd lie awake at night, anxious about whether I was making the right decisions. I didn't know what I was doing, but somehow, I couldn't let myself fail him. I hadn't told my mum he was staying with me. She was beyond sunk and David was trying to get her the help that she needed to keep her with us. She had threatened to take her own life the day that Jack was arrested. She had hit fifty feet below rock bottom and was now dangling on a thread somewhere between life and death. We may have to get her sectioned for her own good but like me, David was patient and hoped that with enough love between us, we could heal her and get her well. I would never burden her with this.

In addition, there was Liams birthday to worry about. His 5th birthday was approaching fast, and I wanted to make it special for him. Liam had been through so much, he deserved something good in his life, something that felt normal and happy, but throwing a birthday party was easier said than done. I had no idea how to plan a party for a five-year-old, I mean games I got covered but do you invite parents? What's the cut off age? Or would people be grateful to dump their little bundles of joy off and leg it for a couple of hours respite? If I did invite parents did I need to feed them too? Did other parents eat ready meals?? plus, I definitely didn't have much money to spend. I drove myself crazy panicking at the thought of letting him down.

I found myself scrolling through the internet late one night, looking for ideas on how to throw a budget-friendly kids' party. Balloons, a homemade cake, maybe some simple games in the park, I looked away from the screen and pictured it, NOPE, I'm not taking ten five-year-olds to the park on my own that sounds like hell. I'll contain them indoors. I could manage that, I told myself. Liam loved dinosaurs, so I started planning a dino-themed party. I stayed up late making decorations out of paper and streamers ready for his big day and practiced how to bake a cake from scratch. I sat with him talking about who his school friends were and who he wanted to invite. For that moment, it felt like everything was going to be okay.

It wasn't easy, not by a long shot. Some days, I still felt overwhelmed and scared that I was not enough for him, but when I saw the way Liam looked at me, the way he trusted me and felt safe, I knew that I would keep going. I would keep showing up for him, he is my family, and no matter what, I would always find a way to make sure he was okay, even if I had to figure it out as I went along. Sometimes, being scared doesn't matter as much as being there, and for Liam, I will always be there.

Since Jack got arrested, I've been drowning in a whirlpool of emotions. Guilt gnawed at me, constantly and insistently, reminding me that I'd abandoned him when he needed me most. There was also relief, at least he wasn't dead. That had been my biggest fear for months, finding him lifeless, a final casualty of the drugs that had already stolen so much of him. Now he was alive, but inside four walls and that terrified me too. How would he cope in prison? I couldn't picture it, the Jack I once knew trapped in that world, isolated from everything familiar. The truth was, I didn't know this new version of him at all.

The newspapers were plastered with the story: "Biggest Drug Sting in Lowcroft," "Eight Arrested in Major Heroin Operation." The headlines were everywhere, glaring, and impossible to escape. The story spread faster than the drugs themselves. I'd known Jack was using, but I had no idea how deep it went – Heroin, A drug ring, importing it! The worst part was that he had been selling it to feed his own habit, helping to push this poison into other people's lives.

Scarlet's breakdown was confirmed by the hospital and they sectioned her for her own good. I couldn't blame her and saw it for myself the day I left her for the second time and I took Liam. She was frozen and numb unable to look or speak I should have stayed and helped her, followed them to the hospital, but I'm just one person myself. She had tried for years to save Jack, to keep their family together, making excuses for him and standing by his side no matter what trouble he brought to her doorstep. He was hers and she was loyal to him, but the arrest was the final straw. She needed time and care to heal and put herself back together. In sync, Mum unravelled too. The shock and shame of it all hit her hard, but David, continued to be solid. He stood by her, kept her grounded, and helped her find a way through. Mum managed to avoid being sectioned for a long period of time and was given medication to assist. She was recommended a support group for families of addicts. The book they gave her, 'Today a Better Way,' became her lifeline. It laid out steps of survival for family members all experiencing the same thing, one painful day at a time.

And me? I retreated into my walls. The ones I'd carefully built, brick by brick, over the years to keep the chaos out. Liam was my anchor, my escape. He was healthy, happy, innocent in all of this. His world was simple and safe, and I was determined to keep it that way. We had a routine, one that felt almost perfect from the outside. Every morning, I dropped him off at school, and at dinner times with the help of a blender, I even managed to sneak vegetables into his food without complaint. Then there was work, I threw myself into it like I was walking into another realm every day, I thrived on being needed and had to keep myself busy constantly. Stopping meant time for thinking and that I didn't have the time for or capacity to deal with. Nathan, my manager allowed me to do admin from home which gave me the flexibility of being able to plan my day around school runs, and that balance was just enough space to pretend life was normal, even though nothing was. I didn't harm myself again though the thoughts were there sometimes, poking at me, but I resisted, and I stayed away from Wes and drugs.

Chapter 13

The air felt heavy as I walked toward Carlingford Prison, the massive stone walls looming ahead like a fortress built to keep out hope. The thought of seeing Jack made my stomach churn. I walked heavily weighing up the fact that he's my brother, but also feels more of a stranger now. How had it come to this? How had the boy I grew up with, who taught me how to ride a bike and pulled pranks on our neighbours, become a man selling heroin to feed a £300-a-day habit?

I had read the articles over and over, hoping that maybe, in some twisted way, they were not talking about my brother. There were eight of them arrested, surely it was somebody else's fault. How naive I had been! It was all there in black and white, CCTV footage had caught him dealing heroin to undercover police of all people. Thousands of pounds worth sold on multiple occasions from the back of a hippy van, somehow, the irony of that made it worse. A freedom-loving van, of all things, tied to the chains of addiction. He was still waiting to be sentenced, he'd be lucky if they didn't give him life for it, especially with being party to importing it. Still, the image was burned into my mind: Jack, hair straggly, face gaunt, handing over bags of poison like they were sweets.

I felt like I was suffocating as I handed over my ID to the guard at the visitors' entrance, and after a few security checks, I was led into a sterile, white-walled room. They sat me down at a table, and I waited, the minutes dragging on. The clock ticked, ticking louder with every second that passed, or maybe that was just my heartbeat, that familiar hammering in my chest that I had somehow become accustomed too.

When the door finally creaked open, my breath caught, and my heart sank. I barely recognized him. He looked awful like he was already dead, his body still there but the rest of him gone. I struggled to find any trace of the brother I used to know. The drugs had hollowed him out, and now, without them, he was suffering even more. They had him on methadone, the real stuff this time, not the diluted rubbish he'd tried to manage with before. It was supposed to help, but all I could see was pain.

He looked emaciated, eyes hollowed out like he hadn't slept in days, skin pale from being locked away indoors. His prison clothes hung off him, and I couldn't help but think how much worse he looked than the last time I'd seen him. I thought back to the day I turned my back on him, a lump rose in my throat at the thought of what I had done. Maybe if I had been there more this wouldn't have happened? Maybe I could have stopped him.

I knew it wasn't true but it's so easy to be an imposter to yourself.

The arrest had forced him to go cold turkey and it showed. But even in prison, I knew there were ways to get it. He had mentioned it in his letter, the half-hearted promise to "stay clean" despite temptations he didn't write it that way as everything gets screened before it goes in and out of those walls, but I knew by the way it was written what he was trying to tell me. However, the amounts he could get inside didn't match the beast of a habit he'd built on the outside. He looked haunted, as though part of him had died when the drugs stopped flowing in the way he was used to.

He sat down across from me, and for a moment, neither of us spoke. The silence between us was deafening. It was strange having so much to say, yet not knowing where to start.

"How are you?" I finally asked, my voice smaller than I expected and a little embarrassed at such a feeble question.

He shrugged, eyes darting around the room before landing on me. "Same as anyone in here, I guess." I was almost irritated by his nonchalance.

We talked about nothing and everything, about Liam, and how I'd taken him in since Scarlet was too unwell to care for him. I wasn't helping the situation, but he needed to know it wasn't just himself he put in a prison by doing this. I told him Liam was doing well, but I could see in Jack's face that he knew I was just trying to keep things light. The truth was, Liam was devastated. Every night he asked when he was going to see his dad, and every night I didn't know how to answer. "Working away" just wasn't cutting it, he'd wanted to know more.

Jack looked at me, then down at the table, his fingers twitching like they were itching for a fix. He apologized, but it didn't feel real, or maybe it felt too real, too raw. The damage he'd caused was insurmountable. He had broken our family apart, broken himself in the process, and yet, there I was sitting across from him, hating him, and loving him all at once.

How can you love and hate someone so much? I stared at him, trying to reconcile the brother I knew with the man he had become. I wanted to scream at him, to shake him, to tell him what he had done, what he had thrown away, but I didn't. I just sat there, my heart breaking in silence. I had mastered this now.

An hour passed quicker than I expected, though it felt like a lifetime. The guard came to tell me time was up, and I felt sick to my stomach at the thought of leaving him there. As much as I hated what he had become, I couldn't stand the idea of walking out and leaving him in this cold, lifeless place.

"I'll send you some money," I said as I stood, my voice trembling. "Whatever you need, you'll be fine. Stay strong you've got this."

Jack nodded, his eyes dull, like he had heard those words a thousand times but didn't believe them anymore. The truth was, I didn't have any spare money. I was barely scraping by as it was, but I knew I'd find a way. I always did when it came to

Jack, whether it was bailing him out of trouble or picking up the pieces of his life.

I promised him I'd come back to see him soon, and he nodded again, his lips twitching into a faint, tired smile.

As I walked out, I felt like I was leaving a piece of myself behind. My heart shattered, each step heavier than the last. It wasn't just the walls of the prison that trapped him, it was everything he had done, everything he had lost, everything I couldn't fix. Still after everything, I couldn't stop caring. Even when he didn't deserve it, I couldn't stop loving my brother. That was the part that hurt the most.

When I left the prison, I drove straight to pick Liam up from school. The contrast between the two worlds jarring. I held him tightly, like somehow I could shield him from the reality I couldn't seem to escape.

In true Lucy style, I took a deep breath and forced myself to switch gears. "Let's plan your birthday party, chicken?" I asked him, smiling as though the weight of everything hadn't just nearly crushed me.

"What? Can I have a proper party? Where? Can Charlie come?" His face lit up, and for a second, everything felt light again.

"Yes, pickle. Charlie can come," I reassured him. We went home and we laughed together, as I explained that no his teachers would not be able to attend. We lost time then as we made lists of who to invite and what games to play.

For those few moments, I tucked all the hurt deep inside, out of reach. For Liam, I could keep up the image of a perfect life, at least for a little while longer. No matter how hard I tried though, I couldn't shake the thought of Jack. How could things have gotten so bad without me seeing it? Without me doing something? I didn't know if he'd survive the prison sentence or the demons he was battling, and that fear lingered in the background of everything I did.

For now though, all I could do was hold onto the little things. Liam's party, his smile, and the hope that somehow, we'd all make it through this mess.

Chapter 14

The day of Liams birthday party finally arrived, and Liam was super excited about the prospect of turning five. He was at that age where making friends at school was a big deal, and his little world was full of laughter, games, and endless curiosity. Whatever "normal" meant, I was doing my best to give it to him, even though I was still only seventeen myself.

We'd invited ten of his friends, and when only six turned up, I felt a flicker of panic. I so desperately wanted it to be perfect for him.

We had set up the dining table with dinosaur-themed plates, balloons, and his homemade cake, which leaned slightly to the side and resembled some sort of pre historic cave blob than a dinosaur or something a little ruder, I thought as I tilted my head suddenly grateful I had decided against inviting the other parents to stay. I had neatly laid out party rings, crisps, sandwiches cut into dinosaur shapes, sausage rolls, pizza, literally enough to feed the entire school let alone 10 friends. I prayed it would all be enough. Liam was ecstatic. His eyes lit up when he saw the decorations, and I could see, for the first time in a while, pure joy on his face.

He ran around with his friends laughing and playing all energy and noise, while I sat back watching. I wanted him to feel like his birthday was everything he hoped it would be, and maybe a little more.

I genuinely don't know how people cope with multiple children, this lot were crazy whirlwinds, like six mini Tasmanian devils all on a sugar rush. Once the cushions started being catapulted off the sofa, I decided it was time to kick off the games.

We started with a 'Dinosaur Egg Hunt.' I had hidden plastic eggs filled with sweets and small dinosaur toys around the garden. The kids, armed with their little pointy party hats, went on a prehistoric adventure to find them I was surprisingly good at playing the big mummy dinosaur chasing them round the garden while they were finding them. The excitement on their faces when they found an egg was priceless, and it actually worked out well that there were fewer kids.

Next up was "Pin the Tail on the Dinosaur." I had a big poster of a T. rex, and the children all took turns trying to place the tail in the right spot while blindfolded. It was hilarious! They all got pretty competitive, but in a fun way. The smaller group meant everyone got multiple turns so there was more laughter than frustration and nobody felt left out or overwhelmed.

We also played a "Dino Stomp" game, where I blew up a bunch of balloons, tied them to the children's ankles, and they had to stomp and pop each other's "dino eggs." This turned into a frenzy of running and laughter although the balloons bursting and the kids screaming was starting to make my left eye twitch (I must apologise to the neighbours later.) We changed game rapidly once the kids started bopping each other's faces with any leftover balloons. Five-year-olds are relentless!

Last but not least came Pass the Parcel, the game that had taken me what felt like a lifetime to wrap. Layer upon layer of newspaper, taped up clumsily, the task growing more tedious with each sheet. As they tore through the wrapping, I found myself holding my breath. It was innocent enough, just newspaper, but as the layers peeled back, I spotted it - Jack's mug shot staring out from one of the crumpled pages.

My heart stopped. How had I not noticed that the night before? It was like time froze as that image passed from child to child, Jack's hollowed eyes glancing up briefly being passed from child to child until I pressed paused on the music and the page was crumpled again. I prayed Liam wouldn't notice, that none of the kids would. They didn't. The music was too loud, their laughter too contagious, and I exhaled in relief when the parcel reached the final child and the toy inside was revealed.

Liam didn't notice a thing. He was having the best time, belly-laughing with his friends as they sat on the floor in their little triangle party hats. They looked like seven dwarves, their tiny figures bouncing with excitement, all smiles, and rosy cheeks.

For a moment, I allowed myself to breathe again. The party was a success.

I sat them in a circle and handed them a plate of sausage rolls, sandwiches, and party rings. I watched one pulled the crust off, one stick an entire square in his mouth, one took the two slices apart and face planted the butter side of the bread licking off the jam and butter. I leapt to get the pack of baby wipes ready to polish their faces when they'd finished eating. These children were more prehistoric than any dinosaur I had ever seen on tv!

I lit the candles on the wonky green cake I had made, and we all sang happy birthday to Liam. I think I felt more overwhelmed than he did, and a lump caught in my throat watching his beaming smile as his friends sang to him. I took some pictures for his memory book and wished I could pause that moment.

When the time came for the children to leave, each one marched out proudly with a dinosaur-themed party bag stuffed with sweets and little toys. Liam gave each friend a hug, his face still glowing with happiness. I couldn't help but smile, watching him so content in this new world I'd managed to build for him.

I was exhausted by the time the last child left, but I felt accomplished. I'd done it. The party was over, and Liam had gone to bed happy, his small body wrapped up in his dinosaur duvet, falling asleep with a smile still on his face.

I shut his door and scanned the room, the mess hit me like a tidal wave. How could seven small people create so much chaos?

Crumbs, empty cups, party hats, and bits of wrapping paper littered the room. I didn't mind. The quiet was nice, and I was lost in my own thoughts content in the fact that I'd managed to pull off something normal, something good.

As I scooped up the carnage into a black dustbin bag, I picked up the crumpled newspaper from the Pass the Parcel, smoothing out the pages. Jack's mug shot stared up at me again, just for a second, "I hope I did you proud bro!" I said to his picture before screwing it back up and it disappeared along with the crisps and party ring wrappers. I looked over at the framed picture of him, mum and that I kept on my mantlepiece and smiled. I didn't need to stare at newspaper stories of him. He was my brother and I loved him. I would remember him like he is in that photograph. I pushed the thoughts of him back down, just like I always did. Today was about Liam. Tomorrow would bring its own worries, but tonight, Liam was now officially five and he was happy, and in turn so was I.

The months after Jack's arrest passed in a blur, a strange mix of chaos and calm. Liam and I found ourselves in an uneventful routine, the kind of normalcy that can feel like both a blessing and a burden. Every morning, we would rush through breakfast, usually cereal or toast because cooking just wasn't my thing, and then I'd drop him off at school. The teachers loved him, they said he was bright, kind, and a joy to have in class. I knew they would have an idea of what had gone on now. It was impossible to avoid. What wasn't plastered in newspapers was shared in playground gossip, a trait that nobody grew out of no matter what age. The staff were kind though and didn't pry, so I didn't need to answer any questions.

At home, I tried to make dinner time more interesting, but cooking was a challenge I just couldn't seem to master. I even went through a phase of trying new recipes, curries, stir-fries, casseroles, but none of them ever seemed to turn out quite right. Ironically, sausages, of all things, were my worst. They'd be raw on the inside and burnt on the outside, I'd literally stand there staring at the frying pan, poking at them with a fork, thinking how is it even possible to make something so simple turn out like charcoal?

Liam never complained though, he was easy like that. In the end I managed to keep him alive on a steady diet of fish fingers, frozen pizza, and the occasional handful of Jelly vitamins when I felt guilty about his nutrition. He didn't seem to mind, for him it was all an adventure, and I guess I tried to see it that way too.

Our afternoons were my favourite time. After school, we would go for walks through the woods, the same woods we used to explore when he was younger. There was a tiny wooden bridge over a trickling stream, and every time we reached it, we'd play the Billy Goats Gruff game. I'd pretend to be the troll, crouching down low and growling, "Who's that trip-trapping across my bridge?" Liam, with that mischievous grin of his, would say,

"It's meeeee!" before tearing off across the bridge, giggling as I chased after him.

In those moments, it felt like heaven, a brief escape from everything. We'd lose ourselves in happiness, if only for a little while. It was just us, the trees, and the game, and I clung to those moments like a lifeline.

Chapter 15

Life kept moving forward, and reality crept in. I visited Jack a couple more times after his sentencing, and each time, it was harder to see him like that. He'd been given eight years, transferred to Belmarsh, a Category A prison, the kind of place you only hear about on the news. He wrote me a letter, trying to prepare me for the next visit. He said there'd be a glass panel between us from now on, and I wasn't sure how I felt about that. Part of me was relieved, knowing I wouldn't have to see him so closely, wouldn't have to smell the stale air of prison clinging to him. But another part of me felt the distance more keenly, as if the glass would symbolize the growing space between us.

Liam had started asking more about seeing his dad. He wasn't pushy about it anymore, but I could see the question forming in his eyes whenever I mentioned Jack. He missed him, in his own quiet way. I knew I would have to take him one day, but I wasn't ready. I needed to see what kind of state Jack was in before I could make that decision.

I just didn't want to shatter the fragile sense of peace Liam, and I had built since Jack's arrest. The memories of police banging on the door, of shouting matches late at night, of the tension that used to hang heavy in their home, those were behind him now. Liam had moved on in ways I hadn't. He didn't have nightmares anymore, he didn't flinch when a loud noise broke the quiet. I wanted to protect him from all the bad, to wrap him up and shield him from the harsh realities that had already seeped into his young life.

However, he was Jack's son, and eventually it would be his choice whether or not he wanted to see his dad. I knew that, and I also knew that I couldn't keep him away forever, no matter how much I wanted to.

As the days blurred together, I kept putting one foot in front of the other, just trying to keep us both moving forward. I had a visit with Jack coming up, and I dreaded it more than I could admit. The thought of him sitting there, on the other side of that glass panel, looking at me with those empty eyes, I wasn't sure how much more of it I could take (and equally his demands had increased and I wasn't sure how much I had left to give either.) How can prison life be so expensive?! I knew I had to go, I had to see what state he was in, only then could I decide when or if it was the right time to bring Liam to see him.

For now though, I held onto our little moments of happiness. The walks through the woods, the games on the bridge, the quiet evenings where it was just the two of us, and the world felt a little bit lighter.

One day at a time, I told myself. Just one day at a time.

The time felt right, I felt anxious, but Liam was too young to understand. He had continued to ask about his dad, wondering why he had to go away to work and why he couldn't come to visit. Now it was time for him to see Jack. Maybe it would give him some answers, some clarity, even if he didn't fully grasp the situation and now Jack had been moved out of that section of the prison, we were now allowed to visit without the glass between us.

The sun was just starting to break through the clouds as we sped down the motorway in my old Vauxhall Nova, the engine humming steadily beneath us. It was one of those drives where the air felt thick, like it was filled with everything that was not being said. I glanced at the rearview mirror and looked at Liam curled up in the back seat, his tiny legs barely long enough to dangle off the edge of the seat, clutching his stuffed rabbit, a comfort item I brought him to replicate the rabbit in our story book and remind him constantly how much he was loved. He was only five, yet there was a weight in his eyes that seemed much older.

A Prison visit was never going to be easy and I wasn't sure how much he understood about where we were going or why. I didn't want today to be heavy, I wanted to keep him happy, to give him at least a little slice of joy before the reality of it all set in.

I pushed in our favourite CD "Smurfs Go Pop!" and it started blasting through the tinny speakers of my car. His face lit up immediately. That grin, the kind only a child can manage, full of pure delight spread across his face, and suddenly I felt like everything was going to be okay, at least for the next few minutes.

"I'm Smurftastic!!" I belted out at the top of my lungs, sunglasses on for effect, glancing back to see if he'd join in. He did of course, matching my enthusiasm, his little voice just slightly out of tune but perfect all the same. (Imagine Mr Bombastic but the words are "Mr Smurftastic." That's your tune right there.) The Cd was a number of songs replicated with the word Smurf in it such as "Its oh so quiet" now replace the chorus with "Here comes crazy Smurf!" and Liams absolute favourite was a replica of the techno song "I want to be a hippy" But instead the words were "I want a little puppy little dog of my own" the chorus was "Pooper, pooper scooper." Anything with the word poo in it was a sure guarantee to tickle a five-year-old!

We were a duo now, my small backseat passenger and I, filling that Nova with a noise so loud it felt like we were pushing away the silence, the worry and the fear. The motorway stretched out ahead of us, grey and endless, but inside the car we were in our own little world. I smiled to myself as I saw his face brighten up with each chorus, the kind of smile you try to hold back but can't.

We kept going, louder with every verse, hands clapping along with the beat on the dashboard as "No limits" came on. The outside world melted away, it was just us, the Smurfs, and the open road. I looked back again and saw him laughing, belly-deep, the kind of laugh that shakes the whole body. It was infectious, and soon enough, I was laughing too, my eyes watering from the pure release of it.

As we neared the turn-off, the grey walls of the prison coming into view in the distance, the song finally faded out. There was a quiet pause as the CD switched to the next song, but we didn't say anything. I didn't want to ruin the moment, to remind him of what was coming next. For those few miles, we had been anywhere but here, and I hoped that when we finally pulled up to those gates a bit of that joy would stay with him.

Suddenly the air in the car was thick with tension. My fingers gripped the steering wheel tightly as I navigated into the car park of Belmarsh Prison.

I glanced at Liam again in the rearview mirror, my chest tightening. How could he possibly understand what this really meant? How could anyone explain to a five-year-old that his father wasn't coming home anytime soon? I had told Liam that Jack had to go away to work somewhere special.

"Are we here?" Liam asked, breaking the silence. His wide eyes met mine in the mirror, and I forced a smile.

"Yes, buddy. We'll get to see Daddy soon." Liam beamed at the mention of his dad. He hadn't seen Jack for three months. In Liam's mind, Jack was still a superhero, larger than life, funny, always telling jokes and carrying him on his shoulders. To Liam, his dad hadn't changed.

The looming concrete walls of the prison were now in full view. Barbed wire curled along the top, and tall, grey watchtowers stood guard. My stomach churned at the sight. I'd been here once before. That day was burned into my memory, my brother sitting behind a glass partition, his face pale and hollow, his hands trembling as he tried to reassure me that everything would be okay.

But it wasn't okay. It was never ok! Now here he was after years of Drugs, bad decisions, and wrong crowds. One mistake after another and now he has found himself in Belmarsh, with eight long years ahead of him.

I parked the car and got out, taking a deep breath as I helped Liam out of his seat wondering if I had done the right thing. He hopped onto the pavement, his little legs bouncing with excitement.

"Is Daddy here?" he asked, looking up at the imposing building with innocent curiosity.

"Yeah, he's here," I said softly, taking his hand. "But remember, it's a little different

here. We can't hug Daddy the way we used to, okay? We can talk to him though and you can tell him all about what you have been up to at school." Liam frowned slightly but nodded. "Okay."

As we walked toward the entrance, my heart pounded. I wasn't sure how Jack would react to seeing Liam. Would prison have changed him even more?

The security process was long and tedious. We had to go through metal detectors, hand over our personal belongings, and endure stern looks from the guards as we were patted down. Liam looked around wide-eyed, holding on to my hand tightly.

When we finally made it through, we were led to the visitation room. It was just as I remembered, harsh, sterile, with thick table separating the prisoners from their visitors. A row of chairs lined the partition, and Liam and I were directed near the middle.

I sat down, pulling Liam onto my lap, anxious that the other prisoners except for my brother seemed to be already sat eagerly awaiting the arrival of loved ones. I panicked for a moment that I had got the date wrong. Liam fidgeted looking around for his dad, then Jack appeared.

He walked in from the other side of the room escorted by a guard and my heart sank. He looked thinner than I remembered if that's even possible, his once bright eyes now dulled by time and regret. His hair, which used to be shaggy and full of life, was shaved close to his scalp. But despite everything, there was still something about him that was unmistakably Jack, his slight smile, the way he carried himself even in the prison uniform.

He still tried to be the big brother I knew. Liams face lit up the moment he saw him.

"Daddy!" he squealed, wriggling off my lap and trying to climb onto the table.

Jack's expression softened, and for a moment, I saw a flicker of the old Jack, the one who had adored his son more than anything. He reached the other side of the table and leaned in to throw his arms around his adoring son. Immediately the guard intervened pushing a baton between Jack and Liam "No touching!" He announced sternly like we'd just committed a crime. I peeled Liam off of him his eyes locked on Jacks face, his chin starting to wobble at the sudden interruption.

"Hey, little man," Jack said, his voice cracking just slightly. "Look how big you've grown!"

"I miss you, Daddy!"

"I miss you too, buddy. I've been thinking about you every day."

I stayed in my seat, watching the exchange with a heavy heart. There was no way to sugarcoat what was happening here. Liam didn't fully understand why there was a huge table between them, why his dad wasn't allowed to hug him and furthermore why couldn't he come home with us. But in his young mind, he was just happy to see his dad.

"Are you coming home soon?" Liam asked innocently, tilting his head.

Jacks face fell, and for a brief second, I saw the weight of the situation crash down on him. He glanced over at me, his eyes filled with pain, before turning back to his son.

"I can't come home just yet dude," his voice was thick with emotion. "But I promise, when I can, we'll do all the things we used to. Remember when we used to go to the park and feed the ducks? We'll do that again. And I'll take you to the zoo one day!"

Liam nodded; his face serious as he listened. "YESSS!! Can I come back and see you again?"

"Of course," Jack said, his voice barely holding together. "You can come whenever you want to."

I shifted in my seat, wiping a tear that had escaped down my cheek. I hated this. Hated that Jack had put us all in this position, that Liam had to visit his dad in a prison instead of running around in the park like other kids his age. But I also knew that Jack loved Liam, that much was clear. Now he had a chance to get clean and stay clean and be the best dad that he can be. The alternative could have and would have been much worse. It was only a matter of time before the drugs would have gotten the better of him.

We spoke more in that hour than we had done for years. Liam filled Jack in on School and his new best friend Charlie. That he can draw the biggest bestest dinosaur ever and that every night when he cuddled Little Nutbrown Hare (his teddy) he would think of Jack.

The visit though an hour felt like both an eternity and no time at all. Eventually, the guard came to signal the end of our time, and Liam's face fell when he realized we had to leave.

"Daddy, don't go," he whispered, his little hands reaching out.

Jack's eyes filled with tears, unable to hold back his emotions any longer. "I love you, little man," he said, his voice breaking. "I'm so sorry."

I stood up gently pulling Liam away, I felt so tense but put my shoulders back, my chin in the air as if concreting my stance would remove the emotions that were threatening to overwhelm me.

"Come on, buddy, we'll come back soon."

Jack looked at me "Lova ya sis."

"Right back at ya" I said barely a whisper as I struggled to look at him for fear of breaking down completely.

Liam looked back at his dad one more time as we walked away, his face a mixture of confusion and sadness. "I love you, Daddy."

Jack stood to watch us leave as the guards impatiently ushered everybody out, his eyes never leaving Liam's face until we were out of sight.

As we walked back to the car, Liam clutched his stuffed rabbit tightly, his usual chatter noticeably absent. When I shut the door, he finally spoke.

"Lucy, why can't Daddy come home with us?"

I swallowed hard, trying to find the right words. "Daddy made some mistakes chicken, he loves you so much, he's just... he's just in a place where he has to work hard and learn how to be better."

Liam was quiet for a moment, then nodded, seemingly satisfied with my answer, though I knew it wouldn't be the last time he asked.

As we drove away from the prison, I couldn't shake the image of Jacks face. It wasn't fair, not for Liam, not for any of us. I knew I had to keep going, for my nephew's sake. I would do whatever it took to make sure Liam felt loved and cared for, even if his dad couldn't be there.

Whatever happened next, we would face it together.

Chapter 16

The factory floor was always bustling, a hive of activity where machines clanged, and workers chattered over the noise. I was still only seventeen. It wasn't glamorous work, but it was honest and paid the bills.

I spent most of my shifts focused on my tasks, but there was one person who managed to catch my attention, Tom. He was a few years older than me, with an easy smile and a laugh that seemed to lighten even the grimmest of days. He worked at the station next to mine, and over time, we began chatting more frequently. Our conversations, initially just small talk, soon grew into something more. We shared stories about our lives (mine obviously made up), we laughed about the quirks of factory life and found ourselves looking forward to each shift more than I ever expected.

Tom had a warmth to him that drew people in. He was kind and genuine, a contrast to the rough edges of factory work. It wasn't long before I found myself looking forward to seeing him, savouring the little moments when we'd chat during our breaks or steal glances across the noisy factory floor. I was falling for him, harder than I'd ever expected.

There was another person who occupied my thoughts, someone I tried to ignore but couldn't completely escape. My Line manager, Mr. Harper, was a striking figure, confident, authoritative, and surprisingly young for his position. He had an air of command that was hard to ignore, and there was something about him that fascinated me. His sharp eyes, the way he carried himself with such grace and precision, it was magnetic.

It was a tangled mess of emotions. Tom was real, accessible, and he made me feel special. With him, everything felt easy and genuine. Nathan Harper however, was an enigma, someone I only saw in brief, formal encounters. The attraction was undeniable, but it felt like a fantasy, something I could admire from a distance but never truly reach.

One Friday evening, as the factory floor quieted down and the machinery began to wind down for the weekend, Tom and I were finishing up our tasks. The end of the week always felt like a small victory, and today was no different. Tom was in one of his rare, reflective moods, and we talked more deeply than usual.

"You know," Tom said, leaning against the workbench, "I've been meaning to ask you, what's the real reason you took this job? Most people are just here for money, but you can do anything. Why a factory?"

I hesitated; the truth tangled with my emotions. "I guess I just needed to figure some things out. I thought this would give me some space, you know? To clear my head."

Tom nodded thoughtfully. "I get that. Sometimes, a change of scenery is all you need."

His gaze lingered on me, and I felt a flutter in my chest. It was in moments like these that I wondered if he felt the same way. But before I could respond, Mr. Harper walked by, his presence commanding the room's attention. He stopped near us, giving us a nod of acknowledgment.

"Everything wrapping up alright?" he asked, his accent smooth and authoritative.

"Yes, Mr. Harper," Tom said, his tone respectful. "Just about done."

Nathan glanced at me, and for a brief moment, our eyes met. There was a spark there—a fleeting connection that made my heart skip. But before I could process it, he was gone, walking back to his office with his usual purposeful stride.

Tom looked at me, a curious expression on his face. "You, okay?"

I forced a smile, nodding. "Yeah, just thinking."

The weekend came and went, and with it, the factory's daily grind returned. My feelings for Tom continued to grow, but so did my fascination with Mr. Harper. It was a delicate balance, navigating the genuine connection I had with Tom while managing the complicated attraction I felt toward Mr. Harper.

One evening, as I was leaving the factory, Nathan approached me. "Can we talk for a minute?"

My heart raced. I knew the conversation would be professional, but there was an undertone to his words that made me nervous. We walked to the break room, where he motioned for me to sit.

"I wanted to tell you," he paused for effect "that you're doing a great job. I've noticed your dedication."

I looked down, blushing slightly. "Thank you. That means a lot."

He studied me for a moment, his eyes thoughtful. "I know it's not easy working here, especially at your age. If you ever need anything, don't hesitate to ask."

Our conversation was brief but left me with a swirl of emotions. Nathans praise and concern were genuine, but they only deepened the complicated feelings I had for him. As I left the factory, my thoughts were consumed by the struggle of managing these two conflicting desires.

In the end, it was clear that my feelings for Tom were based on a real connection—one built on shared experiences and mutual respect. Over the last few months, we had built something genuine, and that was something I didn't want to risk. As for Mr. Harper, he remained a figure of admiration and mystery, someone I could appreciate from afar but not fully pursue.

It was a lesson in navigating the complexities of attraction and connection. I continued to cherish the moments with Tom, savouring our growing relationship and even introduced him to Liam. While accepting the reality of my unrequited feelings for Mr. Harper. Life in the factory was still full of challenges, but it also held the promise of something real—a chance to build a future with someone who truly saw me (The me I wanted to be anyway whoever that was.)

Falling in love with Tom was both a surprise and a comfort. There were no butterflies but he was comfortable like I could say whatever I wanted to and it wouldn't matter. He was quite self absorbed but that made him easy to be around. It was a reminder that, even in the midst of confusion and longing, the most meaningful connections were often the ones we least expected. And as I navigated the delicate balance between my emotions, I learned that sometimes, love finds us in the most unexpected places.

At eighteen, I never imagined my life would look like this, raising my five-year-old nephew, in a tiny house that somehow, in its chaos, had become our home. When Jack went to prison, everything shifted. I went from barely taking care of myself to becoming the person Liam relied on. Our routine was stable, but not without its challenges. Winging it, as always.

Liam was the centre of my world, even if I wasn't ready for it. He loved it when I read him 'Guess How Much I Love You' before bed. Talking about love stretching as far as the moon and back felt real and comforting to both of us. I tucked him in each night, after his Hercules pyjamas were on, and sat next to him, turning the worn pages, trying to make him feel safe. We had built something. It wasn't perfect, but it was ours.

Then there was Tom. He came into our lives without much warning. After getting close to him at work, things kind of just...happened. He'd started to be around most of the time, making himself at home. He was kind to Liam, and that counted a lot. Liam didn't ask many questions when Tom was around, just accepted him as part of our world.

Tom was a stoner, he smokes weed like it was going out of fashion which irritated me but not to the point I was ready to get rid of him. I refused to let him smoke in the house full stop so he would retreat to the garden. It baffled me how he thought no one would be able to smell it. He was laid-back in a way that made me feel like I was always running at full speed while he just coasted through life. The smell of weed lingered through the house sometimes when he smoked it in the garden, and I would kick off like crazy about it. But in a relationship sense he didn't push me for anything. He wasn't interested in the details of my life, which was fine by me because I wasn't interested in sharing them. It worked, somehow. It was a quiet understanding, and at that time, that's all I needed.

I'd been trying to hold it together at work, too. Taking every training course, they offered me, putting my hand up for every extra shift, grinding to make ends meet. It was exhausting, but it was starting to pay off. The previous week, I got promoted. Nothing huge, just a step up the ladder, but it felt like a win.

More money meant I could keep the house, maybe even get a better place down the line. Every time I got a break, I felt like maybe I could finally breathe. Then reality hit, reminding me that none of it ever came easy.

The boss had started flirting with me, and I flirted right back. It felt good honestly. It was like a game, something to remind me that I was still me, still young, still desirable. I wouldn't let it go further. I knew better than to mess up what I'd built for Liam and me. Happy endings aren't real anyway. You just play the hand you're dealt and make it work.

Then there was Jack, always there in our hearts and minds. He called once a week from prison, the same time, the same day, like clockwork. Our conversations were always a strange mix of small talk and heavy silence. He asked me last week if I could take him drugs when I visited. Plug some for him. The thought made me sick. Absolutely not, I told him perplexed that he'd even had the guts to ask. He'd asked in code of course and I wondered how stupid he had to be to think that the prison wouldn't decipher it. He didn't argue with me, just sighed, like he knew better than to push it and to risk cutting off the weekly small supply of money I had been sending him allowing him to buy cigarettes, toiletries and gamble snickers and mars bars. It was always something with him. Someone always wanted something from me.

I was stretched thin but holding it together. Winging life, trying to make it work for us. It wasn't pretty, but it was ours.

Every night, when I sat next to Liam reading 'Guess How Much I Love You,' I reminded myself that that is what matters. His world, his safety, his tiny, trusting smile. The rest? I would figure it out. Somehow, I always did.

Chapter 17

Life felt like a whirlwind of responsibilities and uncertainties. Liam had been living with me for over a year and our series of challenges felt a world away. We had a perfect routine and as Scarlet had started her recovery, Liam had begun spending weekends with her. Scarlet was making huge progress rebuilding her health and her life, whilst Jack continued serving his time. When she came out of hospital she moved into a new house a little further afield. The visits with Liam and her had initially started as a couple of hours with the three of us together. We would eat or go out somewhere and she would talk and play with Liam trying to get reacquainted with him. Those hours turned into a full day, then gradually he began to sleep over there reunited with his mum. The mum who had given birth to him and nurtured the tiny, unexpected bundle whilst battling the carnage that came with my brother.

It was an overwhelming responsibility having Liam full time, but one that I had embraced completely. He was all I had, he was my world, his laughter a daily reminder of what mattered most.

I had grown to love him as if he were my own, and we had built a life together filled with laughter, bedtime stories, and endless adventures.

The call came on a bright, sunny evening. I was folding some clothes when the phone rang. I knew it would be Jack. He had phoned every week at the same time for as long as I could remember. Our love hate relationship continued as he made demands and asked for more luxuries be sent to him in prison, forgetting that I was out here feeding his son and trying to keep my own head above water. Then he would say something funny, and as time grew forward little pieces of the old Jack started to rebuild themselves which made me soften. I continued to struggle to say no to him. I visited once a month with Liam and during that time Tom had well and truly become part of the furniture.

The voice on the other end of the phone that day sounded different though, more distant than the chirpy phone calls I had learned to look forward to and enjoy. I relished listening to the confidence of my true brother returning.

"Luce, I need to ask you something." Oh god. My heart sank.

I braced myself for him to ask me for the umpteenth time to get something illegal into the prison for him. My backside wasn't designed to be a carrier pigeon, I didn't know how many times I would have to explain this!

He'd whispered to me on our visits about launching a dead bird over the fence stuffed with a mobile phone and how handsomely I would be paid for it. Or a tennis ball filled with treats to accidentally find its way into the yard. You can take the criminal out of Lowcroft, but you can't take Lowcroft out the criminal! As tempting as it was to stuff some poor unsuspecting pigeon with an old Nokia in exchange for a thousand pounds there were far too many flaws for my liking. Firstly killing birds not my thing, I couldn't even contemplate it, how do you even kill a bird? Shoot it? I don't own a gun. Poison it? With what? I wasn't even sure why I was asking myself those question. Besides, I couldn't even cook a sausage let alone carry out full surgery on a pigeon or the like, so it just wasn't going to happen. Secondly, I couldn't throw a party let alone a tennis ball. I had visions of being back in school and trying to launch a shotput only to watch it land directly in front of me. I was born with no co-ordination! My throwing was worse than my cooking skills and that takes some doing, so the idea of launching said dead bird over the towering, barbed wire fence of Belmarsh prison was never going to end well for anybody.

However, the news that came was bittersweet and quite frankly I'd have preferred the Nokia option any day.

"She wants him home Luce." I paused to digest what he had just said to me. Searching for anything it could have meant that did not involve Liam.

"Home." I repeated the word and let it roll around my tongue for a minute. I couldn't find any words and as reality set in my eyes filled up and I could already feel the emptiness that I was about to endure. I wanted to protest. I had nursed him through sickness, through his first days of school, thrown his first ever birthday party. I knew who every one of his friends was, his teachers at school. They may have been his parents, but I didn't feel they knew him anymore, not like I did. I let that sink in for a minute. I didn't know who I was without Liam.

"When?" Was all I could muster up. The thousands of questions and protests creating a tornado in my mind.

"Dunno, but soon it's for the best." What the actual fuckery did he know about what is best? He turned all of our lives upside down, I had spent more time nurturing Liam over the last few years than he ever had.

The words hit me like a punch to the gut. For a moment, I couldn't speak. I just stood there, staring at the wall, the phone heavy in my hand.

"Home?" I finally managed to repeat, my voice a mix of disbelief and anger and then let out a laugh that scared even me.

"She wants him to come home," Jack continued interrupting my hysteria, his tone casual, as if this was just a small matter of logistics. "She says she's ready now, that she's feeling better and can handle things. I mean, you've done an amazing job, but she's his mum, you know?"

I could feel the heat rising in my chest, my heart pounding. I'd rearranged my entire life for Liam. I was 14 when I started helping out with him, when no one else was available. I'd shut out my friends, given up my dreams in college, changed my work schedule, put everything on hold just to make sure he had what he needed. I had become an adult for him, learned how to raise a child when I was barely more than one myself. Now, a casual phone call was supposed to undo all of that?

"She can't just decide she's ready now," I said, my voice shaking. "Liam isn't some toy you can pick up and put down when it's convenient. I've been the one here. I've been the one taking care of him while Scarlet got better and while you weren't there!"

Jack was silent for a moment, and I could hear the faint hum of prison life in the background; voices, clanging doors, the hollow echo of a place that never let you forget where you were.

"I know," he said quietly. "But she's, his mum."

Those words 'She's his mum', like I didn't know that. like I hadn't spent every single day of the last few years trying to make sure Liam had everything he needed because his parents weren't there to do it. I had been the one who sat with him when he had nightmares, who knew exactly how to get him to laugh on the days when the weight of everything was too much. I knew his favourite food, the exact amount of ketchup he liked on his fish fingers, the way he loved bubble-gum ice cream to brighten his mood after a tough day.

"I know what he likes! I know what makes him happy! What scares him! What he needs when he is sad" I snapped, my anger spilling over. "I've had him projectile vomit over me like his head was going to spin off. I've been covered in shit, sick and wiped more tears that you could ever imagine! He is MY life Jack!" The last bit slipped out by accident.

"I get it," Jack said, his voice soft. "But we always knew it wouldn't be forever. You knew that! I need to go my time is nearly up."

My time was up too. I knew it wouldn't be forever, but it didn't make the thought of letting him go any easier. He wasn't mine to keep, but God the thought of losing him now was unbearable. How could I just give him back when my whole world had become centred around him?

The thought of Scarlet taking Liam home now she'd gotten over her own grief. It felt like a betrayal, even though I knew deep down that it wasn't. She had the right, but that didn't make it right.

"I'll have to think about when and how to tell him," I muttered, my mind racing and trying to take back some control. How was I supposed to let him go after everything we'd built together? Would he even want to go?

"Take your time," Jack said, though his voice was strained, like he knew this conversation wasn't going to end well "We'll figure it out."

After we hung up, I sat in the silence for a long time, staring at the empty walls, feeling like my whole world had just shifted beneath me.

That evening, I watched him as he came home from school, his face bright as he told me about his day. I made dinner, fish fingers again, because at least I couldn't ruin those and listened, nodding, smiling, all while the weight of Jack's call pressed down on me. Liam was everything I had, and I couldn't imagine my life without him. How would I fill the silence? Who would I be once he was gone?

I sat with him after dinner, reading his favourite book like we always did. My heart ached as I watched him, trying to figure out how to say the words that would change everything. For now, I just held onto the moment a little longer, hoping it wouldn't slip away.

That night I slept restlessly. I could hear Liam's soft breathing from his room, and I thought about how he had made me into something I never expected, someone responsible, someone who had purpose. He had made me grow up. I didn't know who I was without him. I would tell him about Jacks phone call the next day.

"Does that mean Daddy is coming home again?" Liam had asked, his eyes wide with anticipation. I was a little hurt by his reaction it was far chirpier than I had anticipated but I suppose I should have been grateful for that.

"Not quite yet it doesn't" was my reply, my voice catching slightly. His face dropped. "It means you get to stay with mummy always in her new home. You can pick new wallpaper out for your room and make it a nice surprise for Daddy when he comes home. Plus you can still come and stay with me any time you like. He sat silent while I watched his forehead crease and un crease as his little mind tried to work it all out. "How about we plan to spend one last super duper special day together?"

His face lit up with excitement. "What are we going to do?" I smiled, already knowing how I wanted to make our last day memorable.

"How about a trip to the beach?" The beach had always been a magical place for Liam. I remembered the first time I took him there a day filled with laughter, sandcastles, and waves that tickled his toes. It felt right to end our year together with a day that would be just as special.

The sun was already high in the sky when Liam and I arrived at the beach that day. We packed a small bag with snacks, a beach blanket, and Liam's favourite toys. As we neared the beach, Liam's excitement was palpable. He pressed his face against the window, his eyes wide as he spotted the shimmering water and golden sand (Well cobbled stones with a hint of sand but golden sounds better.)

The weather was perfect for us, the warmth of the sun sinking into our skin as we stepped out onto the soft sand (cough stones). The beach was bustling with families and sun-seekers and I found a perfect spot for us near the edge of the water. Liam wasted no time, rushing toward the waves with an exuberance that made my heart swell. I had planned this day for weeks, the last day it would be just the two of us before he went back to live with his mum. Every part of me ached at the thought, but I pushed it down, determined to make the day unforgettable. I wanted him to treasure it forever, to carry it with him no matter what his new life looked like.

"Race you to the water!" Liam shouted, already kicking off his shoes and taking off toward the sea, his laughter carried away by the wind. I couldn't help but laugh too, watching him, full of energy and light, the way only kids can be. His joy was contagious, and for a moment, I let go of the heaviness in my chest and chased after him, sand flying behind me.

The water was cold, shocking at first as it splashed over our feet, but Liam didn't seem to mind. He waded in further, arms stretched wide, the sun glinting off his wet hair as he turned back to me with that mischievous smile. As I watched him play, my heart full of a mix of pride and sadness.

We spent hours like that, letting the waves crash against us, jumping and splashing as though nothing in the world mattered but this moment. I wanted time to stop right there, with Liam's laughter ringing in the air and the ocean stretching out endlessly in front of us. But the sun kept inching across the sky, and I knew the day wouldn't last forever.

"Let's build a sandcastle," I said, pulling him back onto the beach.

Liam's eyes lit up, and we got to work, digging trenches, piling up wet sand, and patting it down to make walls and towers. The castle wasn't perfect it tilted to one side, and one of the towers collapsed almost immediately but to Liam, it was a masterpiece. We decorated it with seashells we found nearby, and when it was done, we stood back and admired our creation, proud of something so simple.

"Will the sea run it over!" Liam said, squinting at the water that crept closer and closer.

"Maybe," I said, smiling at him. "But that's okay. We can always build another one."

He nodded, satisfied with the answer, and ran off to collect more shells while I watched him, feeling that familiar ache return. This was our last day. Tomorrow, everything would change. I'd go back to an empty house, and Liam would be with Scarlet. I wanted him to be happy. I knew he needed his mum but the thought of the void he would leave behind felt unbearable. I wasn't ready to let him go.

As the afternoon wore on, we sat together on a beach towel, sharing a portion of chips coated in ketchup and a slightly melted ice cream. I had bought him his favourite of course, and something I knew Scarlet wouldn't have stocked in her freezer.

As the evening wore on the sun began to dip lower, painting the sky with streaks of orange and pink, and the waves turned golden in the fading light.

"Do you think we can come back here again one day?" Liam asked between bites, his voice so casual, as if he didn't realize what tomorrow meant.

"Of course," I said, though I wasn't sure when that day would come.

We stayed on the beach long after the sun began to set, watching as the sky turned from fiery orange to a deep purple. Liam cuddled into me, staring up at the sky as the clouds blinked into view. I held him tightly, listening to the sound of the waves and his soft breathing, and I wanted to freeze that moment forever, to never let it slip away.

But time didn't stop. The tide had risen, creeping closer to our sandcastle, slowly erasing it piece by piece until it was nothing more than a memory. I knew the same thing would happen with this day with everything. Liam would go back to his mum, and our life together, this chapter we'd written between us, would become part of his past. He wasn't mine to keep, and I'd always known that, but now that the moment had come, I didn't know how to let go.

As we packed up to leave, Liam was quiet, his energy spent from the long day. I watched him as he walked beside me, his hand still small in mine, he'd grown so much in the time he'd been with me. I wondered what his life would be like without me there, how he'd change and grow in ways I wouldn't get to see. Would he remember our walks in the woods, our games on the bridge, our days like this one, spent at the beach, skipping along the sand where nothing existed but the two of us?

As we reached the car, I looked at him and swallowed the lump in my throat.

"Did you have fun today chicken?" I asked, hoping he'd carry some piece of this with him.

"The best," he said, smiling up at me, his eyes heavy with sleep. "I'll remember it forever."

I nodded, trying to keep my voice steady. "Me too."

The drive home was quiet, Liam asleep in the backseat, and all I could think about was the emptiness that would come tomorrow. I didn't know how I'd fill the void he would leave behind. I didn't know how to go back to a life where he wasn't there, where his laughter didn't fill the house, where the days were not built around him.

When we arrived home, I tucked him into bed and read 'Guess How much I love you' for the last time. I stayed by his side watching him as he slept, his face peaceful and content. Tomorrow would come soon enough, but for tonight he was still mine. I closed the door softly behind me, my heart aching with the knowledge that this was the end of something beautiful, I knew, no matter how much time passed, I'd treasure this day forever.

Chapter 18

The day had come. Liam's bags were packed neatly in the back of the car, filled with all the new clothes, toys, and pieces of the life we'd built together over the past year. As I fastened his seatbelt and settled into the driver's seat, my hands trembled on the steering wheel. My stomach churned, a knot of dread tightening with each mile we drove. I couldn't shake the thought of how empty my life would be without him there.

Liam chattered beside me, his voice full of excitement, even though I could sense the nerves beneath it. He didn't fully understand what today meant. To him, it was a new adventure, going back to live with his mum after so long. But for me, it felt like losing a piece of myself. I smiled and nodded along to his stories, trying to keep my voice light, as though this were just another day, another drive.

But inside, I was crumbling.

When we pulled up outside Scarlet's house, my heart felt like it was being squeezed in a vice. Scarlet came out to greet us, a smile on her face, although I could see the uncertainty in her eyes, she looked better, healthier. I had to believe she was ready for this, that she could be the mother Liam needed now, but that didn't make it any easier to let go.

"Do you want to come in for a bit? Stay for a cup of tea?" Scarlet asked, her voice tentative.

I forced a smile, shaking my head. I couldn't. I couldn't sit there, pretending everything was fine, making small talk over tea while inside I was falling apart. I wasn't strong enough for this goodbye.

"No, I should get going," I said, my voice strained but steady. I couldn't let Liam see me like this. I had to hold it together for him. I unloaded my car surprised at how much we had managed to accumulate over that time.

As I knelt down to say goodbye, Liam clung to me, his little arms wrapping tight around my neck.

"Please, stay for a while," he whispered, his voice cracking with emotion. It nearly broke me. Everything inside me screamed to stay, to delay the inevitable, to hold him just a little longer. But I knew I couldn't. I had to be strong for him, and me.

I pulled back, my hands on his shoulders, keeping my voice upbeat, light-hearted, as if I was selling this day to him as another one of our fun adventures.

"Hey, it's going to be great, you'll see! A new adventure with Mum, and don't forget you can always come and stay with me whenever you want to, okay?"

His eyes were glassy, I could tell he didn't want to let go, but he nodded, trying to be brave.

I gave him one last squeeze and whispered into his ear "Guess how much I love you?"

"To the moon and back," he beamed, his little face lighting up and that chin wobbling threatening to allow tears to fall. In that moment my heart shattered.

I kissed him on the forehead, my throat tight, barely able to hold back. I turned to Scarlet giving her a smile and a nod, because there was no way I could say another word without an avalanche of tears spilling out. She gave me a sympathetic look but I couldn't meet her eyes for long.

As I walked away my chest ached so badly I thought it might split open. I could feel Liam's eyes on me, watching me leave. I slid into the front seat of the car and as I closed the door, everything felt so final, like the end of something that had once been so full of life and love.

The second I sat in the car, the tears came. They poured out of me in heavy, wracking sobs, harder than I'd ever cried in my life. I cried for Jack, for the brother I'd lost to his addiction. I cried for Liam, for the sweet boy who had become the centre of my world. I cried for mum who had worked tirelessly to try and keep us safe and warm, but then lost her own mental health battle through all of this. I cried for Scarlet, who had fought her own battles to get to this point, and I cried for myself, for everything I had given, everything I was losing.

It felt like hours passed before I could even think about driving.

By the time I pulled into the driveway of my empty house, the weight of the day still clung to me. That thick fog I'd experienced so many times before slowly engulfing me again. I stepped inside, the silence suffocating. Tom was there, sprawled on the sofa, eyes glued to the TV, oblivious to the wreckage inside me. He glanced at me briefly, noticing my red, tear-streaked face, but didn't say a word. Maybe he knew. Maybe he didn't. Either way, I couldn't face him.

Without a word, I shuffled up the stairs to bed. The bed felt too big, too cold without Liam in the house. I lay there, staring at the ceiling, the quiet pressing in around me. The void he left behind was overwhelming. He had become my entire world. The laughter, the bedtime stories, the little hands that reached for mine, it was all gone, and the silence was overwhelming.

The house was emptier than it had ever been, and so was I.

Chapter 19

I had always been a master of adaptation. From the time I was a child, I learned to mould myself to fit into the lives of others. In school, I was the studious one, following the rules that would please teachers. At home, I had been the perfect daughter, calm and obedient, never daring to let my true thoughts disrupt the fragile balance of my family. With friends and colleagues, I was a chameleon, changing my colours to match their likes, their moods, their desires.

The reality was very different. Deep down beneath the masks, there was a place in my heart where sadness bloomed. It was subtle at first, just a dull ache of longing I couldn't name. But after my brother went away and Liam went home, the ache grew into a storm. Grief wrapped its cold fingers around me, blurring the already delicate sense of who I was. I had spent years pretending to be the strong one, the steady one who could carry the weight of our broken family on my shoulders. Now though, my carefully constructed identity began to crack. There was no one left to be strong for. No one left to tell me who I should be.

The façade of the laughing girl was exhausting. I had no energy to put on a show anymore. I was in that dark place and the door was bolted firmly shut. I did not know what direction the light was in, so I gave into it.

The house felt so quiet. It wasn't like it had been loud before, but now, the silence pressed down on me in a different way, more suffocating than peaceful. I hadn't realized how much of my day revolved around Liam until he was gone. I'd spent just over a year looking after him, tending to the small things, making sure he was alright, and now, there was just... nothing. No one to check on, no one to cook for, no one to keep an eye on.

I'm being dramatic of course Tom is still here, but Tom is just Tom. He moves around the house in his usual rhythm, eating his dinner, reading the paper, smoking weed, and falling asleep in front of the TV. Nods at me if he has to walk past me or speaks to me if he wants me to cook him something, but that's about as exciting as it gets. His presence doesn't fill the void. If anything, it only makes it more obvious. He seems to have no trouble continuing with his life as usual, while mine feels like it has screeched to a halt. I didn't know why I was still with him. I wasn't frightened of being alone I don't think, he didn't offer me anything other than money towards the bills. However, he fit perfectly into the picture that I was trying to paint for the rest of the world. Look at me with my own home, a good job and somebody to love me. I'm assuming this is love. Disney is just a fairy tale isn't it? Something to give us hope and keep striving for better. Reality is a different story though, so here I am being a good partner, cooking, cleaning, telling jokes, showing as much affection as I can muster regardless of whether or not its being returned.

When my alarm went off for work at 6am this morning blasting 'Happy Days' out to me, not only could I not get up, I wanted to rip it out of the wall and launch it across the room. This is even more frustrating when said alarm clock won't detach itself from the wall no matter how hard you pull, so I settled for knocking it on the floor like a petulant child in a bad temper. I just couldn't bring myself to get up. The thought of slipping into yet another version of myself, another mask, exhausted me, so I stayed in bed sinking deeper into the emptiness. I withdrew from everyone. Friends reached out, even Tom attempted to speak to me, but I couldn't find the energy to pretend anymore. I ignored Jacks call that evening. The weekly call had been a part of my Tuesday evening routine for over a year, but now I just wasn't in the mood. I had nothing to say, nothing to share and there was nothing I wanted to hear. I had transferred his weekly twenty pounds that he had become used to, so I'm sure there's nothing more he needs from me.

The evening drew in, and I realised I had laid there festering all day. I sat up in my bed and stared at the reflection in the mirror, I didn't recognize the person staring back at me. I couldn't remember what I liked or what made me happy, had I ever really known? I had been so busy perfecting my roles that I had erased myself in the process. I flopped back onto the bed and buried myself back under the safety of my quilt.

Tom made a sudden appearance upstairs and climbed in next to me prodding me to get my attention. I didn't have the energy for an argument or to deal with him in a bad mood, so I dutifully turned onto my back allowing him the satisfaction that he desired. My expression didn't change and no words were exchanged. It was quick and robotic. I distracted myself by staring at the pattern of the Artex ceiling, taking myself away in my mind. When the grunt came and he was satisfied, I silently shifted back onto my side and shut my eyes again. He got up and whistled whilst heading back downstairs to make himself a drink. I felt nothing, not angry, not used, depleted yes, but that's how it goes isn't it? We offer what we can to keep others happy. Is this my purpose? I didn't know.

When Nathan received my email regarding my absence from work, he didn't question me and told me to take all the time I need. He didn't know my circumstances in detail but seemed to have a quiet understanding for what I needed.

Once Tom left for work the following morning I couldn't take the stillness anymore. After 2 days in bed it felt like the walls were closing in on me, the quiet too loud. I forced myself out of bed, pulled on some clothes, and headed out for a walk. The air outside was crisp, and the sound of my footsteps on the pavement was strangely comforting and for the first time in days, I felt something other than numb. I went for a walk through the woods, seeking solace in the quiet spaces between the trees watching people pass by, some laughing, some deep in conversation. Each of them seemed so sure of themselves, so alive in their own worlds. I felt like a ghost drifting through the edges of my own existence yet was equally getting on my own nerves now with my self-pity.

I wandered without direction letting the streets guide me through the town. The faces of everyone going about their daily business a blur, until I found myself standing in front of a tattoo shop. The big sign outside read 'Walk-ins Welcome,' and before I even knew what I was doing, I pushed the door open.

Inside, the smell of ink and antiseptic filled the air, and the faint buzz of a tattoo gun hummed from the back room. I didn't know what I wanted but I craved something, anything that would make me feel grounded again. I needed to feel something and pain was going to remind me I was still here, still existing. I needed something that would pull me back into the real world, where things hurt and bled and healed.

I flipped through the sample books, looking for something that spoke to me, something that would make sense of the chaos in my head. There was a picture of a feather, delicate and simple, with the words "I'll never forget" woven through it. It was nice, but it didn't feel right. I didn't want a reminder of the past, I wanted to escape it. I wanted to fly away, to disappear.

"Can you do something with this?" I asked the artist, pointing to the feather "but change the words to say 'One day I'll fly away.'" The artist nodded, drawing up a new design with a soft curve in the feather, as if caught mid-flight, and the words woven through it like a whisper of hope.

Sat in the quiet back room of the shop, the buzz of the needle was the only sound breaking through the silence. I lay down on the bench lifting my shirt just enough for him to ink the design onto my ribs. The artist was focused, his hands steady as he worked on the delicate feather that would soon be etched into my skin. It wasn't just a tattoo, it was a prayer, a plea for the freedom I didn't know how to find. The pain from the needle was sharp, but I welcomed it. I needed it. The physical sting of the ink carving into my ribs, was something I could control. It was real. It didn't lie or disguise itself like everything else. I leaned into it, embracing each burn, each tear of skin, because for those few moments, it was a distraction from the suffocating weight that had been crushing me for so long.

I watched the feather slowly taking shape, its delicate lines stretching across my ribs, the words weaving through it like a lifeline. I wasn't sure I believed it, but I needed to. I needed to believe that one day I could be free, that one day I wouldn't feel this way anymore. That one day I could breathe again. But today wasn't that day. Today, I was still trapped. Trapped in this life, in this body, in the silence of the secrets I carried. I didn't know how to escape.

The artist wiped the excess ink from my skin, revealing the finished feather, its pieces slowly fading into the wind, as if they too, were trying to escape. The words were there, stark, and final, a reminder of a hope I wasn't sure I had anymore. The walk home felt different. Every step felt more deliberate, more real. By the time I reached the house, I wasn't thinking about Liam, or Tom, or the silence that waited for me inside. I was just... there.

That evening, as Tom stumbled in from another round of his weed-fuelled escapades. The house felt more suffocating than ever. I broke down, tears streaming down my face, as I struggled to understand how I had ended up in this dark place that I couldn't climb out of. I was drowning in my own life, trapped between the pain of losing Liam, the dissatisfaction with Tom and the yearning for something more. For the first time ever I craved Tom to be the stronger one, to cradle me and tell me everything was going to be ok. I wanted to ask for help but I was frightened he would laugh at me. I couldn't get the words out, I didn't know how to. How could I explain how I was feeling if I didn't know myself. I opened and closed my mouth repeatedly struggling to ask him to hold me. I had spent so long pretending everything was fine that he didn't see the cracks in my armour, no one knew how close I was to falling apart not even me until today.

I stared at him pleading with my eyes. I knew the distance between us was my fault, I sought a relationship that kept everybody at arm's length. Afterall that's how I lost Jimmy wasn't it? I hadn't wanted to be smothered, I didn't want kindness, sympathy or questions. My walls were built to keep people out and keep me strong but those walls were starting to crumble from the inside and I was faced with new emotions that I didn't recognise. I ached to be held, just a hug but instead he said nothing. He looked at me raised his eyebrows like I was offending his vision, yawned, and as if made of pure stone took himself up to bed.

I looked in the mirror of our hallway at the dark circles that had formed under my eyes and realised I was the only person that could help me. Tomorrow I would go back to work. I'd get out of bed and remind myself that I still had a life, that there were people who depended on me. I couldn't afford to stay in bed for days, letting the world pass me by. Live or die I had to make that choice. For now I choose living, this meant I needed to move forward, to keep going even when it felt impossible. I lifted my top up and looked at my tattoo. I'd let the pain remind me that I was still here, still standing. One day I'd fly away, but just for now, I'd just keep putting one foot in front of the other.

Chapter 20

After a restless sleep, I woke up with a strange mix of anxiety and determination swirling in my chest. Today was my first day back at work, and I wasn't sure if I was ready, but I knew I couldn't stay curled up in bed anymore. I had to keep moving. Chin up, shoulders back, and a fake smile firmly in place, that was the plan.

I took my time getting ready, trying to make sure I looked the part. I dressed in my usual work clothes, but today they felt like a costume. My reflection in the mirror didn't look like me, it looked like someone pretending to have it all together. The laughing girl was dolled up and ready for action.

When I arrived at work, I walked through the doors with my head held high. I smiled at the receptionist, said hello to a couple of people in passing and kept my pace steady. It was all about keeping up appearances.

"Morning Lucy" Michelle chirped genuinely happy to see me. I smiled, said good morning and continued walking allowing no time for conversation.

Nathan caught up with me as I was heading toward my desk. His face was soft, concerned, and kind, too kind. "Hey, you alright?" he asked, his voice gentle, as if he knew I wasn't. I forced the grin even wider, putting on my best "nothing to see here" face.

"Absolutely," I said, my voice bright and chipper. It felt like I was pushing the words out through clenched teeth, trying not to break under his kindness. Even though he didn't entirely believe me, he let it go.

Nathan called me into his office a number of times that day and asked if everything was alright. His concern was genuine, and for a moment, I felt seen, understood. I wanted to pour my heart out, to tell him everything, but I couldn't bring myself to do it. Nathan was everything Tom wasn't - driven, charismatic, and sharp. The way he moved through the office with confidence and purpose was mesmerizing. He was also kind, a rare trait in a world where most people were too wrapped up in their own lives to notice others. I found myself drawn to him, and not for the first time, daydreaming about what life might be like if I were in his world. Nathans kindness and attention only fuelled my fantasies, making me imagine a life where I was more than just a struggling employee. But as much as I longed for something different, I knew that dreaming was a far cry from reality. The more I daydreamed about Nathan, the more I felt like a spectator in my own life, unable to take meaningful action. As time passed, I considered opening up to him, confessing my feelings for him, speech comes freely in my sleep but now stood in front of him, I reminded myself I'm nothing and nobody. I was just another face at the factory, he was kind to everyone I chastised myself, I was just clinging onto his warmth.

The following days and weeks went by in a blur, with work flying past me in waves of tasks, emails, and meetings. It was almost a relief to be busy. I didn't have time to dwell on Liam, the emptiness that had taken over the house, or Tom's growing distance. It was easier to just focus on ticking things off a list.

I tried to move forward, to take control of my life and work out what my purpose was, but each step felt like stumbling in the rain. I buried myself in my job, in my friendships, in anything that could give me a sense of being. But every version of myself I created felt foreign. It wasn't long before I lost sight of the lines between who I was and who others expected me to be. It seemed easier that way. The world became less complicated when I tucked my own wants and needs beneath layers of people-pleasing smiles and carefully curated personalities.

My work was the perfect escape. I loved my job, the people I surrounded myself with and I strived for perfection. I threw myself into it, picking up extra workloads and putting in as many additional hours as I could. I was then awarded a second promotion. It was a huge victory in an otherwise bleak landscape, and I was grateful for it. The new role came with more responsibilities and an office of my own, it also brought me dangerously closer to Nathan. He had no idea he was the reason

I now bounced out of bed in the morning, he was the invisible thread holding my head high and keeping me going. His support of me professionally and personally knew no bounds and I was excited at the prospect of being even closer to him, learning more, working harder and drinking him in every day.

Together we built the contract, we found new, more efficient ways of working and was an unstoppable tag team making positive changes to our unit. He was still my boss but treated me like an equal and embraced any new ideas I had, allowing me the freedom to grow in my position. That being said, I was still surprised when talk of the upcoming business awards began to buzz through the office and even more surprised when I heard my name mentioned as an attendee. I looked up from my note pad as we huddled around the white board back out on the factory floor, and sure enough, the lads were gathered around, encouraging me to go. "You've gotta come, it'll be a good night!" Paul insisted, his grin wide and infectious. I hesitated at first, all the directors would be there I'm not sure I could keep up the façade on such an important evening and certainly didn't believe I deserved a place to go. The Senior Management Team paused and looked at me expectantly, so I said yes of course. The prospect of a night out was exhilarating and exactly what I needed, a chance to dress up, feel good, put my best poker face on and drift one baby step further into the new life I was chasing, whatever that may be.

When the evening arrived, I put on the new floor length cocktail dress and black high heels I had purchased especially for the occasion. It hugged me in all the right places, and for the first time in a long while, I caught myself in the mirror and thought, I look nice. There was a flicker of something in my chest, confidence? Pride? I wasn't sure, but I held onto it.

I waited downstairs for Paul to collect me as he had volunteered to drive a group of us. Tom looked me up and down over the top of his phone but didn't move out of his seat. I craved his attention, good attention, I wanted him to get up and hold me and kiss me but nothing. He mumbled under his breath as Pauls car pulled up outside and beeped. I stopped next to Tom laying across the sofa. He stayed fixated on his pone. Spite rose in me and I felt angry at his nonchalance "Don't wait up." I spat my words at him and left the house without glancing back. Paul, ever the perfect gentlemen dressed in a dark blue tux and looking handsome held the car door open for me offering me the front seat of his Ford Focus while the others occupied the back. "Cinderella, your chariot awaits" He joked offering me a hand to help me in. The atmosphere in the car was light, the guys that had become my friends were buzzing with excitement for the night ahead and exchanging congratulations across each other for recent recognised efforts affording the company a place at the business awards for the first time. As we drove, Paul pulled over into a car park I assumed he needed a wee or something so didn't ask. However he reached into the glovebox and pulled out a CD case and placed it on his knee. Opening a small paper wrap he tipped some white powder onto it then proceeded to pull his bank card out of his wallet and began chopping the powder finely, separating it into neat lines.

I froze for a moment, watching him, feeling like time had slowed down. He rolled up a twenty pound note and sniffed a line, then handed it to me without a word, as if it was the most natural thing in the world, it was adult pass the parcel and it was my turn for the sweets.

I should have said no. I should have handed it back, laughed it off, or made an excuse, For a second I flashed back to the flats, the ghosts and shadows and Jack. A flipbook of images played in my mind reminding me of the hundreds of situations I found myself in too many times. That dark underworld that I hated the sight and smell of, but Paul did not look like that. He was together, sophisticated and would catch the eye of any woman with his striking eyes and crisp new suit. I looked in the back seat at the other guys from work all dressed to the nines. Bow ties perfectly placed, hair combed into position. Not a pale face or dark circled eye to be seen. They all started at me in anticipation of their turn with the powder. They were clearly familiar with this routine but they still looked young and fresh, alive and in control. I wanted that. I didn't want to be the misfit. I didn't want to be the person the other side of the wall so I took the CD case without hesitation. Taking the rolled up note like I'd done it a thousand times before. I leaned over to inhale before my brain could catch up or protest and made myself an outsider. I inhaled and passed the case on to the guys eagerly awaiting behind me. The powder burned sharp and fast in my nose and throat, but there was a rush too, something charged and almost instant, like somebody had cast a spell and suddenly the air was electric. Paul winked at me and started up the car again to finish our journey. I knew this wasn't me, this wasn't who I was supposed to be, but at that moment the part of my brain that chastised me went silent and for the first time in forever I just didn't care.

From that moment it felt like everything was happening in a dream. The coke gave me a buzz, a confidence I didn't know I was capable of. We walked into the Grand Theatre where the awards was being held with my arm linked through Pauls on one side and Marks on the other. Nathan was already inside when we arrived and he paused as he noticed us and his smile twisted up at the sides. My stomach flipped betraying me and I couldn't help but smile back at him, I held his gaze as he strode over to me kissing me gently on the cheek. "You look gorgeous" he said making me blush. "Come on let me introduce you to some people." Nathan smiled and nodded at Paul like I had dutifully been delivered and if I wasn't wrong Paul looked a little disgruntled about it. I on the other hand was hand as a kite so floated away on Nathans arm breathing him in and trying to decide if I had pins and needles or was melting at being on his arm. He took my hand (eekk my hand) and led me to a smartly dressed group of people gathering to sip champagne and talking business. Nathan introduced me proudly and before I knew it we were knee deep in conversation and KPI's, margins and new tender proposals. It was thrilling and I felt an air of importance that I had never felt before. I felt like I mattered, but Nathan always had a knack of making me feel special I had to keep reminding myself that was just his way and ignoring the stirring in my stomach.

By the time our company was announced as the second winner of the night, I was flying. Nathan grabbed my hand and pulled me up with him to collect the award. The local paper was there snapping photos of the winners and I felt Nathan's hand slide around my hip as he leaned into me smiling for the camera, the trophy gleaming between us. Something about the way his hand lingered, the way he looked at me, sent a rush through my body. It turned my stomach in a good way, something I hadn't felt before. I didn't know why, but it unsettled me, made me feel alive, unsteady and reckless all at once.

The rest of the night was a blur of dancing and laughing, the buzz of the cocaine making everything seem brighter, sharper, better. I stayed on the dance floor feeling invincible, like nothing in the world could touch me. Every now and then I'd catch Nathan's eyes on me and each time, my heart skipped a beat. There was something there, something unspoken, and I wasn't sure what to do with it. 'Dancing on the Ceiling' came on and I danced with Nathan singing ridiculously out of tune to each other, our eyes locking as we laughed, that invisible hunger between both of us suddenly audible. He took my hand and spun me under his arms as the others joined in singing with us. Everyone else in the room blended into shadows as we all lost ourselves in the euphoria of the night. It was medicine and I didn't want it to end.

When Paul pulled me away from the dance floor to leave for the evening. I wanted nothing more than to cling to Nathan and go home with him. I knew he had a beautiful girlfriend and perfect home but I wanted it to be me on his arm. I looked back at him as Paul offered me his arm once more patting my hand as I linked my arm with his. "Don't worry boss" he winked "I'll look after her." With that we left and Paul drove me home. I wound the window down leaning my head into the fresh air. I couldn't remember the last time I had such an incredible night. I felt euphoric.

When we reached my house my high was fading but still pulsing through my veins. I opened the door quietly, slipping inside and kicked my shoes off. Tom was asleep on the sofa, in his usual spot, the TV still on. I stood there for a moment, looking at him, feeling the divide between us grow wider with every second. But I was too high and happy to think about it.

I turned off the TV and gently shook his shoulder. "Come to bed," I whispered. He stirred, mumbled something, and followed me upstairs, still half-asleep.

I tried to be romantic with Tom as I slid in bed next to him lost in my high from Cocaine and business talk and drunk on a night with Nathan offering me a new expectation of caring connections. I was hazy and hopeful that love making you see on tv could be real as that was the feeling inside me that the evening had left me with. However, that was short lived as I began to run my hand down Toms body he grabbed my wrist, flung me on my back and pinned my arms down calling me a drunk whore. He told me not to move, put his hand over my mouth and satisfied himself taking me roughly, enjoying every second of me trying to fight against him. When he turned over I lay still, my heart racing trying to adjust my blurred vision and found myself staring at the ceiling once more. As the high faded away I wondered who I was becoming. The answer felt like it was just out of reach, and I wasn't sure if I wanted to catch it.

I had enjoyed being out, really enjoyed it, I felt like a new door had opened and as I focused my thoughts on those eyes, those hands, the dancing and that smile, I felt alive, regardless of how it had just ended, I couldn't be brought down. With the buzz of the evening still lingering in the background whispering promises of escape I turned over and fell asleep dreaming about bright lights, music, blurred faces and Nathan.

Chapter 21

I started tagging along with the guys from work whenever they went out. I just didn't want to be home. Tom didn't like it. He didn't want to go out, and he didn't want me to go either. He'd grumble, trying to convince me to stay home with him, but I shrugged it off. I could feel him getting more controlling, but the more he tried to keep me in, the more I pushed back.

The nights out started off harmless enough, just drinks, a laugh, an excuse to forget the mundane reality of everyday life. I loved it every second of it. Dancing with a drink in hand, not clock watching to get home to Tom and no chid to look after so no panic about morning packed lunches or school runs, just innocent fun. When handed a straw, the same as before I didn't hesitate. With a Vodka and coke in hand I would spin around the dancefloor, the guys from work all keeping an eye on me like protective big brothers from another mother. Never mind the fact they fed me cocaine before we left and topped me up during our escapades. When they saw men approach me they would appear by my side from nowhere ushering them away. Someone offered me some pills and Marcus pounced on him in a nano second. The irony of it wasn't lost on me. Drugs had destroyed my brother's life, my family's life, but I shut all of that out. I didn't want to think about Jack, or the mess he'd made, or the fact that I couldn't look at Tom without picking a fight every time he lit up a joint. I wasn't ready to face how much I resented him for sinking into the same lethargy day after day, yet here I was high as a kite following Pauls unspoken rules. Cocaine and speed were ok, pills were not. Drink lots of water, don't accept drinks from strangers. He was never more than a few feet away from me ready to save me from anyone going in for a quick grope or handing me drinks I hadn't ordered.

When I inhaled coke, it felt like everything in my head went quiet. The noise, the clawing feeling that I couldn't escape, the endless, gnawing anxiety about who I was or what I was supposed to be doing, the resentment for Tom, the resentment for Jack, the missing limb syndrome I felt since Liam went home, it all just disappeared. It was euphoric, like the world suddenly made sense again. I felt alive. I danced in the clubs until my legs ached, until the music was pounding in my chest. I didn't ever want to leave, didn't ever want to go home. Night after night I would end up being shoulder carried out by Paul. It was a running joke now on who's turn it would be to drag me out. Home was a place I didn't know how to be in anymore. Every time I left the house, it felt like I was running from something, but I didn't know what. Every time I snorted that line, I was trying to escape the suffocating emptiness, the confusion about who I was without Liam or Jack or mum, I couldn't fix any of them and couldn't fix me either. The more we went out the more I chased that high, sniffing a line or six, and losing myself in the haze of it all. The thought I was fun, always up for a dare, always the life of the party. Little did they know that inside, a storm was brewing, one I couldn't stop. I told myself it wasn't a big deal, that it was just a bit of fun. But the truth was, I was unravelling and I could feel it happening. Underneath all the highs, the lows were always there, lurking just beneath the surface. I'd wake up the next morning, my head pounding, my body aching, and the guilt would settle in like a that heavy fog I knew all too well. I knew what I was doing was dangerous. I knew where this path could lead, I'd seen it firsthand. But after a week of pussy footing around Tom, pandering to his every need, praying for a glimmer of affection and attention, so when the weekend rolled around again, I'd go back to the same routine, because in those few hours, the chaos in my mind went quiet. The longer it went on, the more I realized I was spinning out of control, but I didn't know how to stop more to the point I didn't want to stop. That storm was there inside me, and I didn't know how to calm it down.

During my prison visits, with Jack I'd tell him stories about raves and taking lines, things I thought he'd never agree with me doing. But he laughed. He actually laughed and listened, like he was amused by this version of me that was suddenly bold, reckless, and maybe, in his eyes, a bit cool. The deeper I sank into the world of cocaine and speed, the more I felt like I was connecting with my brother. It was strange, ironic, even that in the haze of drugs and chaos, I finally found common ground with him. For once, I felt like I wasn't the odd one out. I was part of a world that I could understand, and it felt good. It was surreal, like some twisted version of bonding.

Jack filled me in on his life inside where he was receiving counselling and had started a plastering course. He joked about evening card games and how they'd trade chocolate bars like they were gold. He looked fit and well and was no longer using at all just smoking cigarettes. Yet there I was sat the opposite side of the table high as a kite at two in the afternoon, warming up for the evening ahead restless and excitable. Soaking it all in and feeling, for the first time in forever like I enjoyed his company. Like I belonged somewhere.

I knew it was wrong. It wasn't lost on me. But the craving to be a part of someone's world, to not feel like an outsider for once, was too strong. I couldn't be like Tom, the stoner who could sit still for hours, letting the world pass by in a cloud of smoke. That was never me. I needed to move, to be distracted, to run away from the constant noise in my head. The drugs made me feel alive, made me forget. I felt happy, even if it was all a lie, and even if deep down, I knew the happiness was built on something dangerous.

I started seeing Liam less and less, as he settled into his new life at home. I tried to give him distance while I strove to be better at work. I would always be here if he needed me but my new found freedom was thrilling. Nathan had begun joining our weekend shenanigans. Late nights filled with more drinking, more cocaine and more attention from Nathan was riveting. I was being reckless. It was a train of disasters waiting to happen, and I was driving full speed ahead.

Chapter 22

Nathan always made me feel like I mattered. I leaned against the door of his office chatting to him as he typed away discussing how near he was to completing his masters degree in Engineering. He was already a Senior manager and was hungry for more. I felt inspired by his drive and determination to progress and wanted to be a part of that journey and learn as much as I could from him. Conversations with him were easy. He invested in me a lot at work and I appreciated him for it. Nathan opened doors for me offering me endless training and opportunities to build something of myself. He had attended more nights out with all of us recently and each time I allowed myself to believe we had become a step closer to each other.

"You need to slow down Luce."

"What?" I stepped back shocked and offended and had the audacity to look confused even though I knew exactly what he meant.

"The drugs. Slow it down a little, you're so good at what you do here. Don't let it take over your every day life!" He continued to tap away at his computer. I felt small again. I smiled at him I knew I was teetering on the edge. I wanted to fall into him, to let it out, to start again, for him to wrap those big manly arms around me and tell me it will be ok, but I daren't. We were work colleagues, he had a girlfriend, I had a Tom and managers didn't fall apart. He glanced over at me as if looking inside me and suddenly I felty like I could fall apart. He walked over to me, his smell was incredible. I turned away from him willing myself to walk back to my desk. If I looked at him in close proximity I would break for sure. He stood too close to me and squeezed my shoulder. I took a deep breath closing my eyes and readjusting myself and walked back to my desk.

I felt silly and weak. I was stupid thinking he had feelings for me he just felt sorry for me. I didn't need feeling sorry for though. But I did need to get my shit together. In a moment of clarity, I realized that I needed to face my emotions rather than hide from them. I couldn't lose my job out of stupidity but knew I didn't trust myself to stop drinking and taking drugs. I was afraid of totally unravelling and ending up a ghost myself so I decided to google counsellors on the work computer -

Seeking professional help to navigate the overwhelming feelings of loss and confusion?

'Yep, that sounds about right' – booked.

Counselling was a small step, but it was a start. The door was opened by an older lady with a soft looking face, her hair in a neat low bun and glasses with a chain attached to them. The décor was minimal with some framed artwork and motivational quotes. An odd plant had been carefully placed and there was a bookshelf containing hundreds of books about psychology. I was excited about being fixed, about finding the new me. I wanted to sit in her chair and have her tell me what the problem was and make it go away. I was looking forward to walking out feeling fresh and newly motivated.

I sat back in a single leather chair in the clinical uninviting room and took myself to a faraway place. I explained that I felt uneasy. That I woke up every morning with a burning anxiety that squeezed my chest and stole my oxygen. I explained that when I woke up every day I immediately wished I hadn't. I told her that I craved pain and went out a lot to avoid that feeling. I told her of my fear of facing every day until I got dressed and put on my make up. That was my mask allowing me to become the 'laughing girl' again until bedtime when I could scrub it all off and I was left with the nothingness that was me. I craved darkness, I enjoyed it, and if I couldn't sleep... I stopped talking. I was about to tell her that the drugs did the same thing. Sleep made things dark and non existent but drugs took me to the clouds in a completely different way. But fear crept in as I heard myself speak and suddenly I wasn't comfortable offering that part of myself to this strange lady. I wanted help yes, but I didn't want her judgement. I didn't want her to think I was 'that person' so I stopped abruptly in my tracks and told her I couldn't pinpoint the reason that I felt this way.

"Tell me about your family?" She started.

"I don't see my dad, he works abroad." I left out *he beat my mum senseless and is the reason that our close nit tiny, loving family fell apart at the seams.*

"I see" she nodded "and your mother?"

Currently sat in a rehabilitation centre dosed up to the eye-balls just to keep her alive - "Oh she's incredible! The strongest woman I know! (she really is) We're so close (not a lie) we see each other regularly (again the truth) We go shopping all the time, she loves shoes, we talk on the phone every night..." OK stop. I chastised myself for going on a fantasy tangent.

"mm hmmm" she took more notes. "Siblings?"

"Oh I have a brother" I said bursting with pride "and my nephew Liam, he's funny and cute, so loving. When he comes to stay.." Suddenly I caught my breathe. I couldn't go down that road, I was here to heal not cry. "So that's me" I stated putting a big fat full stop in place. "Work, family, life, everything great its just me, I'm the problem!" I said smiling sweetly having managed to contain my reality from her. Then I sat back, took a deep breath and listened waiting patiently to begin healing, already debating how I would carefully construct my answers...

"So" She said with a sympathetic smile "When your life is perfect, that is to say what we perceive perfection to be"

Wait what?

"...our minds tell us that something bad is going to happen."

Again what?

"...It happens to us because we are programmed by fear of the unknown, so because Miss Lawson you are so settled and content right now, your mind is playing tricks on you. It's looking for something to go wrong so that it can protect you when it does."

Eeeerrrmm

"As you grow older and experience more, your emotions will change."

AGAIN WHAT? My eyes nearly popped out of my head at the sheer audacity. The patronising old cow knew nothing. NOTHING! I'm not sure what I was expecting from a counselling session, but it wasn't this. I wanted a chez long where I could lay stretched out, massaging my temples, fanning myself and she could sympathise with the life I was going to make up. She paused for a sip of water then continued softly.

"Your hormones will balance out and your anxieties will make sense to you. We just need to enjoy all the wonderful things we have and feel grateful for them. You are only..." She glanced at her paperwork while I picked my jaw up off the floor and I took a mouthful of my own glass of water trying to reflect on what she was saying.

"Nineteen!" She continued, peering at me over her glasses like I'd just skipped out of preschool.

I looked her square in the eye as I sat back in my seat and contemplated hitting her with that clipboard she was holding. She wasn't done...

"You're still a baby, there is a big wide world out there that you haven't experienced yet…" On hearing her words, I choked on my water, it came firing out of my nose at such speed you'd have thought the coffee table was on fire!

I was stunned at what she said and irritated that I was now choking and couldn't protest. *Should have gone for the clipboard not the water!*

That all too familiar volcano was bubbling inside me, and I wasn't sure how it was going to come out. I wanted to laugh hysterically but was concerned that if I did, I'd laugh all the way to the funny farm. Maybe that's what I needed? Maybe I should get up and dance like a crazy woman around the room letting out the loudest most harrowing laugh and never stop until they take me away. Maybe I genuinely was losing my mind? Maybe this is it? Numbness that sends you into craziness. What an absolute pile of shit this was!

I was perplexed to the point of winded and now choking was in the equation. For the actual love of God - can I do anything right??? I fidgeted as my anxieties were heightened.

"Imagine a cupboard…" She continued and I still hadn't stopped choking…

"And if we fill that cupboard up with too many toys."

Did she just say toys?

"At some point that door is going to pop open."

Did she just say pop??

I stayed silent almost intrigued at the most patronising speech I had ever been delivered. I smiled taking a deep breathe slowly regaining my composure. I considered offering her a life lesson of her own but of course I stayed quiet.

At the end of our session I was mystified. I politely told her that her theory was interesting, and I hadn't looked at my life like that before. Then out of nowhere as I put my coat on I started giggling like a child, instantly followed by an uncontrollable loud, ugly laughter. Even though I was screaming and protesting inside I just couldn't stop laughing. The more I laughed the more embarrassed I felt. My counsellor stood in front of me bemused but said nothing. I scrambled through my handbag trying to stifle my laughter, handed over my £50 (FIFTY ACTUAL POUNDS) and headed for the door.

"Shall I book you in for next week?" I nearly choked again – (on air this time) I plastered my well-rehearsed toothy smile on my face, I forced my shoulders back to stop my laughing fit or choke again (me or her I hadn't decided). My 19-year-old, inexperienced, untarnished, unknowledgeable baby face announced loudly and proudly that I felt a thousand times better. I Lied.

"Well," she smiled patting me on the arm. "Sometimes we just need someone to remind us how lucky we are." I nodded and left swiftly before my reflexes could throw my glass of water at her and before my mouth could catch up with my brain. For someone that makes a living from reading people and helping them, she was clearly oblivious to the fifty nine subtitles coming out of my face! As I walked home irritated, I made a conscious decision that counselling clearly wasn't for me.

That night I lay in bed suffocating on my own thoughts as usual. I knew I couldn't continue living like this. I had to find a way to reclaim my life, to make peace with my past, and to build a future where I could truly be myself, or somebody else. I didn't need help.

I had mastered being a perfect mix of chameleon and laughing girl and applied this whenever I met anybody new. This was me taking control. I continued drifting further and further away from myself as the actress in me settled in, I laughed carelessly around my audience, pretending to be the happy laughing girl that everyone had come to know and love. I liked that her, I liked that other people liked her.

My journey was far from over, but I was learning to navigate the complexities of my emotions and the challenges of my life by trying to transition into someone, something completely new. I was starting to accept that while I might not have all the answers, I had the strength to keep moving forward, one step at a time.

Chapter 23

The morning had been dragging, and I must have looked as deflated as I felt. It had been one of those weeks where everything seemed off, and apparently my boss had noticed. He was always reading the room, always aware. As I was reviewing some reports, he casually approached my desk and leaned in slightly, lowering his voice.

"You've been a bit quiet this week," he said, his eyes filled with genuine concern and placing that all too familiar comforting hand on my shoulder. "If you need someone to talk to, I'm here." His moods were giving me whiplash. Five minutes ago he was reminding me of my place at work and telling me to sort myself out and I had listened. I booked counselling that turned out to be crap and made me feel worse about myself. Now I had no drugs, still wasn't healed and I wasn't impressed with either of these outcomes. I fought my frustration and stayed silent.

"Why don't we get some fresh air at lunch? There's a meadow just outside town I like to go to sometimes." I hesitated, unsure of my mood or how to respond, but something about the offer seemed comforting.

"Yeah, that sounds nice," I relented mastering a smile but still secretly still blaming him for my counselling escapade. Lunch came around faster than I'd anticipated. I'd tried to look put-together, smart even, in my pinstripe trousers, loafers, and a fitted blouse that felt both professional and slightly daring, with the top button purposely left undone. Id show him unravelled!! It gave me confidence, although I was already feeling flustered.

Nathan walked with me to his sleek car, and the adrenaline hit me. It wasn't like I hadn't ridden in a car with a colleague before, but something about this felt different, thrilling even. As I slipped into the passenger seat, I became intensely aware of the proximity between us. His aftershave was subtle but unmistakable, a mix of cedar and something else that lingered in the air between us.

He glanced at me before turning on the ignition, his eyes catching mine for a moment longer than usual. He smiled, soft but deliberate, and suddenly, I wanted to kiss him. The thought startled me, and I shifted awkwardly in my seat, trying to push it out of my mind. This was just a friendly gesture, nothing more.

We drove making small talk. I was a dithery mess and was irritating myself for the hundredth time. When we pulled up to the meadow, I fumbled, literally. As I went to step out of the car, I caught my foot on the seatbelt and, in the most graceless way imaginable, fell out of the car and face planted the floor.

So much for the poised, professional image I'd been trying to maintain.

Nathan burst out laughing, and though my cheeks burned with embarrassment, his laughter was contagious. I couldn't help but join in.

"Smooth," he teased, still chuckling as he held out a hand to pull me up.

"Thanks," I mumbled, brushing off my knees, already noticing the faint green stains. He smiled, his laughter softening

"It barely notices" he said glaring at my knees. I rolled my eyes,

"subtle really subtle." He couldn't help but snigger again at my expense. "We'll have fun explaining it when we get back to the office that's for sure!"

We started walking along the path and I was surprised at how easy it felt to talk to him. The conversation flowed naturally, like we'd known each other much longer than just a couple years at the factory office. He told me about his passion for music, how he played guitar to unwind, something I never would have guessed about him. We talked about work, but it drifted into deeper topics of life, dreams and aspirations.

"I always thought about taking a break from the corporate world and just... living off the grid for a while. Playing guitar in the mountains somewhere," he mused. In the middle of a mountain listening to him play a guitar was instantly my vision of heaven and an image I'd use at night to help me sleep.

I found myself sharing things I didn't normally talk about (and didn't really know about me until I said them out loud), things about my own ambitions, what I wanted out of life. He listened intently, not just nodding along but actually hearing me. I wanted to be somebody, I wanted to manage a team, to make a difference. For a while, I forgot that he was my boss, that we were colleagues, and I let myself just be in the moment.

By the time we made our way back to the car, it was way past my usual lunch hour. I glanced down at my grass-stained knees and felt a pang of embarrassment. Seriously, how was I going to explain this?

Back at the office, I tried to make a quick, inconspicuous entry, but the frowning faces that greeted us both didn't seem convinced by my hurried explanation about tripping over the seatbelt. They exchanged knowing glances, as if there was more to the story than I was letting on. I could almost hear the whispers starting to form behind me as I made my way back to my desk. Nathan just caught my eye from across the room, that same smile flickering at the corner of his mouth as if he found the whole thing amusing. I couldn't help but smile back.

It had been just a walk in the meadow, but something had shifted. There was a quiet understanding between us now, something unspoken but undeniably there. The grass stains on my knees and the new rumours were a small price to pay for that.

After the counselling, the grass stains and my mass pity party
for one, I decided to get over myself and reconnect with my
friends. It had been years since we'd all been in the same room.
Life had pulled us in different directions: new jobs, new cities,
new relationships. We hadn't fallen out, just drifted apart, each
of us tangled in our own lives. As I'd been feeling a little lost, like
I was standing on the edge of something, not knowing which
way to go. So, on a whim, with my new found determination
to recover a part of myself I sent out a message: Come round
tonight? Takeaway and wine? Let's catch up like old times.

To my surprise, the replies were quick and enthusiastic.
Within hours, my house was full again with voices I hadn't
heard in so long. When the doorbell rang, I felt a knot of nerves.
Would it feel awkward? Would we have anything to say after so
much time apart?

The second I opened the door, I was hit with a rush of familiarity. There they were smiling, arms outstretched. Hugs were
exchanged, a few awkward laughs at first, but it didn't take long
before the years between us melted away.

We gathered around the table, takeaway boxes spread out,
the smell of Indian food filling the air. Someone poured wine,
and with that first sip, it was like a switch flipped. Conversation
flowed easily. We talked about what we'd been up to, the jobs
we hated, the ones we loved, the people we were seeing, and
the people we had let go. It felt like therapy without the ap-

pointment and was certainly more effective than that other silly cow! The kind of calm you get from people who've known you for years, who've seen every version of you (well almost every version) and still show up.

As the night went on, we began reminiscing, laughing about old nights out and embarrassing moments we'd tried to forget. Someone mentioned that song we used to blast on every get together or car journey to a bar and before we knew it we were all singing 'Country Road' together, wine glasses in hand, sat together in the living room like no time had passed. It was ridiculous, off-key, and absolutely perfect.

The music from the old days became a soundtrack to our reunion. We played all the favourites, the ones that had shaped us, the ones we knew all the words to even now. For those few hours, we weren't just adults navigating complicated lives, we were us again, the version of ourselves that had once felt invincible.

There was something about that night that went deeper than nostalgia. It reminded me of who I used to be, carefree, ambitious, and maybe a little reckless, but happy. Sitting there, surrounded by people who knew the real me, I realized that I didn't need anything more than this. No distractions, no false highs, this was what I'd been missing. The laughter, the warmth, the shared memories. As we talked and laughed it was like all the pieces of me that had been scattered came back together. This wasn't about reliving the past, it was about remembering that some things, some people, are worth holding onto.

By the end of the night, my heart felt lighter. We promised not to let this much time pass again, and it didn't feel like an empty promise. As I sat there in the quiet after they'd all left, surrounded by empty wine glasses and half-eaten food, I smiled to myself. This was the kind of high I'd been searching for, not from distractions, but from something real. Reconnecting with old friends was like hitting reset on my life and I knew then that everything was going to be okay. I didn't need anything else, just this, just them.

Chapter 24

I pulled up outside my mum's house, engine idling as I took a breath. She'd been out of rehab for a week now, and while she looked better, stronger, I couldn't shake the worry. There was still something fragile about her, something that made me feel like if I spoke too loudly, it might shatter her all over again. Today was going to be hard, we were visiting Jack in prison.

When she opened the front door I noticed the change immediately. She was dressed neatly, her hair combed, a far cry from the person who had been admitted to rehab. But her eyes, her eyes gave her away. She was anxious, fidgety. She'd been to the prison before, but the thought of seeing Jack behind bars still got to her every time.

"You ready?" I asked, trying to sound more casual than I felt. She gave a sharp nod and got into the car without a word, her hands twisting the strap of her bag in her lap as we drove.

The drive to the prison was quiet, both of us lost in our thoughts. I could feel her tension building as we neared the gates. It was either going to be a smooth visit or a meltdown. There wasn't much in-between with Mum.

Once we got through the usual checks, IDs, UV stamps, clanging of doors the familiarity of the prison atmosphere settled over us. Cold, clinical, like the place drained warmth out of people as soon as they walked in. When we reached the X-ray machine, we had to take off our shoes and belts. I had done this a thousand times so it had become second nature and I didn't question the injustice of it anymore. A guard, tall and expressionless, told mum to remove her brooch, a small silver dove with a diamond for an eye that Jack had given her one Christmas. Stolen or not, no one ever asked. It was her pride and joy, a symbol of something purer than what had come since. I swallowed hard when I clocked the look on mums face and I knew we were in for an episode.

Mum froze. "What if I say no?" she asked, her voice trembling on the edge of fury. The guard looked at her with zero patience. "Then you don't go in," he said flatly, signalling for the next person in line to come forward as if we were just an inconvenience.

It happened quicker than I could stop it, her nerves snapping like a rubber band stretched too tight. "Fine!" she snapped, hands shaking as she struggled to unpin the brooch. "Look, it's off!" she said, her voice rising, waving the tiny pin around. "What a dangerous weapon eh?" she shouted jabbing the brooch toward the guard and in the air towards the audience queuing patiently behind us. The pin was barely a centimetre long. "You must feel safer now - Careful all of you..." She was shouting now "I might Stab you with it!"

The guard towering above her at easily six-foot-four didn't even flinch as she waved the little dove inches from his face threatening to stab him with it. "Sound the alarm." She continued yelling "I have a dangerous weapon!" If it wasn't so serious, it would have been funny. This tiny woman standing up to a prison guard that looked like he worked out daily with the hulk. But prison officers aren't known for their sense of humour and I had just driven an hour and half to get here, I was not in the mood to be chucked out.

"Calm down, Mum," I said, stepping between them. I tried to meet the guard's eyes pleading for some understanding. "She's just anxious, it's been a really difficult time. We'll be fine okay? Can we just get through this?" I turned to mum and held her hands looking into her eyes trying to beg for calm but saying nothing.

Thankfully The Hulk grunted and finally waved us on, clearly done with the theatrics. Mum, though still fuming managed to hold her tongue, for now.

When we finally saw Jack he was already sitting at one of the tables looking amused. He had that cocky grin, the one that never quite left him even in here. "What happened out there?" he asked, clearly having heard the commotion.

Mum still looked like she was on the verge of losing it, but when I told Jack what happened he chuckled, and suddenly we all started laughing uncontrollably. I looked around the room and watched as the visitors that had been queuing behind us had taken their seats nodding their eyes towards us, clearly mum has given them a topic of conversation for their visit. She'd be talk of the prison later no doubt. It was nice, different, to laugh together, even in this bleak place. For a moment it felt like we were just a normal family again.

Mum was still upset though, her fingers twitching where they should have been clutching her brooch. "I don't know why they do this," she muttered, her eyes darting around the room still ruffled.

Talking to Jack in the prison visiting room always felt like losing time in the best and worst ways. He caught us up on the latest card games being played inside, what people were betting and what the real stakes were. Mars bars and cigarettes had become currency. It was a kind of underground economy where the price of a pack of Benson and Hedges could rival anything you'd find on the outside. Jack was never short of schemes either. Once it was heroin he wanted me to smuggle in, these days it was tobacco. Years of trying and he still hadn't given up and even joked at mum to have a go. She winced at the thought and thankfully laughed it off.

The new two hour visits on Saturdays were a blessing, though they still slipped away so quickly. In those moments, it was easy to forget we were sitting in a prison visiting room talking across a bolted-down table. I told him about seeing my friends and how good it felt to feel human again. I asked about Scarlet and whether she'd brought Liam to visit recently. His response was brief, Liam was doing okay. It was one of those things that neither of us wanted to dig into. The topic of Liam was always delicate, always avoided as quickly as it came up, like something fragile we were too scared to break.

The worst part was always when the time was up. I was never ready to leave, even if I told myself I had nothing more to say. As I stood up, he thanked me for the money I'd sent him and immediately placed his next order with me. He never needed much, usually tapes or something to trade inside, but it felt like a piece of normality for him in a place where nothing was, so I really didn't mind.

Jack leaned in toward me when Mum wasn't looking. "Look after yourself," he said, his tone shifting, serious now. "You look like shit!" He gave me a knowing look, the kind that said more than he could out loud. His comment stung. I was hearing this a lot lately. It was irritating coming from him but I chose not to retaliate in defence. We'd had enough drama for one day so I just nodded and told him I loved him.

When we left, the brooch was handed back to Mum at the gate. She clutched it like a magpie that had just discovered something new and shiny to take back to his nest, she smiled at it like it anchored her in some way. We managed to get through the rest of the exit without any more drama, though I could still feel her simmering underneath.

As I drove her home the streets passing by in a blur, I couldn't help but wonder, was she healing, or was she just balancing on the edge of something worse? The visit had been a distraction sure, but there was no telling how long that would last. All I knew was that for now, we had made it through another day. I hugged her tightly as I handed her back to David at the front door.

Driving back to my own house, the weight of Jack's words settled over me again. I played music loudly, trying to drown out my thoughts, but they wouldn't go away. I walked into the house and saw Tom sitting on the sofa, staring at the TV, not even looking up when I came in.

"Where have you been?" he asked, his voice flat, his eye staying fixed on the screen.

"You know where I've been," I said kicking off my shoes and heading for the stairs.

"Don't get narky with me," he shot back, his voice sharp. There was an edge to it that sounded almost like a threat. I ignored him, went upstairs and filled the bath. The water was hot, steam rising up around me as I sank into it trying to clear my mind. But Jack's voice was still there, asking me the questions I didn't want to answer.

Was he right? Was I ignoring the signs? I didn't know but I knew one thing, I didn't want to think about it.

Chapter 25

At twenty-one the promise of adulthood had morphed into a chaotic reality. The house I shared with Tom was a mess of discarded takeaway containers and empty beer bottles, a reflection of the disarray in my life. Tom, perpetually high and unmotivated was more a burden than a partner. Our relationship was strained, held together only by the thin thread of familiarity.

My job at the factory had become both a sanctuary and a prison. Work was demanding but it provided a semblance of stability amid the whirlwind of my life. Nathan had become more than just a figure of authority, he was a beacon in the storm. Our affair had started innocently enough, late-night work sessions, shared frustrations and unspoken connections, that day in the office working late he had put his hand ever so softly on the side of my face and leant in for that kiss, neither of us had the strength to stop it. My feet felt like they would lift off the ground. It quickly spiralled into a full-blown secretive relationship. It was thrilling and dangerous at the same time, an escape from the suffocating reality of my daily existence and I was falling for him more and more every day.

Liam, now nine years old was a constant thought in my mind. I missed him more than I could express. The joy he had brought into my life was something I struggled to recapture. I knew that he was growing up without me and the guilt gnawed at me every day that I didn't make the effort to see him more regularly. I thought about him often, wondering how he was adjusting and feeling overwhelming guilt at the way I had shut myself off over recent years.

The emotional turbulence of my life drove me to return to seeking more solace in cocaine and speed. The initial euphoria was a stark contrast to the numbness I felt otherwise. I began using more frequently again in the week not just weekend escapades, trying to keep up with the demands of work, the responsibilities I couldn't quite manage, and the chaos of my relationship with Tom. The drugs gave me a temporary escape but they also fuelled a dangerous cycle. My highs were followed by crushing lows and I struggled to maintain a façade of normalcy.

Nathan's affection, though intoxicating, was a double-edged sword. Our affair became a reckless pursuit of pleasure and distraction. The moments we shared in secret were exhilarating, he was a perfect mix of authority coupled with gentle touches and dare I say it love. He was the only person after Jimmy to turn my stomach into butterflies and my body responded to his hungrily every time we were together. However, these feelings also left me even more disconnected from reality. It was easy to lose myself in his world, where I was desired and valued but the real world was never far behind, waiting to pull me back.

Letters from Jack arrived as regularly as our calls and visits. His words were increasingly demanding and filled with frustration. He wrote about his struggles in prison, his need for more money and his anger at how his life had turned out. His demands only added to my stress, making me feel trapped between my obligations to him and the crumbling remnants of my own life. Each letter was a reminder of the past I couldn't escape and the responsibilities I felt I was failing to meet.

Amidst this turmoil I discovered I was pregnant. The news hit me like a ton of bricks, leaving me paralyzed with fear and confusion. I knew it was Toms child. Even though I saw Nathan daily, the time to be intimate with him was few and far between as those private undisturbed moments were difficult to find.

I wasn't ready to be a mother, not in this chaotic, drug-fuelled environment and allowing this to happen was stupidity at its best. The prospect of raising a child while fighting to be somebody more at work, Tom's increasing dependence on drugs (and mine), and an affair with Nathan seemed overwhelming. I was stuck in a cycle of self-destruction unable to see a clear path forward.

My pregnancy became another secret to hide, a new layer of deception. Lying to myself while trying to block it out and hide it from everyone else. I continued to use drugs, convincing myself that I needed them to cope. I avoided discussing my pregnancy with Nathan, who was oblivious to the reality of my life outside of our affair. I also avoided confronting Tom, who was too lost in his own world to notice the growing strain in our relationship. The more successful I had become at work the more hostile he became towards me.

As the months passed, the weight of my choices became unbearable. The drugs, the affair and the demands from Jack, the promise to Liam broken as I was no longer there for him, all converged into a perfect storm. I felt like I was yet again spiralling out of control, unable to keep up with the demands of adulthood and the expectations placed upon me. The once-hopeful prospect of a new life was now a source of dread and despair.

I had to face the reality of my situation. I was alone, sitting in our cluttered house staring at the pregnancy test in disbelief. The decision to confront Nathan was inevitable, and when I finally did, his reaction was a mix of shock and confusion.

We spent a day walking hand in hand in the woods where we knew we wouldn't pass anybody that knew us. He squeezed my hand and turned to me gently stroking the side of my face. His words cut harder than any abuse that has ever been spat at me.

"You have to choose now Luce." He was supportive and willing to sacrifice the comfort of the mundane but safe and steady relationship he was in. He chose me and wanted me to choose him back. He offered me the world I craved, a secure job, financial stability and knowing the baby wasn't his had promised to love it like his own.

Panic rose in me and I found myself in unfamiliar territory. Nathan was everything I could have ever wanted. We lost time together, his affection was something I had never experienced and craved day after day. It was overwhelming and terrifying at the same time. My stomach was a mix or want and fear and now I had this tiny seed inside me that would depend on me forever. He pulled me into a gentle embrace with one strong arm around my back and the other stroking my head. A tear sneaked out and I suddenly felt vulnerable, like I couldn't breathe but I didn't know why. I wanted him more than anything but those oh so overpowering thoughts lingered in my mind

What if he leaves me

His house is HIS house not mine

His money is his security not mine

Did I want to be responsible for separating him and Saman-tha? I hadn't even given her a second thought when I was sat spread eagle on his desk at night. I suddenly hated myself AGAIN. He didn't really know me! He didn't know about Jack, about Liam, about mum. He had suspicions but they were all brushed away by my ability to smile and wave and joke because that made everything ok. What if he didn't / wouldn't/ couldn't love the real me? I didn't even know who that person was.

We stayed close together, our hands embraced, while I tormented myself with the what ifs and we continued walking and talking about possibilities before returning to work. For the coming days he was like a wolf protecting his pack, he'd leave post it notes on my computer every morning and would constantly make me drinks and kiss me on the head. The affair was obvious to everyone at work but they daren't question either of us.

At home the decision swirled around my mind as I watched Tom, thinking about how I was about to turn his world upside down. He was so easy, just blatantly ignored me most of the time and would love me one minute and hate me the next. Sex was rough and fast with no emotion attached just animal instinct kicking in whenever the need arose.

Over the next 2 weeks Nathan began to become distant, he was ruffled by my inability to let him sweep me off my feet which made me panic even more. When sat in his office one morning trying to have a conversation with him he was stressed as his dissertation was due for his masters degree. He was 10 years my senior and the company had high plans for him in mind.

"Do you need help?" I asked tip toeing around him, searching for something else to say as I knew he was waiting for my decision.

"Yes fucking clever clogs write my dissertation for me!" He'd never sworn at me before. His words stung and made me feel five years old. I stood up suddenly and stormed out of his office. He followed me apologising and offered to take me out to lunch. I declined like a petulant child still speed walking back to my desk. He was desperate and sorry and all it had taken was that few seconds for my entire emotional system to shut down and detach myself from him. As he followed me into my office and closed the door gently behind him he got down on both knees no care given that the entire factory could see through the window. Anyone outside would have thought he was proposing as he spun my chair to face him and held both my hands in his.

"Lucy please. You drive me wild, you've got inside my head. I want you. You make me feel alive. I want to go and watch football matches together putting my scarf around you and sharing a cone of chips. I want to walk along the sea front with you losing time. I want to dance with you always like we did at the Christmas do. You light up my world. There is nothing I won't do for you."

"I can't" I said my voice nothing more than a whisper. My words surprising me as much as him. I was doing it again. It was Jimmy x 2 on a billion times bigger scale. The enormity of his gentleness was too much. I didn't know how to cope with it. Small fleeting moments were incredible with him but the fear of allowing someone to look after me was too much. I didn't belong in his world and he didn't belong in mine. He didn't know me not really. Tom was a safe bet. He was familiar and he loved me in his own way. Nathan was a dream and the thought of a fairytale life with him was all I ever wanted. But the possibility of him maybe leaving me one day was something that would surely break me for good. I retreated back into myself. I didn't deserve his love, Samantha did. She took herself to the gym every morning and kept herself slim and beautiful. I got out of bed looking like Worzel Gummage and needed three cups of coffee to function on a daily basis! She was far better suited to him than I ever would be. I could offer him nothing.

His face sunk and he looked the most upset id ever seen him. He squeezed my hand and made a promise to always be there for me no matter what which nearly made me completely unravel, change my mind and beg him to look after me until my dying day, but I held it in. I held my breath and stared robotically at my screen. He stood up, walked back out of my office closing the door gently again. I felt like every face in the factory was watching us but of course that was my paranoia, they were all too busy I'm sure but I felt judged, felt eyes piercing I knew a baby bump appearing would set off new rumours and I didn't want that kind of attention. I looked out of the office window across the bustling factory floor to see who was staring but nobody was. Heading back to my computer I focused on my screen trying to block out what I had just done.

I was hoping to seek solace in Tom that evening and had even convinced myself in some imaginary place in my mind that he would be pleased with my news. That he'd wrap his arms around me and kiss my stomach, professing his undying love for me when I announced my pregnancy to him. The reality of his reaction though was devastating. When I showed him the little stick with two pink lines on, his face was indifferent, and his response mired in his own drug-induced haze. " You keeping it?" He asked like a stranger id just met in a bar although I was thankful his temper seemed to be dormant for now.

"Of course" I answered touching my stomach and allowing myself to really absorb the reality of our situation now I had said it out loud to him. He sniffed, got his coat and went out. The realization that I really was facing this alone, hit me hard. But that was where I was safest – on my own. I didn't need anything from anybody I resolved.

Eventually, I reached out to Jack on our Tuesday call. I needed to explain my situation and ask for help. The response I received was a mix of sympathy and anger, reflecting his own struggles and frustrations. It wasn't the support I had hoped for, but it was yet another reminder that I was entirely alone.

In the midst of this turmoil, I knew that change was necessary for this baby to survive. The drugs had to go, and I had to find a way to navigate the complexities of my life. I began attending counselling sessions once more, seeking new help to address my addiction and the overwhelming feelings of guilt and fear. It was a painful process, but it was a step toward reclaiming my life and preparing for the future. They were carefully constructed sessions where I portrayed my self as an unruly young adult who just happened to dabble. I still left out Jack, Liam, Mum and Nathan, those were topics I didn't want to confront.

The road ahead was uncertain and fraught with challenges, but I was determined to make a change. The pregnancy was both a burden and a blessing, a catalyst for confronting my demons and finding a path forward. As I prepared for the arrival of my child, I hoped to build a better future, one where I could be a responsible mother, find stability, and make amends for the mistakes I had made.

It wasn't an easy journey, but it was a journey toward healing and redemption. Through the chaos and the heartache, as I allowed happy memories of days out with Liam to re-enter my mind. I began to see a glimmer of hope, a chance to rewrite my story and create a future that I could be proud of. Maybe this something would replace the hole that Liam had left inside me the day I returned him home. Maybe this was my purpose – to be a mum.

Chapter 26

I was buzzing with a newfound excitement at the thought of our first holiday. Sun, sea, and sand was exactly what Tom and I needed. The sun had begun to set over the turquoise waters of Montego Bay, casting a golden hue across the horizon. We finally arrived in Jamaica after a long flight, a holiday we both desperately needed after months of non-stop work and worries. The warmth of the breeze, the scent of saltwater and tropical flowers, and the gentle sound of the waves were everything I had hoped for. It felt like paradise.

From the moment we stepped off the plane, I could feel the tension easing out of my body. I was excited to explore, to meet people, and to embrace the carefree energy of the island. Tom, on the other hand, seemed a little quieter than usual, but I chalked it up to the travel fatigue.

On our first night, we headed down to the resort bar. I could feel the lively atmosphere from a distance, laughter floating in the air, reggae music playing in the background. I felt alive, eager to chat, to share stories, and to make the most of this time away.

We found a couple of seats at the bar, and I immediately struck up conversations with a few other guests. Most of them were couples like us, enjoying their own tropical escapes. A few of the men were talking about scuba diving trips they had planned for the next day, and soon enough, I was laughing along with them, swapping travel stories, and enjoying the friendly banter.

Tom stayed quiet beside me, his hand resting on his drink, his gaze occasionally drifting over to the group. I didn't think much of it at first. He wasn't as outgoing as I was, and I figured he was just taking in the atmosphere. I was having such a great time that I didn't notice his growing frustration.

The men I was chatting with had wives who were nearby, laughing and chatting with other women. It was all friendly, light-hearted fun. But as the evening went on, I noticed Tom becoming more withdrawn, his jaw tightening each time I laughed a little too loudly or shared another story with the guys.

When the evening drew to a close and we made our way back to our room, the air felt heavy. I could tell something was wrong, but I didn't know how bad it was until we walked through the door.

Without warning, Tom turned on me, his face a mask of anger. "Why do you always have to talk to everyone? You're such an attention seeker?" he snapped, his voice low but seething. I was taken aback, not expecting this outburst.

"I was just being friendly, Tom. They all have wives you're overreacting!"

But my words didn't seem to matter. Before I could say any more, he slapped me across the face. The sting of it shocked me, both physically and emotionally. My cheek burned, and for a moment, all I could feel was the ringing silence that followed. I stared at him, disbelief washing over me. I wanted to say something, to demand an explanation, but I was frozen in that moment of hurt. He stood there, his chest rising and falling, his anger simmering just beneath the surface.

And then, just as quickly as it had happened, he softened. He reached out, pulling me into a tight embrace. His arms wrapped around me, but there was no apology in his voice, no sign of remorse. Instead, he whispered, "You shouldn't have wound me up like that. You know how it makes me feel when you flirt. Now tell me you love me."

I stood there in his arms, feeling his warmth, but the words cut deeper than the slap. It was my fault, he was saying. I brought this on myself? Those words settled in, and I didn't know how to respond. Part of me wanted to push him away, to demand an apology, to stand up for myself. But another part of me was exhausted, emotionally drained by the sudden turn of the night and the decision I had made only a couple of weeks previous. I had chosen this.

So, I stayed there, in his arms not returning his embrace but not pulling away either, letting the silence grow between us.

He held me tighter, as if his embrace could erase what had just happened, but all I could feel was the sharp edge of his anger still lingering in the air.

I had always thought of Jamaica as a place where we would find peace, where we could reconnect ready to embrace the next chapter of our lives and become parents. But now, as I lay next to him in bed, my baby growing in my tummy, I realised we had only brought our troubles with us, and if they were far deeper than a tropical holiday could fix.

I spent the remainder of the week keeping myself to myself, I made the most of the swimming pool and jacuzzi and buried myself in books. If people spoke to me I was short and unsociable and quickly returned to my pages wherever I could. Tom would go to the sports bar, go for walks, I never really knew what he was doing. But he knew where I was and I knew where he wanted me to stay. I resonated that the rest would do me good. The fear was always lurking if someone spoke to me, especially if I was in a bikini, I was always turning my head to see where he was and if he was watching ready to pounce or accuse me of anything. The flight home was silent. I didn't feel happy, or sad, I didn't feel anything. Nothing at all. When I unpacked at home and prepared us some dinner I stared too intently at the steak knife. I long for the sharp edge of it just to create something small, just a little prick somewhere on my skin to make me feel something again. As I twisted it in my hand a little flutter in my tummy made me feel something else entirely. It was warm and tingly, a gently reminder that I had another life growing inside me. I could feel after all. I smiled slowly placing the knife back in the drawer and placing a hand on my tummy, feeling a new wave of love for something I didn't yet know. We would be ok.

Watching a tiny heart beat on a screen in front of me was up there with the best feelings in the world. I found out I was having a girl and was absolutely over the moon. The regular flutters in my stomach made me connect to my unborn baby with emotions completely new to me that I wished I could bottle up and keep.

The morning air was crisp, a chill that bit lightly at my cheeks as I left the hospital clutching my scan pictures and I made my way to Mum's house. My heart fluttered with a mix of excitement, nerves and nostalgia as I entered my childhood road, I was about to tell mum the biggest news of my life. A new baby, a new life that we could all celebrate together. I couldn't wait to see her reaction.

Mum opened the door before I had the chance to knock, her face lighting up with joy. "Luce! It's been too long, love," she said, pulling me into a warm embrace. I breathed in her familiar scent, the kind of comfort that only a mother's hug can bring.

"I've got some news," I said, my voice barely able to contain my excitement. Her eyes lit up immediately, her hands flying to her mouth as her eyes followed my hand to my stomach.

"Oh my God, you're pregnant, aren't you? A little one!" She was beaming, her face almost childlike with happiness. "I'm going to be a Nan again. What does Tom think?"

I froze for just a second, the smile on my face becoming just a touch stiff. "Yeah, well, you know…" I trailed off, brushing over the subject like dust on an old mantelpiece. Best to avoid that landmine.

She gave me a look, one of those Mum-knows-everything looks, but didn't press the issue. "You look well, Mum," I said quickly, changing the subject. "It's good to see you like this."

David appeared behind her, resting his hands gently on her shoulders. "She's been doing great," he said with a smile. His hands moved tenderly, rubbing away any tension she might've been holding. I hadn't quite gotten used to seeing her like this, happy, looked after, loved. It was more than I ever thought possible for her, after all we'd been through. Here she was, well and truly on the road to recovery finally with someone who cherished her the way she deserved.

I sat back into the chair sipping my tea and took in the walls around me suddenly feeling a little claustrophobic. I never could stay long in this house. I couldn't ignore the restlessness growing inside me. The house, the rooms, even the air felt heavy. The memories here, were thick, almost suffocating with the ghosts of the past still lingering in every corner. I gave Mum a big squeeze and a kiss on the cheek, promising I'd visit again soon, then I left, walking away feeling light, happy and genuinely proud of her at how well she looked and how far she had come.

The next stop for me was the prison. The guards all knew my face by now. Every time I visited Jack, it was a strange mixture of routine and emotion it was second nature to me now. The buzzers, the metal detectors, the clink of doors locking behind me, all of it was too familiar.

Jack greeted me with his usual swagger, though there was something softer in his eyes these days. "Hey sis," he said, giving me a quick, awkward hug. "How's things?"

"Good," I said, feeling the nerves creep back in. "How about you?"

He grinned. "I've been keeping busy. Finishing this plastering course, you know? And counselling's almost finished. They reckon I'll be moving to an open prison soon. Get my own key, day release, I'm even allowed curtains and a rug." He sounded proud, hopeful even. "Once I'm out, I'm going to propose. Don't think I've ever appreciated her more than I do now." Scarlet had stood by his side throughout his time away, loyal through everything, his only constant, she had never turned her back on him despite her own collapse in the beginning.

"That's amazing Jack I'm so happy for you!" I smiled, genuinely over the moon for him, my mind spinning, wondering how I was going to drop my news without stealing his thunder. Finally, I just blurted it out. "I'm pregnant."

Jack's eyebrows shot up. He took a second to process, "Shit who's is it? And what's twat-head say about it?"

I shrugged. "Its his" I spat a little too harshly having the front to feel offended. "Not much. Never has been a man of many words has he." There was no point sugar-coating things with him. He knew me better than most.

Jack shook his head and sighed. "God, Luce. You've got your work cut out for you." I let out a little laugh.

"Yeah, tell me about it." His face softened, and he looked me straight in the eye.

"If you're happy, I'm happy for ya. You're gonna be a great mum."

That hit me harder than I expected. His blessing meant more than I could put into words. I rubbed my belly absentmindedly, already feeling that growing sense of purpose, of excitement for this new chapter. Despite the challenges that were sure to come, I was ready for it.

Jack smiled at me, his usual tough-guy bravado slipping just a little. "You'll be alright, Luce. You've always been tough." We joked about ridiculous baby names and how she could be a bridesmaid at his wedding one day. For a while we both forgot where we were.

As I left the prison that day, I felt lighter, more sure of myself. The day had been a whirlwind of emotions, but it felt good. Mum was over the moon, Jack gave me his blessing, and despite the complicated path ahead, I knew one thing for sure, I was ready for this new life growing inside me. Ready for whatever came next.

Chapter 27

The day started with an early drive, a slight knot of nervousness in my stomach, but also excitement. It was Jack's first day release since being moved to an open prison, and I wanted everything to go perfectly. The idea of seeing him out in the world, even if just for a few hours, filled me with hope. Before picking him up, I swung by Scarlet's house to collect Liam. It had been a while since he'd seen Jack, and I wanted them to have a real father-son day, one that Liam could remember for a long time.

Liam was waiting at the door when I pulled up, bouncing on his toes with his small backpack slung over his shoulders, face beaming with that innocent excitement only kids have. His mum gave me a tight smile as I leaned out of the car window. We hadn't said much over the past year, but today wasn't about all that. Today was about family.

"Lucy!" Liam shouted, racing to the car. "We're going to see Dad, right?"

I nodded. "Yep, buddy. You ready?"

He jumped into the back seat, grinning from ear to ear. As I drove, I could see him in the rearview mirror, his eyes darting out the window like he was searching for the first glimpse of his dad. I couldn't help but feel his energy seeping into me, replacing the nerves with excitement.

The car hummed beneath us as I drove toward the prison, my hands gripping the wheel a little too tight. Liam was talking about school, his words distant yet steady. He wasn't the same little boy I had raised when things were different. He was nine now, and there was something almost teenage in the way he spoke, short answers, occasional shrugs, a kind of quiet detachment. It tugged at my heart, the way time had passed without us really acknowledging it, without talking about those days when it was just him and me.

I missed him terribly, but I didn't want to open that box. Not today. Today was about Jack. Liam shifted in his seat, glancing at me before his face softened. "How's the baby?" he asked, and there was a flicker of excitement in his eyes. I smiled.

"She's doing well," I replied. "Not long now before she's here."

"You'll bring her to see me, won't you?" he asked, his voice brightening. "I can't wait to meet her."

"I'll bring her the second she's born. I promise." Another promise. I should learn to stop making those. A grin tugged at his lips, and then he said it, words that landed with a force I wasn't prepared for.

"You'll be the best mum ever." For a moment, I couldn't breathe. My chest tightened, and I stared ahead at the road, blinking away the sting behind my eyes. It wasn't the words themselves that got me, but the way he said them, like he already believed it, like he knew something about me that I sometimes doubted. I glanced over at him, my voice thick.

"I love you, little man." He gave me one of those rare smiles, the kind that broke through the teenage veneer he was beginning to adopt.

"I know," he said simply. "Love you too."

We drove in silence for a while after that, but it wasn't an uncomfortable silence. It was the kind that settles when there's nothing left to say but everything's been understood.

We arrived at the prison just before 10 a.m. It was strange seeing my brother come out through those gates, wearing his usual clothes but looking somehow different. Prison does that, I guess. Takes pieces of you and changes the way you move, the way you see the world. But when he saw us, especially when he saw Liam, a wide smile broke out on his face, and for a moment, it was like nothing had changed at all.

Liam leapt out the car and bolted toward him, wrapping his small arms around my brother's waist. I hung back a little, letting them have their moment. There was something raw and pure in the way they looked at each other, like the world outside of that embrace didn't matter.

"Let's go!" I said eventually, clapping my brother on the back. "We've got a full day ahead of us." The plan was simple: Brighton Pier. It wasn't far, and I figured the sea breeze and wide-open spaces would be a welcome change from the confined walls Jack had been staring at for the past 4 years.

When Jack got in the car, there was a moment of awkwardness, all of us caught between the past and the present. He put on his usual big bravado, cracking jokes and giving Liam a playful nudge, but I could see through it. There was something fragile underneath, the same thing I felt, this odd mixture of joy and sadness that came with knowing this day had limits. But we didn't focus on that. We hit the road, the three of us, and somehow it felt like we were piecing something back together, at least for today.

As the journey went on Jack relaxed and we chatted about everything and nothing. It was almost easy, falling back into the rhythm of being brother and sister, with Liam in the back peppering us with questions about the rides we'd go on

When we reached Brighton, the pier stretched out in front of us, a colourful, buzzing playground of lights, sounds, and smells. The sun was out, and the sky was that perfect shade of blue that made everything feel lighter, like we had left all our troubles behind.

Liam was tugging at Jack's arm before we even got to the end of the pier, eyes locked on the rides. "Dad, can we go on that one? The big one?" he asked, pointing at the roller coaster. Jack laughed, ruffling Liams's hair.

"Alright, alright, let's start with that." He looked at me. Obviously I was funding the day but I didn't mind. Today was everything.

Seeing them together, I realized how much my brother had missed. But for those few hours, it was like they were making up for lost time. We went on every ride Liam wanted, the roller coaster, the dodgems, and even the spinning teacups, which had my brother and me laughing like we were kids again. I couldn't help but think of the baby, how she was already experiencing her first roller coaster before even being born. The laughter, the adrenaline, it all felt so real, like a dream we were all clinging to, even if just for a few more hours.

After the rides, we grabbed some doughnuts from one of the stalls. They were warm, sugary, and just what we needed after all the excitement. We sat on a bench overlooking the water, watching the waves crash against the shore. Liam was busy devouring his doughnut, his face a mess of sugar and happiness. My brother took a deep breath, the kind that seemed to release months of tension.

"This is perfect," he said quietly, not looking at me, but out at the sea. "I needed this."

I nodded, not wanting to say too much and ruin the moment. It was perfect. For a few hours, it felt like we were a normal family, enjoying a normal day. But as the afternoon stretched on, the clock started ticking louder in my mind. We had to get him back by 6 p.m. That was the deadline. And as much as I wanted to keep this day going, the reality of it was looming closer.

We walked back to the car in the late afternoon, the sun casting long shadows across the pier. Liam was tired, resting his head on my brother's shoulder, but still grinning from ear to ear. I caught my brother glancing at him every now and then, that mixture of pride and sadness in his eyes, knowing he'd have to say goodbye again soon.

The drive back to the prison was quieter. The laughter from earlier had faded, and there was a heaviness settling in. My brother didn't say much, and neither did I. What was there to say, really? Liam had fallen asleep in the back, worn out from the day.

As we pulled up to the prison gates, my brother sighed deeply, turning to me. "Thanks for today," he said, his voice thick with emotion. "It means more than you know."

I nodded. "We've got plenty more of these days to come, alright? One step at a time."

He smiled, but it was sadder now. He kissed Liam's forehead gently, then got out of the car. I watched as he walked back toward those gates, the world around us suddenly feeling smaller. The guards nodded to him, and just like that, he was gone again.

The drive to Liam's mum's house was quiet. He was still asleep, his little face peaceful in the fading light. When I dropped him off, his mum looked at him, then at me, with a soft understanding in her eyes.

"I'll see you soon, buddy," I whispered squeezing his hand. He looked at me through tired eyes, giving me a sleepy nod.

As I drove home, the sun finally setting, I felt a strange mix of emotions. Taking my brother back had been hard, saying goodbye was harder than I thought it would be now wed had a taste of him outside in the real world, but knowing that today was the start of many more days like this, filled with freedom and family, made it easier to bare. We'd made it through today, and we'd make it through the rest, one day at a time.

Chapter 28

Turning twenty-two had been a quiet affair since I had cankles and a baby bump the size of a small country. I had barely slept the night before, my thoughts consumed by the whirlwind of emotions surrounding the birth. My life had been a chaotic mix of choices and consequences, and now with my due date fast approaching, I found myself at a crossroads.

The past year had been a blur of struggle and pretence. My relationship with Nathan had crumbled in the wake of my pregnancy. The affair that once seemed so exhilarating had ended in disappointment, disillusionment and a marriage proposal to his long-term girlfriend as if that would seal their affections and teach me a lesson. Tom was as distant as ever, lost in his own world of drug-induced escapism with no sign of let up. I had hoped that having a baby would offer some semblance of purpose and fill the void in my heart.

In the weeks leading up to the birth, I worked hard to maintain the façade of happiness. I attended prenatal classes, decorated the nursery and smiled through friends' gatherings where everyone congratulated me on my impending arrival. To them I appeared like any other young woman eagerly awaiting the joys of motherhood. They saw the outward signs of contentment, my carefully chosen maternity clothes, the glowing smiles, the excited chatter about baby names.

Inside however, I felt a profound emptiness. My relationship with Nathan had ended in secrecy and silence. He had moved on and I was left with a lingering ache that no amount of external validation could soothe. Tom's indifference to the pregnancy and his own descent into drug abuse left me feeling isolated and unsupported. Everyone thought I was living the dream, but the reality was far different. I was struggling to keep up the pretence of a happy, fulfilled future while battling feelings of doubt and loneliness.

The night I went into labour was a whirlwind of activity and emotion. I had been having irregular contractions for days, but when they became stronger, more frequent and I realised I needed more than the toilet, I knew the time had come. I went to the hospital alone, the ache in my heart matching the contractions that seemed to come in waves.

The labour was long and painful, a gruelling process that seemed to stretch on forever. The moments of discomfort and fear were punctuated by fleeting thoughts of what could have been, a different life, a different love. I pushed through the pain, driven by a mix of determination and hope. Despite the struggles, I knew that this baby was my chance to create something good, something that might fill the emptiness inside me.

Tom made it to the hospital just as the baby was finally born. The rush of emotions was overwhelming. I held my daughter in my arms, her tiny face scrunched up in a sleepy yawn. In that moment all the pain and uncertainty seemed to fade away. She was perfect, a small, fragile being that needed me. I was filled with a new sense of love and responsibility. This was the beginning of a new chapter, one where I hoped to find the purpose and fulfilment that had eluded me. Even Tom when he eventually made an appearance, seemed enthralled at the tiny new being.

In the days following the birth, I was surrounded by congratulatory messages and visitors, each one reinforcing the image of a new mother on cloud nine. I played the part well smiling through the exhaustion, accepting the well-meaning advice and showing off my beautiful baby to friends and family. I wanted to believe that this was the life I had always wanted, that the baby would make everything better.

But behind the scenes, the reality was more complex. I struggled with postpartum emotions and the daunting responsibilities of new motherhood. The loneliness of my situation became more pronounced as I faced the challenges of raising a child with little support. I felt trapped in the role of the happy, successful mother while grappling with the disillusionment of my personal life and that ever niggling thought that if I had chosen differently how it may have felt.

Despite the challenges there was a small undeniable truth, my baby was a source of joy and love that I had never experienced before. The nights were long and the days were filled with a mix of joy and exhaustion, but every time I looked at my daughter I felt a glimmer of hope. She was a reminder that life could still hold beauty and purpose.

As time went on I began to confront the reality of my situation. I realized that while my baby brought me immense joy, she couldn't fix all the problems in my life. I needed to address my own emotional and mental well-being, to find a path that would allow me to grow and heal as both a mother and an individual.

In the quiet moments, when I rocked my baby to sleep or watched her sleep peacefully in her crib, I found solace. She was a beacon of hope and I was determined to give her the best life possible. I knew that my journey would be fraught with challenges, but I was committed to navigating them with strength and resilience.

Though the emptiness inside me hadn't vanished entirely, I found that my baby gave me a renewed sense of purpose. In caring for her, I was learning to care for myself as well. The journey was far from perfect, but it was mine to embrace, one step at a time.

I sat in the soft glow of the nursery, watching Charlotte's tiny chest rise and fall as she slept. Her little hand was curled into a fist, her cheeks flushed with that sweet warmth only babies have. Every time I looked into her beautiful, wide eyes; I was reminded of just how much I loved her, a love that eclipsed anything I had ever known. She was everything. Her laughter, her innocence, the way she discovered the world around her with those delicate fingers and curious eyes, she filled every corner of my heart. Nothing else mattered anymore. No high could ever compare to this.

I promised myself and her, that I would never touch drugs again. I'd be strong for her. I wanted her to grow up surrounded by laughter, joy and the kind of adventures Liam and I used to have, before life became so tangled. I imagined showing her the world with all its beauty and wonder, not the darkness I had once known.

Tom was a different story. Far from embracing new beginnings and parenthood he had spiralled deep into his own world, smoking weed like it was as casual as breathing. His mood swings were wild and unpredictable. At first it was just words - vicious, biting insults flung at me when he was frustrated. Then it escalated. He'd smash glasses against the walls, throw the remote across the room or yell at the tiniest provocation. I stayed calm, pretending it didn't affect me, cleaning up the mess he left in his wake. The behaviour was not new to me. I had watched my own mother get punched and pushed. I'd seen plates of dinner thrown and watched her quietly clear up the carnage. My brother would try to intervene but he was never a match for my dad. I mimicked my own mothers actions silently clearing the mess around me, keeping everything perfectly clean, I wished my brother was near, wished I could call him. I wondered what he was doing now. I had to remain focused on the present. All that mattered was keeping my beautiful little bubble Charlotte safe.

As his temper got worse my silence around the house increased. I could bear the bruises and the shoves against the wall as long as he wasn't hurting Charlotte. He didn't mean it anyway, I told myself this, the more frequently it happened, not really. I learned to brush off his rage and when he'd apologize, say he loved me, and pull me into him I lapped up the scraps of affection like a starving dog waiting for treats.

Chapter 29

The day Jack was released from prison was one that had filled me with both hope and anxiety. I had been preparing for it, thinking through every moment, but nothing could have prepared me for the emotions that came when I saw him step out of those gates.

I picked Mum up on the way. She'd been quiet in the car, her fingers twisting in her lap again, a sure sign she was nervous. We had visited him constantly over the last four years, but it wasn't the same. Behind the grim walls of the prison, Jack had been distant lately as panic set in. Now, out here in the open world, I wondered if he'd still be that way.

Charlotte was in her car seat in the back, oblivious to everything. She was just a few weeks old, her tiny face scrunched up in sleep, completely unaware of the gravity of the day. My heart swelled at the sight of her. She was my new beginning, and Jack deserved his.

When we pulled up outside the gates, Jack was standing there, clutching a small carrier bag, looked unrecognisable compared to the day he went in, but he's still my big brother. His eyes were darting around, nervous, as if he wasn't sure what to do with all the space. I could see the fear in his face, fear of the outside, of freedom. Prison had been safe for him, predictable. This was all unknown.

I stepped out first, leaving Mum in the car for a second. I knew she needed a minute.

"Hey, Jack," I said softly as I approached him. His eyes locked onto mine, and for a moment, we just stood there, staring at each other. Then, suddenly, the tension broke, and he pulled me into a hug. He was trembling, and I squeezed him tight, hoping he could feel that I was still here, still his sister.

"It's so good to see you," I whispered, feeling a lump rise in my throat. Jack nodded, too overwhelmed to speak. When we got back to the car, Mum finally opened her door and stepped out. Jack stiffened, looking down at his feet as she approached. But Mum, being Mum, just wrapped her arms around him, her small frame somehow giving off the strength of a giant.

"Welcome home, love," she murmured, and I could see the tension begin to melt off his shoulders. Back at Jacks house, Liam rushed to the door the moment we pulled into the driveway. He was so eager to meet see his dad again, and to meet Charlotte. Liam took to her immediately.

"Can I hold her? Please?" he asked, eyes wide as I lifted her out of the car seat. I smiled and handed her over carefully. Watching him, it was like seeing a new generation of love and innocence right there in my living room, so pure and untouched by the heaviness of the world Jack and I had known for too long.

We all settled into the living room, and Jack sat beside me on the sofa. It felt strange and yet so familiar, the two of us sitting side by side like we used to when we were kids. But now everything was different. I had Charlotte, my baby, my new life. And Jack... he had freedom, but it was fragile. He was excited, but I could see how overwhelmed he was. His eyes kept darting around the room, his foot tapping restlessly.

"How's it feel?" I asked, nudging him gently with my shoulder. He exhaled, running a hand through his hair.

"I dunno," he said quietly. "It's good, but... it's weird. Out here, it's all there's no routine, no one telling you what to do. I don't know how to be... out here anymore."

"You don't have to figure it all out today," I reassured him. "You'll find your way. And I'm here, Jack. You're not doing this alone." We sat like that for a while, side by side on the sofa, a silent promise passing between us. I had become a mother, finding my own strength through the newness and chaos of having a baby. Now Jack in a way was like a newborn too, stepping into the world for the first time in years.

As the day wore on the sky outside began to darken. I didn't want to leave him, not yet. Jack still looked like a man lost in an ocean, just barely staying afloat. He kept smiling at Charlotte, cooing at her and pulling faces at her. He was using her a distraction from his new found freedom but I could see the weight behind his eyes.

"I'll come back soon," I promised as I stood to leave cradling Charlotte in my arms. "You won't be on your own." Scarlet linked her arm into Jacks almost protectively. I felt they would be ok together, they have come so far, they would find their new normal.

Jack stood and hugged me again, tighter this time. "Thanks, sis," he murmured into my shoulder. "I don't know what I'd do without you."

"You'll never have to find out," I replied. It was true. No matter what, we had each other. As I got into the car and drove away I knew Tom would be waiting at home, probably in one of his moods. He hadn't come with me today. He had waved it off, saying he "couldn't be bothered," and I knew he would start when I walked in the door. But I didn't care. Today wasn't about him. Today was about Jack and his new beginning.

In those first few months of motherhood my world became a bubble of baby giggles, tiny clothes and quiet moments where I'd just sit and hold Charlotte for hours. Her warmth against me filled a dark hole I hadn't realized had been growing inside me for years. I hadn't felt truly complete until her. Every fear I had before her birth dissolved the moment she looked into my eyes, and I promised I'd protect her forever.

I enjoyed every second of being a new mum. I never knew love like that could exist. It was overwhelming, raw and pure. The moment Charlotte came into my life, everything shifted. She became the centre of my world and I was more than happy to orbit around her. Her tiny fingers, the way her eyelids fluttered when she slept, even her cries felt like a song I'd been waiting to hear all my life.

Tom, took a little longer to warm to her. I suppose I had expected that. He wasn't the nurturing type but I caught glimpses of his tenderness at odd moments. The way he would stroke her head absentmindedly or the slight curve of a smile when she babbled at him. They wasn't picture-perfect moments, but they gave me hope. For a while it felt like our family was finally coming together.

One day, I decided to take her to the office to meet everyone. I was excited and proud to show off my beautiful girl to people who had known me for years. As I walked into the building, the familiar scent of coffee and the low hum of printers filled the air. It felt strange to be back, after only a few months away it felt like I had lived an entirely different life here, one where I wasn't the woman I had become since Charlotte.

Nathan was the first to greet me. He walked over, his smile broad, arms outstretched in an offer to hold her. My heart did an odd little flip as I passed Charlotte into his arms. He handled her with such care, gently bouncing her in a way that made her giggle softly. My throat tightened. That was the relationship I wanted, the tenderness I had dreamed of for my family.

Nathan's eyes were soft as he looked down at her and in that moment I saw something I couldn't ignore.

He caught my gaze and the air between us shifted like it always did. It was subtle but undeniable. That glance sent electricity through me, a spark of something old, something unfinished. We had never crossed that line again but there was always this undercurrent between us, something that hummed beneath every casual conversation, every laugh. I swallowed the feeling, forcing myself to focus on the present.

Charlotte was passed around the office, from one eager pair of arms to another but my eyes kept drifting back to Nathan. I wondered briefly what might have been different if life had taken another path. If we had met under different circumstances, if timing had been kinder, would we have had that connection? The kind that I so desperately longed for in my own home?

But this was my reality. I had a family, a beautiful baby girl, and a husband who, despite everything, was trying. I couldn't afford to entertain fantasies. Still, as Nathan handed Charlotte back to me our fingers brushed for the briefest moment, and I knew he felt it too.

The moment passed, the tension lingering for just a second before life returned to its steady hum. I bundled Charlotte close to my chest and gave her a soft kiss on the forehead, her tiny hand curling around my finger before I passed her to others eagerly awaiting a quick snuggle of my tiny perfect bundle.

I left the office that day feeling more confused than I had in a long time. My love for Charlotte was absolute, consuming. But love, I realized, could come in so many forms. It could fill your heart and still leave parts of you aching for something else, something more.

Chapter 30

The night had started with such promise. I'd put Charlotte to sleep with the familiar routine: bath, bottle, lullaby, and then the soft click of her door as I backed away from the crib, knowing she was down for the night. I'd even prepared a bottle just in case so Tom could feed her if needed. It was the first time I was going out since having her, and I was beyond ready. Nervous, yes, but excited. I wanted to feel like myself again, the version of me that existed before late nights were defined by nappy changes and feeding schedules. Tonight was my night.

The Chinese restaurant we picked wasn't just for the food. By day, it served dim sum and sizzling noodles, but by night it transformed into something else - a full-blown disco with neon lights and a dance floor. I hadn't felt this free in ages. My friends and I ordered drinks, laughed too loudly and toasted to "me time," to the first night out in what felt like forever. I got drunk too fast on cheap wine and empty stomach, a dangerous combination but I didn't care. The music swirled in the air, the lights dizzying, the laughter infectious.

At one point, while stumbling toward the bathroom, I heard an amazing tune come on, something that immediately made me stop. I turned right around and, forgetting my original destination, rushed back to the dance floor. Whitney Houston's "I'm Every Woman" blared through the speakers, and before I knew it, I was belting out the lyrics at the top of my lungs. My friends joined in, egging me on, laughing and cheering as I twirled and sang like I was the queen of the night.

By the time the evening was winding down, we were all a mess of giggles, clinging to each other as we stumbled to the exit, promising to do it again soon, hugging too tight and whispering secrets we probably wouldn't remember tomorrow. I was so drunk I struggled to get the key into the lock when I got home. Tom had to open the door for me, standing there in his sweats, arms crossed. His expression was sour, like I'd just ruined something.

"You're drunk" he said flatly, pulling me inside too fast. I laughed, stumbling over the threshold and into the hallway. He didn't laugh.

"Yeah, I'm drunk" I giggled, trying to keep the mood light, but there was a tension there that set my nerves on edge. Something in the way he grabbed my arm as I tried to steady myself. I told myself I was imagining it, that he was just helping me because I was a mess, but my stomach twisted all the same.

I stumbled toward the kitchen to get water, hoping it would help me sober up. But then, Tom's hand clamped around my arm again, harder this time, and he yanked me back, pushing me against the wall.

"Where the hell have you been?" His voice was low, cold. I tried to laugh it off, but the tight grip on my arm was no joke.

"We were at the Chinese place, remember? Just a night with the girls. Your games are getting boring now Tom" Alcohol obviously made me brave. He cut me off.

"You smell like men," he growled, his eyes flashing. I knew he was wrong. I knew I hadn't been near anyone but my girlfriends, laughing, dancing. I rolled my eyes, hoping to defuse whatever this was.

"Oh, for God's sake Tom. Seriously here we go again your jealousy is becoming a little boring. Charlottes got a hand puppet upstairs why don't you stick your hand up its arse and amuse yourself with that instead of trying to control me. I'm not a toy you can pick up and break when you feel like it!" That was when it happened. Faster than I could process, I was on the floor. His fist had come down so fast I barely registered the pain before I felt his foot connect with my stomach. The air rushed out of my lungs and the next blow came before I could blink. I curled up, instinct taking over, trying to protect myself from the blows raining down on me but they just kept coming.

"Slag," he spat. "Whore." I wasn't even sure where the words were coming from. My brain couldn't catch up. He was furious and I didn't understand why. It had been one night. One night with my friends but here I was, on the floor, my body convulsing with each hit, trying to make sense of the madness.

It turns out alcohol makes me stupid not brave, not brave at all. I should have stayed quiet. I should have begged him to stop and apologised but instead, something inside me broke and I laughed. I laughed even though it wasn't funny, even though I was terrified, even though my body was screaming out in pain. I laughed because my brain didn't know what else to do and that only made him angrier.

He grabbed my hair holding my head in place and swung his arm back fist clenched, I don't remember what happened after that. Everything went black.

I woke up to the sound of Charlotte crying. For a moment, I thought it was a dream, but then the pain hit me. My face felt swollen, my stomach throbbed and I realized I was still on the kitchen floor not far from where I'd fallen. Slowly I dragged myself along I needed to get to the kitchen side to pull, my self up on it. It seems far away as my who body stung with each moment . I urged myself to get there made stronger by Charlottes cries. I had to get up. Hand, hand, knee, knee, hand, hand, knee, knee, hand on the side, other hand on the side, good god this hurt I need to gather the strength to pull myself up, every inch of my body was aching. The pre-prepared bottle was still on the kitchen side. I went through the motions on autopilot, scooping powder into water and shaking it, the simple act of making my baby's bottle grounding me in a way nothing else could.

As I climbed each step a sharp pain rushed through me reminding me of the evenings events, Charlottes cries like an invisible rope pulling me up each step at a time, coaxing me through the agony I was in. I somehow reached the top. Tom emerged from the bathroom, his face a mask of concern that felt sickly and wrong.

"Oh, my poor baby," he said, pulling me into a tight embrace that hurt. "You must've had too much to drink last night. You're so silly." His voice was sticky-sweet, but all I could think about was the sharp grip of his hand, the blows, the pain.

"I love you. Tell me you love me," he whispered, his breath hot against my ear. I couldn't speak. I just stood there, limp, dazed. He pushed me away offended by me not attempting to return his affection. "Fucking slag" he spat as he turned back toward the bedroom.

I rushed into Charlotte's room scooping her up from her cot ot caring that my arms felt like they might snap away from my body at any moment. I needed to feel her warm soft body in my arms. She stopped crying instantly, her tiny fingers wrapped around the bottle as she drank, her perfect face content and peaceful. I rocked her, even though my whole body screamed in pain and for that moment my head was quiet.

Chapter 31

Three months after Charlotte was born, I went back to work, craving the control, the stability and the affection of my colleagues and the life I'd known before everything shifted. I brought Charlotte with me to the office again, eager to cling to anything that felt familiar.

Nathan met me at the car, his face lighting up as soon as he saw us. His arms enveloped me in a bear hug, warm and steady and I was overwhelmed by a thousand emotions. I never wanted him to let go. In that embrace, I realized it all too clearly. I loved him! And in a cruel twist, I knew I had chosen wrong. But I was too proud to ever admit it out loud, though I'm sure Nathan felt it too, standing there in that moment, holding me in a way that made me feel both safe and shattered.

I adjusted my cardigan, the same way I adjusted my emotions, trying to smooth them over, tuck them away. Nathan smiled down at Charlotte, still sleeping in her car seat. Without asking, he lifted her up, carrying the seat with such care, as though she was his own. Once in the office when everyone gathered round to see how much she'd grown in the few weeks since they'd met her. She was still like a little doll. Nathan took Charlotte out of the seat and cradled her in his arms, eyes soft. Everyone in the office shared glances, the silent question in their eyes, was she his? It was almost an unspoken truth, though we knew the answer. Charlotte wasn't his. But in every aching part of me wished she was.

Watching Nathan with her did something to me. It thawed the coldness I'd built up, almost cracked the shell of numbness I'd been hiding in. But we never crossed that line again, even though I could feel the weight of unspoken words between us. The truth lingered like smoke, present, heavy, but impossible to grasp.

Charlotte was a ray of light in my life, the brightest part of my world. I enrolled her in the nursery next to the office, a small comfort knowing she was close by while I worked, pushing myself up the career ladder, trying to distract myself from the emptiness that gnawed at me. Nathan would meet me every morning, carrying her car seat like he always did, walking beside me in quiet understanding. His hugs became my anchor, but they never became more

than that. I don't think either of us had the strength to make the break from our separate lives, no matter how much I wished for it.

Since Jacks release we drifted further apart. The weekly calls stopped, and it became painfully clear that I was just another part of his old life he was trying to erase. After everything, I had become a reminder of the past, and Jack needed to move forward. Whenever we spoke, it was strained, each conversation a reminder of how far we had fallen from who we once were. I was on one side of a wall he had built, and he had no interest in looking back.

Tom, on the other hand, grew more distant and volatile. His temper flared, not to the point of that night, no, we never spoke of that night again. But the violence simmered beneath the surface. There were broken dishes, smashed glasses, and the occasional slap or shove into the wall, but he never kicked me again. I think that scared him more than it did me. He knew he'd crossed a line that night, but he also knew I wouldn't leave. I was trapped by the life I had built, good job, home, partner, baby. On paper, it was all so tick box perfect. I had the checklist life, everything I thought I was supposed to want. But inside, I was floating through it all, a ghost clinging to the illusion of control.

I absorbed every moment with Charlotte, as if by holding onto her, I could keep myself grounded. Her first words, her first steps, they were bright, golden memories in an otherwise bleak and grey world. She was my sunshine, my everything. And yet, even in those precious moments, a part of me wondered what it would have been like if things had been different. If Nathan had been the one waiting for us at home, if my life had taken another path. But the what-ifs were endless, and so I swallowed them down and continued to float through the days.

I had built a life that looked picture-perfect from the outside. But the cracks were there, just beneath the surface, threatening to split me open. And in the quiet moments, when Nathan hugged me or held Charlotte like she was his own, I could feel those cracks widen, just a little more each time.

For the next two years Tom and I carried on our rollercoaster of love and hate and I fell deeper for Nathan. I was all consumed by work and charlotte and my pretend life outside of our home kept me sane.

The day inevitably arrived that I found out I was pregnant again. I should have felt joy, but instead, I felt fear even though I knew I was being careless and another pregnancy was always a possibility. I told Tom the news when he was out of weed, and the anger in his eyes was immediate, like a storm gathering force. His words cut deep:

"How could you be so fucking stupid? You're already fat!" He didn't even know where to put all his rage, and when I braced myself for a shove, he did something new. He grabbed the skin under my arms, squeezing so hard I thought he'd tear it. The pain was intense, but I stared him down, refusing to flinch, refusing to cower. I didn't care anymore. I was used to it. Let him hurt me.

When he finally let go, he threw my arms down with disgust.

"If you don't want this baby, I'll leave. I don't need you." My words dripped with venom.

"You do fucking need me," he spat. "You're nothing on your own. Who's ever going to want a fat, disgusting pig like you?" He laughed. A sick, twisted sound that made my skin crawl, and I waited for the next blow. But it didn't come. Instead, he grabbed his keys and stormed out of the house, leaving a trail of tension in the air.

I stood there for a moment, numb, before making my way to Charlotte. She was still curled up, fast asleep in her chair, her peaceful little face a stark contrast to the chaos around us. I knelt down beside her, gently tucking the blanket around her tiny body. I felt nothing, not the pain, not the fear, not the sadness. All I cared about was protecting her, this small, perfect person who had saved me without even knowing it. Only she mattered.

I loved Charlotte more than I ever thought possible. Every moment with her filled me with a deep, soul-anchoring warmth, and it only grew with time. I wanted more of that, more love, more connection, another baby. Charlotte deserved a sibling, someone to share her world with, someone else for me to pour my love into. It seemed like a simple decision, one driven by the purest of instincts. But I didn't anticipate the ripple effect it would cause.

When I told Nathan I was expecting again, it broke something between us. He had always been my constant, even in the silence and unspoken tension that bound us. But the news of the baby was like a wall crashing down. After that day, he couldn't even look at me. At work, he became a shadow of his usual self, distant, guarded. He stopped meeting me at the car. Stopped carrying Charlotte in from the car park. His hugs were gone, the warmth replaced by a void I couldn't fill. I could see the hurt in his eyes every time we passed each other in the office, but neither of us had the words to fix what was broken.

Then I received the news that shattered what little thread still tied us together: Nathan married Samantha in a shot gun wedding. I found out the same way everyone else did, through social media. My heart sank when I saw their wedding photos. Samantha was radiant in white, her eyes sparkling with happiness, and Nathan stood beside her, smiling for the camera. Together, they were the picture of a perfect couple, laughing as if their love was boundless.

I knew Nathan better than anyone else, or at least, I thought I did. As I scrolled through the endless gallery of their day, I picked apart every detail. His eyes, those eyes I once found comfort in, looked empty. His smile was there, but it didn't reach the warmth in his gaze that I used to know so well. And when they posed together, he didn't lean into her like a man truly in love. It felt staged, like a perfectly crafted advertisement meant to sell the world a vision of happiness. A masterpiece of appearances. But I saw through it.

The jealousy tore through me like a raging storm, waves of anger and longing crashing inside me. That could have been me. No, that should have been me. I could feel the ache of that reality, the regret. The missed chances. If I hadn't chosen the path I had, if I had been brave enough to admit how I felt, maybe Nathan and I could have had that happiness. I could picture myself in that white dress, standing beside him, smiling at the life we could have built together. But I'd chosen wrong, and now, Nathan had chosen her.

I stared at their photos for too long, the images of them etched into my mind, taunting me. Each one felt like a dagger, and no matter how much I tried to justify it, I couldn't shake the feeling that it was my fault. Nathan had loved me once, and I had let him slip through my fingers.

Eventually, I peeled my eyes away from the screen, but it was too late. The damage was done, and the pictures stayed with me, haunting the quiet corners of my thoughts. I knew then that I couldn't continue like this. I couldn't keep working alongside him, pretending like everything was fine, when every glance in his direction was breaking me a little more. The wanting, the longing for something I couldn't have was tearing me apart.

So I made the decision. Once I had this baby, I wouldn't go back to work with him. I needed to move on. I needed to find a way to live without the constant reminder of what could have been. As much as it pained me, I knew leaving was the only way to heal.

The new baby would bring change, a fresh start. It would be my chance to break free of the past and focus on what mattered most, my children. They needed me, and in that, I found some comfort. I could pour all my love into them, into building a life for them that was full of happiness, even if my own was marked by the cracks of what I had lost.

When I sat with Tom I brought up the topic of marriage. "What's the point?" He shrugged.

"Its nice, it shows that we love each other and id like to have the same sur name as you and our girls. It makes our little family whole." It was the biggest lie to him and to myself. I didn't want his name, didn't want him full stop. It was a childish revenge on Nathan. Desperate to steal a little of that staged happiness. To show him and everyone else that I had chosen correctly. I was making a mockery of marriage and I knew it. But I was so desperate for my happy ever after even if it was just on paper.

"If you want." Tom said non-committal. I did want and the thought filled with excitement. I ordered my own engagement ring and started planning what our special day would look like, sharing our news with everyone and anyone that would listen.

But the ache for Nathan, the jealousy that rippled through me when I thought of him with Samantha, it would never fully fade. It was a part of me now, like an old wound that never quite healed, a scar left by the choices I made, another wound of my own making that I would need to put an emotional plaster over.

When I went to Collect Charlotte from play school, she was sat at a table drawing with a set of worn-out colouring pencils. She was beautiful and so content. How was she growing so quickly. I watched her lost in her own world. She was focused, her brow furrowed as she scribbled furiously on the paper.

"What are you drawing?" I asked softly trying not to make her jump. Charlotte looked up, her eyes wide with excitement.

"It's me." My breath caught in my throat. I glanced at the drawing. It was a colourful mix of wild dreams, a stick girl in a superhero cape, a crown perched on her head, holding a book in one hand and a sword in the other. It was messy and chaotic, but it was free, full of life. A memory came to me of the day I picked Liam up and he had drawn a fly swat for a dinosaur. It made me smile.

"That's awesome!" What a perfect world little minds live in all princesses and super heroes. I stood there for a long moment, watching her. There was no fear in her expression, no pressure to be anything other than what she imagined herself to be. I realized, for the first time in a long while, that I had been going about it all wrong. Maybe the answer wasn't in pretending to be someone better. Maybe it wasn't about living up to anyone else's expectations. Maybe it was about giving myself permission to be messy, to not have all the answers, to be lost and still moving forward.

As we walked away from school that day, something in my heart began to thaw. I didn't have a clear picture of who I was or who I wanted to be, but for the first time that didn't scare me. I wasn't pretending anymore. I was just Lucy, a girl still learning how to live.

The thought of bringing a second child into the world was an experience both familiar and new, filled with moments of joy, anticipation, and deep connection. Nurturing my growing bump, I found myself constantly amazed by the thought of another little person developing inside me. This time, though, I had Charlotte by my side, her curiosity and excitement adding even more magic to the journey.

Charlotte loved to place her tiny hands on my belly, eagerly waiting for those special moments when the baby would kick or roll. Her eyes would light up, and she'd giggle with amusement. We'd spend quiet afternoons reading together, her nestled beside me, occasionally stopping to feel the movement in my bump. I could see the beginnings of a beautiful sibling bond forming even before they met. Charlotte would lean in close, whispering to my belly as if sharing secrets with the little one inside.

Growing a second child was an even deeper experience of love than I imagined. Feeling the kicks, the stretches, the hiccups, it was a daily reminder of the new life on its way. But it was also a reminder of the life already in front of me, the incredible bond I had with Charlotte. I knew she would make the best sister, gentle, kind, and full of wonder. I promised myself I would nurture their connection, ensuring they would always be close, always kind to one another, no matter what.

When the time finally came, the birth was agonising but mercifully quick. Every moment felt like a surge of intensity, but

I focused on the thought of holding my baby. And when she arrived, she was perfect, tiny, warm, and everything I had been waiting for. In that instant, the pain faded into the background, and all I felt was overwhelming love.

As I looked down at her, I could already picture her and Charlotte growing together, each other's first friend and greatest ally. The journey of raising two little souls had just begun, and I knew, no matter the challenges, it was going to be the most rewarding adventure. Baby Lily a beautiful name chosen by Charlotte.

Chapter 32

The day of my wedding dawned bright and crisp, the kind of day that was supposed to be full of joy and celebration. I had spent months planning every detail, from the flowers to the music to the seating arrangements each item trying to erase Nathans perfect wedding pictures from my mind and replace it with my own pretend happy ever after. Everything was set for what was meant to be a perfect day. But beneath the surface of this carefully crafted celebration, I was struggling to keep up a facade that was growing increasingly difficult to maintain.

The night before the wedding had been fraught with tension. Tom had lost his temper yet again when I dared to forbid him from taking drugs on what was supposed to be 'the happiest day of our lives,' his anger manifesting in a way that left me with dark bruises under my arms where he had pinched me so hard for so long, his favourite choice of inflicting pain exactly where nobody else could see it, challenging me because I wouldn't buckle and beg him to stop. It was his favourite choice of inflicting pain where no one else could see it. If I twisted or tried to escape my strength was no match for him and it only made the pain worse. I had to stand and take it. Keep my chin up, don't cry. That was the best way. Not letting him get to me. I had learned to hide these marks over the years, but on a day when I was supposed to feel elated, the pain was a constant reminder of how far from perfect my life truly was.

As I dressed in my wedding gown, I carefully adjusted the sleeves to cover the dark bruises. I used layers of makeup and fabric to mask the discoloration, hoping that the marks wouldn't be too noticeable. Little did the inventor of the foundation tattoo cover up know that their recipe also works a treat on bruises, even the deepest purple ones. My heart pounded with anxiety, not just about the appearance of my bruises, but about the entire charade I was about to participate in.

The ceremony was taking place at a picturesque venue, chosen for its beauty and elegance. It was everything I had dreamed of a fairytale setting that seemed worlds away from the reality of my daily life. The guests arrived, and the atmosphere was filled with the sounds of laughter and cheerful conversation. My two beautiful girls, now aged two and four, were dressed in their beautiful flowy pink dresses, their faces beaming with innocent joy. They were the light of my life, and I wanted this day to be as special for them as it was supposed to be for me.

The day was the picture of perfection, or at least that's what everyone saw. Behind closed doors, nobody knew the truth about Tom, his temper, his fists, the way his words cut through me like daggers. He was charming and sociable when we were out, a perfect partner to the world. My friends were in awe of what they thought was an ideal setup: the house, the kids, the loving husband. I had become a master at painting that picture, of wearing a mask that sold the fairytale. But the real story lay hidden behind smiles and wedding vows.

It was a grand event that any girl would dream of. Planned as if Nathan, not Tom, was the one waiting for me at the end of the aisle. But Nathan wasn't there. He hadn't been for a long time, and I was marrying Tom, the man everyone believed was my perfect match.

Charlotte and Lily, were beaming as they swished their beautiful dresses. Charlotte was growing up so fast, her wide eyes taking in the day like she knew something more about it than I did. Lily was still so small, clutching her flower basket, oblivious to the complexity of the life we lived. They threw petals ahead of them as we made our way down the aisle, and for a moment, everything looked just right.

Jack was there, too. He had been out of prison for 4 years now, but suddenly we felt like strangers, the distance between us lingered, like a gap neither of us could quite bridge. We barely saw each other, our once close bond now fractured by time and life. When Lily was born, he sent a card, no visit, no conversation, no brotherly advice like before. He had his own battles to fight. And though he was physically there on my wedding day, the unspoken tension hung in the air between us.

Liam was almost a man now. Fourteen and nearly as tall as me, he greeted me with the biggest hug, like we hadn't been apart for months on end. His enthusiasm and affection were genuine, a stark contrast to the pretence that surrounded me. He had changed so much since Jack came back into his life, adjusting to a father he barely knew. But Liam had grown into his own, and I was proud of him. In the absence of my dad, I had asked Liam to walk me down the aisle. He looked so handsome in his suit, and when he offered me his arm, I almost forgot the mess behind my smile. For that brief moment, walking beside Liam, I felt the warmth of family again.

Mum sat in the front row, her face beaming with health and happiness. She had been through so much, but now, here she was, strong again. All the cracks in my life seemed to have healed for this one day. Everything looked mended, except for me.

I walked down the aisle, Liam by my side with a smile fixed on my face. The vows were exchanged amidst tears and applause, and for a moment, I allowed myself to believe in the illusion of happiness. I kept my focus on Charlotte and Lily. They were my light, and I needed that light to get through. The ceremony was full of "oohs" and "ahhs," our friends and relatives many of whom we barely knew cooing over the spectacle. It was a show, after all. We smiled for pictures as the photographer directed us like puppets, moving us into the right poses, creating the illusion of a dream.

The evening reception was where Tom started to unravel. He got drunk, so drunk that I couldn't stand to be near him. I watched him spiral from across the room, but instead of intervening, I lost myself in dancing with my mum and friends. For a while, it felt real like a true celebration.

The song "We Are Family" came on, and there we were, me, Jack, Liam, Mum, and the girls holding hands, laughing, dancing together like we hadn't been broken for years. That moment, in the middle of the dance floor, was the kind of joy I hadn't felt in a long time. For just those few minutes, I forgot everything else.

As the night wore on, the crowd thinned. Jack and Liam were the last to leave, long after the music had stopped and the staff had begun tidying up. Jack gave me a hug, a hug that said a thousand things without either of us needing to speak. I missed him, missed the chaos of him, the closeness we used to have but I knew he was carving out a new life for himself. He pulled away, looked at me with a soft smile, and said, "Love you, sis." It felt like a goodbye that stretched deeper than the moment.

Liam hugged me next, taller than I remembered, his teenage arms wrapped around me like he was already grown up. I squeezed him tight, fighting the urge to hold on too long. "Thank you for being amazing," I whispered, knowing I probably wouldn't see him for a long time again. He was another part of a life Id had to let go of, even if I wasn't ready.

As I looked around the emptying room, I realized no one had said goodbye to Tom. No one needed to. He had made his grand exit hours before, vomiting near the bar in front of everyone. I hadn't seen him since, and frankly, I didn't care. The evening belonged to me, to my family, to the illusion of happiness we had briefly shared. Tom was just a shadow in the corner of that memory.

After everyone had left, I started picking up plates, waiting for the taxi. Tom was asleep on a row of chairs, oblivious, while I moved through the motions of tidying up the remnants of our perfect day. The day everyone would talk about, the one where I played the bride in the storybook wedding, the one I had always wanted. Except the story wasn't real, and now the day was over.

We left the venue in silence. Tom looked out one window, I looked out the other, and we went home to the life that waited for us behind closed doors, the one no one else could see. The day had been a beautiful lie, a carefully crafted illusion of happiness. But as I thought about my children and Liam, I found a glimmer of hope. They were the genuine joy in my life, the real and unfiltered love that I held onto despite everything.

My life revolved around my children, and I cherished every moment with them. Charlotte was blossoming into a gentle, thoughtful girl, always full of kindness and curiosity. Her eyes sparkled with the wonder of the world around her, and every new discovery made me fall in love with her all over again. Lily, on the other hand, was a whirlwind of energy, always on the move. Independent and fierce, we affectionately called her "Mowgli," a nickname that suited her wild spirit. She would run around the house in nothing but her pants, climbing anything she could find, causing mischief and laughing with the kind of joy that filled our home with light.

Together, they were my heart, and loving them felt like the purest thing I'd ever known. They brought so much happiness into my life that it was impossible not to be swept away by it. The sound of their laughter, the way they held my hand or curled into my lap at the end of the day, it was all I ever needed. Tom, though distant, was kind enough to them, never crossing the line with his anger or his cruelty when it came to them. But he wasn't the father they needed. He couldn't connect, couldn't give them the warmth and affection they deserved, and I knew it. They never seemed to notice, though. I loved them enough for all of us.

Sometimes, I'd catch them witnessing the darker moments between Tom and me. His sharp words, the way he shoved me when his temper flared, they saw it. I thought I could protect them, shield them from the ugliness. They'd run to me when it happened, little arms wrapping around my leg in comfort, their love acting as a balm. I convinced myself that my love would be enough to protect them from the emotional storm we lived in. I was wrong, of course, but I couldn't see it then. I was too deep in the illusion. I wanted to leave I thought about it everyday but how could I?

My new job working in social services became more than just a job; it was a lifeline. I spent my days helping children who had seen the worst of what the world could offer. I supervised their visits with parents who had hurt them, watching as they tried to rebuild something fragile, something broken. Every time I saw a child's pain mirrored in their eyes, I thought of my girls. I thought of how much I wanted to keep them safe, to love them enough to heal anything they might have seen or felt. But deep down, I knew I was lying to myself. No amount of love could fully shield them from the cracks forming in our life. Equally Toms cruelty was nothing compared to what some of these children endured so I never saw it as abuse. I thought it was just a short fuse, just me that irritated him when I kept getting things wrong.

Mum had become a steady presence again, healthy and full of life. She adored the girls and would take them to the park whenever she could. I watched as they laughed with her, pushing each other on swings or running through the grass. It was nice to see my mother this way, so different from the woman I had known in my own childhood.

Jack, on the other hand, had disappeared again. After my wedding, we drifted further and further apart until he stopped reaching out altogether. It was like he had vanished into the background of my life, a memory that stung every time I thought about him. But Liam, now a teenager, had his own phone, and every few months, I'd gather the girls and take him out with us. Those days were always special, watching him play with Charlotte and Lily. He chased them across the woods, pretending to be the troll from "Billy Goats Gruff" as they squealed in delight, their laughter filling the air. It was the same game I had played with Liam when he was little, and seeing it now, with my own girls, melted me in ways I couldn't explain.

But even on those good days, anxiety had taken root in me, tightening its grip in every corner of my life. I had morphed into a control freak without even realizing it. Everything had to be done in a specific way - my jewellery had to come off in a particular order, and if I got it wrong, I would start again. If I didn't follow these rituals, I was certain something terrible would happen. It was a small comfort in a world where I felt so out of control. I stirred my tea a specific number of times, opened the curtains the same way each morning. Every small task became a pattern, a ritual, something I could control when everything else in my life felt like it was slipping through my fingers.

Nights out with friends were rare. Tom's jealousy kept me on a tight rope, and I didn't trust him to be alone with the girls. Not because he would ever hurt them, but because of his emotional detachment. I didn't want them to feel that coldness, the way he could stare right through them like they wasn't even there. So, I stayed, watching over them, controlling every little piece of our lives to try and keep things from falling apart.

However, the fear and the anxiety was always there just beneath the surface. I thought I was keeping it all together, that I was holding our lives in place. But in reality, I was drowning in it. Every day, the weight of it pressed down harder, making it more difficult to breathe, and harder to see what was really happening around me.

Chapter 33

The day started like any other, an uneasy tension hung in the air. My car tax was due. Without it my insurance would be void and id be trapped at home. I needed my log book but Tom had it. He kept it hidden away for no other reason than another little tick off his control list. Every time I asked for it he acted like I was asking for the world, turning something so simple into a power play. Today was no different but today my tax officially runs out today and tomorrow I had my MOT booked in, so after days of asking (begging) for it I was out of time and needed it pronto.

"Tom can I have my logbook please? I have to tax my car today I'm out of time!" I was trying to keep my tone calm. He barely glanced at me from the sofa, eyes locked on the football match. I asked again, then braved a 3rd time and a 4th hovering by the door ready to react quickly to whatever would come my way.

"Its my logbook," he said flatly the familiar edge in his voice returning. "I own everything that's yours!" I felt so small which was a familiar sensation after years of control and narcissism.

"Can I have it please? I need it! I have to get my car taxed!" Without looking at me he spat his words

"No. Now Fuck off!" Anger bubbled away inside me but I swallowed it. I wasn't asking for much. My mind raced with the consequences, no tax equals no MOT and void insurance which equals no driving. I would be Stuck asking him for lifts, asking his permission for everything. My car was what little freedom I had left I couldn't let this happen and for some bizarre reason I just wasn't going to back down on this.

"Tom I need it." My voice was quieter now, whiny and pleading, but he wasn't listening. I wouldn't stop, knowing full well he'd be teetering on the edge by now with my persistence. He paused the TV, finally turning to look at me

"I said fuck off didn't I? are you deaf? Go on - fuck off!" I stood there staring at him something inside me shifted. I was tired, tired of the games, the control, the constant humiliation. I knew from previous experience fighting back was never a battle I could win, but as usual I wasn't going down without a fight.

"Ok" I said, my voice steady, my heartbeat absolutely not steady in the slightest. "I will when you give me my logbook how's that?" I watched him shift, irritated that I hadn't just slunk away. He stood up fast, his intention to make me buckle but I stayed strong. He was in front of me in seconds and towered over me bracing himself ready to intimidate me into submission. It had worked before countless times but this time I just didn't care. Something inside me had snapped, I was numb inside and I wasn't backing down.

I yawned in his face knowing it would get a rise out of him. It was stupidity on my part but I was sick of his games.

"That's fine you're clearly busy I'll just get it myself." I continued as I slowly turned away from him. My heart pounded in my chest as I headed for the stairs. I knew the logbook was kept in the drawer inside his wardrobe. The forbidden drawer, god only knows what he kept in there. Today though I didn't care about the rules I was getting my logbook back whether he liked it or not.

"Go in that drawer and I'll kill you." I couldn't help but laugh. I don't know why. I shocked myself! It's like my mouth had suddenly managed to detach itself from my brain. I always did this, laughed in the worst situations with absolutely no self control. But it was funny wasn't it, the whole situation was ridiculous.

His threat bounced off me and I headed up the stairs not looking back whilst equally bracing myself to be pounced on, navigating the stairs quickly as I imagined how rapidly I could be pulled down them and wasn't in the mood for broken limbs. I slid the wardrobe door open loud and deliberate making sure he could hear it. He hadn't followed me up the stairs like I had expected. I strained to listen for his movements, the tv hadn't been un-muted,I hadn't pulled me back down the stairs by my hair or arms. Maybe I would win this after all?! As I opened the drawer slowly, my heart in my mouth, his footsteps as predicted came thick and fast up the stairs like lightening. He flew into the bedroom yanked me by my arms forcing me against the wall and pinning me there. Both his hands holding each one of my arms above my head against the wall, pressing himself against me. His strength was no match for me as I tried to kick out he pushed himself into me harder. I laughed again. The people in my head sounding the alarm at my sheer bravado. I don't know what made me snigger it was a reflex in a situation I was never going to win. With that, quicker than I could say my prayers he wrapped his hands around my throat. His grip was tight cutting off my air supply as he continually pulled me away from the wall and slammed me back into it again using my neck to navigate. Panic flared inside me as I struggled, my fists flailing trying to connect with his body, my legs kicking out but he was strong. The harder I tried to fight the tighter he squeezed. My vision started to blur but I wasn't done trying to get him off me.

"Daddy noooo!" A tiny voice broke through the chaos as Lily ran into our bedroom, her small fists pounding on his leg as she tried to get him off me. Charlotte was standing in the doorway and let out a scream. She cried and called lily to go to her, too afraid to join in the fight. Lily was frantic and as her fight to get him off me led to no avail without hesitation she bit him, a feral desperation in her actions. Tom roared in anger and in one swift motion picked her up by her forearms and launched her flying across the room into the radiator. Charlotte stood frozen crying and screaming but too scared to move in towards us. Lily sprang back up off the floor like a rabid Chiwawa and charged at him again ready to pick up the fight as I used the break in being choked to inhale sharply and stop her.

"Lily NO!" I screamed my voice raw. I threw myself at Tom desperate to stop her from getting hurt but Lily was relentless in her actions to hurt him. Charlotte still crying ran over as I lashed out at Tom and she grabbed lily and dragged her out of the bedroom thrashing her arms, kicking her legs out and shouting for him to stop hurting mummy. A lioness had been released inside me after watching him throw her like she was nothing and I was ready to kill him. The anger of the years previous, all spilling out in one go. I couldn't stop lashing out, I was screaming at him kicking and punching and trying to go for his face, his stomach, literally any part of him I could connect with but he was too strong for me and kept throwing me on the floor daring me to go again, which I did multiple times.

The girls stood at the door crying and in a sudden change of tactic after slamming me face first into the wall for the umpteenth time, he walked slowly and breathless to the girls. I collapsed in a heap on the floor wracking sobs coming out of me. Tom picked Lily up and had changed demeanour in a nano second. His voice was sickly sweet as he shushed the girls trying to calm them down, stroking their hair out of their faces just like he did to me whenever he crossed that line.

"Its ok girls, ssshhh. Your mums gone crazy I had to fend her off! She needs help but don't worry daddy's here."

"Let them go" I demanded as I stood up heading towards him. Tom ignored me, his focus on his gentle calming tone. The same one he always used when he had gone too far and wanted to reverse it. He couldn't reverse this.

"Daddys got you." He continued to soothe, wiping their tears away. Lily admitted defeat and nestled into him sobbing. "Don't worry babies Mummy's just upset. We need to get her some help, she started this I don't know what's wrong with her, but daddy loves you and I'm here. Its ok, everything is going to be ok."

The girls cried into him exhausted and confused and I couldn't breathe, I had nothing left, this wasn't ever going to end, I wasn't ever going to make it stop. I grabbed my car keys and ran outside without stopping for shoes. My hands were shaking as I turned the key in the ignition. I didn't know where I was going but I needed to get away. As he flung the front door open in an attempt to come after me I sped off. I headed for the main roads, the speed blurring everything around me. My mind was racing, suffocating under the weight of everything that had happened.

I couldn't do this anymore. I was done.

The road stretched out in front of me, black and endless, as I gripped the steering wheel tighter and veered onto the dual carriageway. The speedometer crept higher, but it wasn't fast enough. The world rushing past in a haze of headlights and streaks of concrete, but none of it could outpace the storm inside me as my sobs continued and memories pocked at me like surges of electricity zapping me one image at a time.

My brother's eyes flashed in my mind, the hollow look they held when we went to those flats, the places where the air reeked of despair and chemicals. Every time I watched the life drain from him a little more, smoke curling around him as he disappeared into that dark space. I told myself I was helping by being there, but I knew better. His addiction pulled him away, and I couldn't hold on. I could never pull him back. The look in his eyes, that distant, haunted look followed me. He faded into smoke as my vision returned to the road blurred by further tears and heaving sobs.

I pressed my foot harder on the accelerator. The engine roared beneath me, but it couldn't drown out the memories. The past came at me thick and fast like a tornado fuelling the storm inside my mind.

The blur of the road drifted into a picture of Liam's face the day I picked him up. He looked so small in that moment, so broken. I remember the way he barely met my eyes, tired, confused and lost in his own pain. I wanted to fix it but I couldn't, now I have shut myself off completely and there is only distance and silence between us, so thick it choked me. His face was burned into my mind, those big eyes and the way his chin wobbled the day I walked away from him and gave him back to his mum Scarlet. God, Scarlet. The look on her face when everything froze around her, when the world she thought she knew crumbled in an instant. I can still see it, the disbelief, the hurt that stretched over her like a shadow. She was trapped in that moment, and I could only watch. I couldn't save her, either. I made a promise to go back and help her and I never did.

The speed of my car climbed higher. My hands trembled, but I couldn't stop. Not yet. The faster I went, the more I understood that the feelings were not left behind they were with me, carried in the passenger seat, impossible to evade.

I blinked allowing my tears to drop onto my chest as Mum's face surfaced, pale against the whitewashed walls of the hospital her eyes hollow and pleading. I could still smell the disinfectant, hear the echoes of the patients down the hall, their cries of pain, their sobs of confusion. I would visit her, sit in that sterile room with her, and she would look right through me lost in her own mind, and I couldn't reach her. I couldn't bring her back, no matter how many times I sat there, hoping, waiting. It was the medication, the family group and David that stabilised her not me, I wasn't enough. I saw what my dad did to her when we were children. I should have called the police, should have asked for help but I didn't I stayed scared and silent. I ran away telling myself she was in the best place when she went into rehab and I left David to pick up the pieces on his own.

I coughed as I tried to catch my breath feeling like my car was closing in on me. I pressed the accelerator again, as if I could leave it all behind to outrun it all and make it go away. But it didn't.

The sounds came to me next, piercing through my mind... glasses smashing against the wall next to where I was standing just missing me, splinters of glass flying into my face as it connected with the wall and shattered. Plates being smashed on the floor because they were not cleaned properly. His voice, sharp and venomous, calling me names, twisting my insides with each word. The rage, the heat of it, filled the room until there was no air left to breathe.

I gasped as I gripped the steering wheel even tighter and struggled to find my breath.

I thought about the blows – strong the kick in the stomach, his hands tightening around my throat. Squeezing in my memory as my knuckles went white squeezing the steering wheel. My children's cries echoed in the background, their terrified voices breaking through the chaos. I wanted to protect them, to shield them from all of it, but I couldn't. I failed them. I failed myself. I failed everyone I really was nothing.

I opened the windows I was suffocating and I couldn't bare it.

My tears were hot and blinding. I wiped them away, but more fell. I couldn't stop them any more than I could stop the flood of memories that raced alongside me, faster than the car, faster than anything I could ever outrun.

I wanted it all to stop. The hurt, the memories, the voices, everything it was too much. I had tried so hard to fix things, to keep the pieces together, but I couldn't anymore. Something had broken inside me, something that had been holding it all in place. Now it was gone, and everything was falling apart.

I didn't slow down. The speed wasn't enough. Nothing would be enough. The car raced forward, but I felt like I was standing still, caught in the middle of a storm I couldn't escape. And in that moment, I realized that I didn't want to fix it anymore. Maybe I just wanted it all to end. The road stretched on, and the memories chased me, relentless.

Suddenly a bridge came into view ahead and for a second my mind went quiet. The idea formed quickly, like it had always been there waiting. In a moment of madness as his words cut into my brain shouting at me.

"You are fat, you are useless, you are nothing!" There was nothing coming around me only God could stop me now. As I sped towards the bridge something switched in me. I lost all control and pulled hard on the steering wheel sending my car screeching into the barriers.

As the car skidded and the metal split, time slowed. There was a strange relief knowing the end was coming. Finally it would all stop. As the land blurred either side of me and the white painted lines stretched out ahead of me something bright was coming fast – Shit! Headlights.

The impact was sudden and everything went black. In that moment just before everything faded one thought lingered in the darkness. My girls. What had I done?

Then, Silence.

Chapter 34

When I opened my eyes, all I saw was white, blinding, sterile, and unfamiliar. My body felt like it had been crushed, every muscle screaming with pain. For a moment, I didn't know where I was. And then, like a flood, it all came rushing back.

The bridge. The rain. The sound of screeching tires. The feeling of weightlessness as the car broke through the guardrail and plummeted. The cold terror that wrapped itself around my chest as though the world itself had opened up and swallowed me whole. I remembered the silence after, the crushing, suffocating silence, and the last thought that flitted across my mind, clearer than anything else.

Maybe this was it. Maybe it was finally over. But here I was, waking up. Not dead. Or maybe I was dead, I couldn't tell? My thoughts were foggy, and the pain was so sharp that it felt like it was coming from a distance, like it didn't belong to me.

There was a blinding white light, the sound of machines beeping all around me. The brightness was overwhelming, like the headlights I remembered seeing right before everything went dark. My thoughts scrambled am I still here? Was this the afterlife?

"Well, blimey, she's awake!" That voice. That sounded like Jack, but he couldn't be here, could he? If I was dead, was he dead too? The thought filled me with dread. Had life become too much for him? Typical, I thought, I'm dead, and he's still with me being a pain in the backside! I tried to move, but a sharp sting in my arm and the cold sensation on my cheek kept me still. Pain shot through my chest and stomach. How could I still be in pain if I was dead?

"Alright, twathead," I heard again, unmistakably Jack's voice, "Welcome back to the world." My heart jumped, and I tried to turn my head to see him, but I couldn't move. There was something in my mouth stopping me from speaking. I twisted my head ever so slightly, and through the haze, a figure stood over me. Was it God? Slowly, the shape came into focus—it wasn't some divine being. It was Jack, looking down at me.

"Hurrah," he announced. "What the hell were you thinking?!" It really was him. I blinked, trying to piece it all together. I don't think I've seen him for years. Is he actually here? Am I dreaming? The white walls, the blue chairs, the curtain, the incessant beeping, and the muffled chatter in the background was a little too familiar. I wasn't dead, I was in a hospital.

The vision of headlights flashed in my mind again. My stomach dropped. Did they survive? What did I do? Memories of the night started creeping back. The car, the crash, the panic.

"Rise and shine," a new voice called, and someone in a white coat stepped into my view. The beeping from the machines quickened as the panic inside me surged. I felt something cold enter my hand, and I closed my eyes again, retreating into the darkness for a while.

When I reopened them hours later, everything was still the same. The beeping machines, the hospital room, the ache all over my body. But now, it was quiet. I twisted my eyes to look to the side without turning my head. Jack sat in a chair next to me, his head resting on one side, snoring softly. I tried to move again, just a little. My body was stiff, and I couldn't speak with the tube still in my mouth. The other car, I had to know. What had I done?

The machines must have noticed my change in heart rate because someone entered the room again. "Morning, Miss Lawson. Are you back with us?" The nurse's voice was gentle, but I wasn't sure how to respond. I couldn't speak, couldn't even nod. My mouth was dry, and my stomach throbbed with a deep, aching pain.

Jack was awake again in an instant, his hand on my arm, smiling at me. He looked different, healthier. He had gained weight, his skin brighter than I remembered. Was I imagining it? I tried to smile back, but I wasn't sure if my body was responding.

A team of nurses soon gathered around me. Someone held my wrist, checking my pulse. Another took my temperature. I could hear numbers being read out, and finally, one of them slid the tube out of my mouth. I gasped, panicking for a moment, but a soothing voice, calm and steady, guided me through how to breathe. "Slowly, Lucy. You got this," Jack whispered, his voice steadying me. I exhaled shakily as the beeping slowed. The nurses smiled, relieved, as if I had passed some kind of test.

Over the next few hours, I drifted in and out of consciousness, each time waking to find Jack still there, his same blue jumper and jeans, keeping vigil by my bedside. How long had he been sitting there? I had no idea how much time had passed since the accident.

Then, another voice familiar and warm. I blinked and saw my mum walk towards me. She looked... different. Beautiful. Healthier than I had seen her in years. Her skin was tanned, her eyes bright and full of life. Was I dead after all? Had we all crossed over together? She smiled down at me, but I still couldn't speak. She rested her hand gently on mine. Her eyes were red-rimmed, her face worried. But she was there. Just like she always had been. I couldn't tell if it was relief or guilt that tightened my chest when I saw her. I had shut her out for so long, so afraid that if she knew what I was really going through, it would break her heart. And now here she was, by my side when I needed her most.

I tried again, forcing out a whisper. "The... other car?" The words came out as a croak, but I had to know. It was all I could think about.

"He's fine," Jack said, his voice quiet but reassuring. "Managed to spin off the road. His car's a wreck, but he walked away with a scratch on his finger and a little neck pain."

Relief flooded through me. Somehow, by some miracle, I hadn't caused anyone's death. I closed my eyes again, sinking back into the fog. The relief was short-lived, though, the pain in my leg and chest throbbed, a reminder of the damage done.

I felt the tension release, but it didn't bring any comfort. Instead, the weight of what I had done, what I had almost done, settled over me like a heavy, suffocating blanket. I didn't want to die. Not really. I just wanted all the hurt to stop. I had lost control, my mind spiralling out of the darkness that had been creeping up on me for months, years even. And in one split second, I had let go, let the pain and the hopelessness take over, until I was plummeting off that bridge, wondering if the fall would be enough to end it all.

But now, here I was. Alive. And I didn't know whether to feel relief or dread.

My thoughts wandered, flashing to my children. My heart ached as I thought of them, their faces, their smiles, the way they looked at me with trust and love. What had I done to them? What had I put them through? They didn't deserve this, this mess of a person who couldn't even keep herself together, let alone be the mother they needed.

I remembered Jacks hands around my throat. The fear in their eyes and the way Tom had tried to soothe them. As if reading my expression Jack said "The girls are at mine with Liam and Scarlet."

What? How? I couldn't piece it together. What happened after I left. How did everyone know?

"They're ok Luce I promise." Jack meant it. His voice was soft and caring. Tears filled my eyes, but I was too exhausted to cry, too overwhelmed to let them fall. Jack squeezed my arm and mum squeezed my hand, their warmth grounding me for a moment. "I'm sorry," I whispered, the words barely audible. "I'm so sorry."

In the days that followed, I learned the extent of my injuries: a broken leg, four cracked ribs, my back was broken and I had a small bleed on my brain. But I was alive. Jack stayed with me the entire time, never leaving my side, like a watchful protector, making sure each time I gave in to sleep that I came back to the world. He didn't say anything for a long time. Just sat there, his hand on my arm, as if he was afraid to let go. Finally, he spoke, his voice thick with emotion. "I'm glad you're still here."

I closed my eyes again, the weight of those words pressing down on me. I had almost not been here. I had given up. But now, as I lay in that hospital bed, the reality of it all hit me. I hadn't just almost up on myself. I had given up on my children, my family, the people who loved me even when I couldn't see it.

I wasn't sure what came next. The road ahead felt long and painful, and I knew it wouldn't be easy. But lying there, bruised, and broken, with my mum and Jack's hand in mine and the knowledge that I was still alive, I realized that maybe, just maybe, I hadn't lost everything yet. There was still time to try. Time to heal. Time to be the person, the mother, I needed to be.

Chapter 35

The first morning I woke up in my new home, I didn't know where I was. For a split second, my heart raced, that familiar surge of anxiety flooding my chest, and I held my breath, waiting for the dread to settle in. But then I remembered I wasn't in that house anymore. I wasn't with him.

The sheets were rough against my skin, and the room was bare except for a couple of boxes and a mattress on the floor, but it was mine. Our new home. My children were still asleep in the next room, nestled in a mess of blankets on makeshift beds. The house was far from perfect, no furniture yet, not even a proper table but it was ours. I felt the smallest flicker of freedom deep inside me, like the first breath after holding it in for too long.

I tried quietly lifting my plastered leg out of the bed, careful not to wake the kids, and hobbled to the window, looking out at the world that felt new to me now. Everything was different. There was no more fear, no more waiting for his voice to echo through the house, no more calculating every move to keep the peace. We were safe. But somehow, that freedom felt terrifying. The anxiety still thumped in my chest.

I had spent so long living for someone else, for him, for my children, for everyone but me, that now, with no one controlling my every move, I didn't know what to do with myself. It was ironic, really this peace, this safety, the thing I had fought so hard for, felt like the most uncertain place I had ever been.

I sat on my bum and shuffled down the stairs to make a drink. Something moved on the sofa and I jumped so much I was nearly sick. It was Jack. Unwilling to leave me, frightened I wasn't well enough not to do something stupid. He refused to leave no matter how many thousands of time I told him I was fine.

He took the girls to school and came straight back. Careful not to get in my way but never wanting to leave me alone. Truth be told I didn't trust myself either. One minute I would be full of hope and motivation. The next I would feel like I was drowning in a storm and craved pain to get me away from it.

The day stretched ahead of me, empty and full all at once. There was so much to do, yet none of it felt real. We needed furniture, proper beds for the kids, chairs, a table, all the things that made a house feel like a home. I spent the morning scrolling through second-hand sites with Jack, looking for anything we could afford. A couch that was a little too worn, a kitchen table with mismatched chairs, Jack arranged collection using his truck from work, never letting me lift a finger. The furniture wasn't perfect but it was ours. Pieces of a life we were trying to rebuild from scratch.

Jack took the girls and I shopping after collecting them from school. I hadn't been a passenger in a car with him since we were teenagers. It was strange, walking (hobbling) through the aisles without feeling like I was being watched, without that constant pressure of Toms voice in my head, telling me what I could and couldn't buy. For the first time in years, I could choose what I wanted. We picked out dishes, simple ones, nothing fancy but I loved them. The girls helped choose towels, bright, mismatched colours they each liked, instead of whatever was "good enough" for Tom like we had become so accustomed to.

With every small freedom came a wave of unease. I had spent years measuring my worth by how well I kept him calm, how I tiptoed around his anger, how I made sure everyone else was okay. I had lived for others for so long, I wasn't sure how to live for myself.

At the checkout queue, the girls were laughing, full of excitement about their new towels and dishes. I smiled at them, but inside, I felt like I was floating in unfamiliar waters as I continued to ask Jacks opinion about every purchase. I had learned to need that approval and jack would just smile and say whatever makes you happy or if you like it, get it.

That night, after the kids were asleep, I sat in the empty living room, surrounded by boxes, staring at the pieces of furniture we had scavenged. I should have felt proud, I told myself. This was the beginning of something new. We were safe. The girls were happy. But all I felt was a heavy emptiness I couldn't explain.

Who was I now, without the role of keeping him happy? Without the constant need to manage someone else's emotions, I didn't know where to place my energy. I had spent so many years living for others that I had forgotten how to live for myself. And now, sitting in this new house, with nothing but space and time ahead of me, I felt lost.

Being okay was harder than I had expected. I had grown so used to the chaos, to the constant need to make sure everything was in order to avoid bad tempers and upset, that this quiet, this peace, felt unsettling. It was like I had lost my compass, the thing that had driven me, even if it was a toxic, suffocating force. I kept thinking I had seen him in the isles earlier that day, startling every time my eyes played tricks on me. Even now sat in my own home I felt watched and vulnerable like life was easier when I knew what curve balls were coming my way.

Jack talked me through my emotions. He spoke of techniques the counsellor in prison had taught him to gain control over imposter thoughts. We talked about the night it happened and I released the tension as I spoke honestly for the first time in my life about what had been going on behind closed doors in number 64. As fate would have it, the night I broke down and left the house, Jack had decided to break the ice and call me after months of us not speaking. He heard the girls crying and distressed in the background and would not accept Toms excuses of my absence he followed his instinct and went round to the house unannounced. Charlotte whether in innocence or bravery had announced to Jack "Daddy tried to kill mummy, is she ok? When is she coming home?" Jack punched Tom square in the face and promised to kill him if he ever came near me and the girls again. Tom was a typical bully. He could hurt me behind closed doors knowing my strength was no match for him but he daren't pick a fight with anyone his own size let alone bigger than him such as Jack. Jack packed bags for the girls and piled them into his car taking them to the safety and love of his own home.

The police visited me in hospital and took a statement. I filed for a non molestation order against him that was granted by the court without notice to keep him away from me and the children.

Exhausted after my conversation with Jack but relieved to be able to speak openly with someone. I heard the soft sound of footsteps. Lily, still half-asleep, padded into the living room, clutching her favourite blanket. Without saying a word, she climbed onto my lap, her small body warm and familiar. I wrapped my arms around her, and for a moment, the emptiness lifted.

I didn't have all the answers. I didn't know who I was yet, or how I was supposed to rebuild my life from the ground up. But I knew one thing - I was here. I had made it out the other side. I hated myself for walking out that day and being selfish enough to try and end my life. That guilt I will have to live with and work on but right now I had given my children safety, a warm roof over their head and unconditional love. That was everything.

In the quiet of the night, with my girls curled up against me, I realized that I didn't need to figure it all out right now. I didn't have to know who I was yet. I knew they would forgive me even if I hadn't forgiven myself. All I needed to do was put one foot in front of the other, day by day, piece by piece. I would find my way. We had freedom, even if I didn't know what to do with it yet.

We would be okay. I would be okay.

Jacks stayed with me for weeks. Navigating school runs, doing the shopping, cooking, even cleaning and was constantly checking on me. We spent many an evening with a cup of tea and a box of tissues as we talked through the traumas of the past and how we can be grateful for each other and our children and how we can navigate the future. He would bring Liam over to visit when he could. It was so lovely watching playing with the girls, reading books with them and never tiring of their questions. "You should be proud of him Jack. He is an absolute credit to you." I smiled.

"Right back at ya sis. We didn't do too bad did we!" He smiled. We clinked our mugs and sipped our tea as we watched the wonder that was our children that by some miracle appeared unscathed and happy in their own worlds.

Every morning when I woke up the anxiety would still be there, lingering like a shadow. But I would remind myself, like I did every morning - we are safe, this is our home, and no one can get to us. I took a deep breath and was grateful to still be here starting a new life with my girls. That was a good place to start.

Chapter 36

After a two years of being single and navigating our new life, the idea of dating again felt about as appealing as a root canal. However my friends, relentless and well-meaning kept on at me, convincing me that maybe, just maybe, it was time to dip my toe back in. Apparently, the solution to my woes was Match.com. Great. Internet dating. Because nothing says "I'm thriving" like anxiously trying to pick a profile picture that doesn't scream, I'm out of my depth here.

I stared at the camera, trying to find an angle that didn't make me look hideous. I had a face like an Easter egg with a backside the size of a small country, how on earth do people make this look so effortless? I resorted to the classic move: arm stretched high up, chin tucked, hoping to eliminate at least nine of the ten chins that seemed to have appeared since my last attempt at flirting.

Headshot only. No one needed to see the rest of the chaos. At least, not yet.

Writing the profile was the next hurdle. How do you sum up who you are, when you've spent the past few years hidden behind the curtain of motherhood, routine, and the quiet safety of single life? I tapped the keys slowly, mentioning that I had children. I left out the part that one of them (Lily aka Mowgli) was feral and would catapult the goldfish out of his tank for fun! One hurdle at a time eh. No need to scare anyone yet.

I didn't want a relationship, God no. The very idea made me shudder. Been there, done that, got the emotional baggage. But a little fun? Maybe. Someone to flirt with for a night, share some laughs, a few dinners and nights out, maybe even a bit of excitement, before retreating to the quiet sanctuary of my four walls. No strings, no complications. Just a brief escape from the mundane.

Profile sorted. Picture posted. I hit "save" and waited.

That's when the messages started to roll in. My inbox lit up with hellos, awkward compliments, and the occasional cringe-worthy pick-up line and photos of the length of their manhood – WOW yes exactly what a woman wants to see before she even knows your name. I put my hand over my face multiple times as I scrolled through. I'd scan through them, smile politely, and then park them there. Some were nice enough through text, but I wasn't exactly feeling the need to engage in lengthy conversations. Just dipping my toe in, remember?

And then, there was Ben. His first message made me smile a real, genuine smile. Something about the way he didn't try too hard, how his humour seemed effortless, caught my attention. It wasn't long before we were exchanging playful banter, and it wasn't long after that when he started sending me videos. I winced and clicked play thinking id got him all wrong and I was about to watch something x rated but not even close. The video was of him singing he loved entertaining and mucking about on his guitar. His voice was rich, warm, and somehow... comforting. He was fun, easy to message, have banter with and phone calls were far from awkward, never any silent pauses. I needed fun.

Without noticing after a short time I found myself looking forward to his messages. He wasn't like the others. He didn't feel like some faceless man on the internet. He felt real, approachable. I could see myself having a drink with him, laughing over something ridiculous without the weight of expectations hanging in the air. So, I decided to take the plunge.

"Fancy meeting for coffee?" he typed, my fingers hesitating on the heart button for just a second before I pressed it. "Absolutely" I said my confidence hidden behind a screen.

I sat back, heart racing a little, waiting for his reply. It was just coffee. No big deal. But there was something about Ben that made me nervous in a good way. The way that good nerves flutter in your stomach. He didn't feel like one of those fleeting, one-night-flirt guys. I ignored that feeling. This wasn't about starting something serious. I wasn't ready for that. I didn't even want that... did I?

When his reply came, it was quick and playful, just like him. "Coffee sounds great. But only if I can serenade you the whole time." I laughed out loud, sitting there in my kitchen as I opened another of his videos, and thought to myself. This could be fun. Just coffee. No pressure. No strings. As I prepared to meet him, something in the back of my mind whispered that maybe, just maybe, this wasn't going to be as simple as I thought.

By the time we met I had gone full circle. Decided I wouldn't let him in, he would only end up in disappointment. I didn't want to waste anyone's time so I showed him the real me whatever that was. I made no effort to impress. No makeup, hair pulled back in a messy ponytail, jeans, and a plain hoody. I was done pretending to be someone I wasn't. Ben, on the other hand, greeted me with an easy smile, a warm hug, and a casual charm that caught me off guard.

We walked for hours that day, wandering through Hayborough Castle, talking about everything and nothing at the same time. He told me about his job, the kind of work that gave him structure but still left him plenty of time to pursue his passion.

The more we spent time together walking, I found myself talking more than I expected. I told him about my children, my life (just a taste of it. But this time it was the truth. I had nothing to hide, no one to protect by lying, he wouldn't stick around anyway so I drip fed him tiny segments to see how he reacted.) I told him about the struggles of starting over. Ben listened, really listened, without interrupting or offering solutions. Just there, a steady presence beside me. It surprised me how natural it felt to be with him, like we'd known each other far longer than a few messages and a single walk. I figured after giving him a glimpse of the chaos that was me he'd run a mile. Yet when I arrived home after our walk I already had a message from him saying how much he enjoyed my company and that he'd like to meet up again – Wait what, how? Why?

Over the next few weeks we spoke every day and started meeting regularly. More long walks, quiet coffees, and conversations that always seemed to stretch late into the day. I still kept my guard up, not ready to let anyone in. But slowly, over time, something shifted. I started looking forward to his messages, my phone lighting up with his name. I found myself smiling at his words, and looking forward to when we'd see each other again. I started anticipating the moments we would spend together, even planning my day around them.

One day, as we walked down a quiet path in the park, Ben stopped turning to face me. There was something in his eyes, gentleness, care, that made my heart skip. Then, without saying a word, he leaned in and kissed me. It was soft, careful, like he was giving me the space to pull away if I wanted. But I didn't. Instead I felt something stir inside me that I hadn't felt since Nathan all those years ago but even stronger! Those butterflies, the sweet nervous flutter that filled me with warmth.

As time passed I introduced Ben to Lily and Charlotte. The ultimate test! They loved him, he joked with them and played games with them. When he turned up to meet me Jack was babysitting. He stood bulked out analysing every inch of Ben and ready to put him to the test. "Play nice!" I said to Jack as I let poor Ben into the house. He'd brought some colouring bits for the girls, they were thrilled. He talked to Jack and the tension soon eased as Ben's humour thawed Jack and before I knew it they were laughing together like old friends, not like two strangers that had just met.

Over the coming weeks and months we met up multiple times. Ben joined us for dinner at home and we would go on long walks with a coffee in hand. Being around him was so easy. I was falling for him without warning. Not just with the way he made me feel, but with the way he cared for the people I loved most in the world. I decided I would enjoy it one day at a time, one foot in front of the other and see what happened. I had no future expectations I would just enjoy the now.

One evening the girls were having a sleepover at Jacks and I was having a quiet night in and one of my low days. The living room felt cold, not because of the temperature, but because of the way the world had drained me. I had become accustomed to this space the way the couch sagged beneath me, the soft glow of the lamps that never quite brightened the room enough, the muted sounds of the street outside. My evenings had turned into these empty pockets of silence, a time to sink further into the quietness of my mind and just exist without expectation. Tonight was no different. Knowing I had no company I had pulled on my old jumper, worn but familiar, paired with jeans that had seen better days, and tied my hair back with little thought.

I lay on the sofa flicking through the television watching nothing in particular. That was the plan until Ben messaged. Ben was fast becoming a highlight in my life aside from the girls of course. He was perfect in his own right. One of those people you don't expect to meet let alone to care about you. He was tall, confident, funny, and had the kind of good looks that felt way out of my league. I almost didn't respond when he asked if I was free. I could have said no. I should have, honestly. But I didn't. So now here he was, standing at my door.

When I opened it, I could see the flicker of surprise in his eyes. I wasn't the vibrant version of myself I sometimes managed to be when we met up. No makeup, hair scraped back, the slump in my posture betraying the heaviness I carried. He smiled though, as if I were some sort of beautiful mess.

"Hey," I said, voice flat, feeling embarrassed but too tired to apologize for my appearance. I kissed him, quick and uncertain, and immediately retreated to the sofa, pulling the blanket up around me like a shield.

I half-expected him to take one look at me, laugh it off politely and leave me alone. He could still walk out that door and save himself from whatever dark, swirling storm was brewing inside of me today. I didn't have much to offer, nothing that would last, at least. A few jokes, a kiss here and there, but long term? Who needed the grief of dealing with someone like me? I was too tired, too messy, too unsure of everything. He deserved someone who radiated warmth and excitement constantly, not the hollowed-out version of me that appeared some days curled up in a blanket.

But he didn't leave. Instead, he followed me into the living room and stood there for a moment, towering above me, all six foot four of him, with that amused tilt to his head and his handsome side smile.

"Blimey" he said staring down as me bundled on the sofa in my old clothes and a blanket. "I don't know whether to give you £20 or a cuppa soup!" he said, his voice light. I wasn't expecting it and I couldn't help but chuckle, the sound surprising me as it escaped my lips. There was something about the way he said it, the way he didn't judge, just teased me with an affection that was unexpected.

Then, instead of walking out the door like I expected, he lifted the edge of the blanket from my feet and sat down at the opposite end of the sofa, so casually like he had been doing it for years. It was a small gesture, but it felt like a kindness I didn't know I needed. We didn't talk about how I looked or how I felt like I was failing at everything. Instead, we just talked about anything and nothing. The hours passed and we laughed more than I thought possible in one evening. His humour was effortless and it cut through the fog in my mind like sunlight breaking through clouds without me even realising it.

The pessimist in me kept waiting for the moment he'd get bored or uncomfortable with this version of me that he hadn't seen up until now, but he didn't seem fazed. There was something different about him. He didn't expect anything from me. He was just there, fully present, talking to me as if I wasn't crumbling from the inside out. And for the first time that I could remember, I wasn't trying to be anyone else.

"Why haven't you left yet?" I asked suddenly, blurting out the thought that had been circling my mind all night. He looked at me, his face softening with a smile that reached his eyes.

"Why would I?" I shrugged, feeling vulnerable and exposed in a way I hadn't planned.

"I don't know, look at me" I gestured vaguely at myself, my words small but heavy. Ben shook his head, leaning back into the couch, completely at ease.

"You're not as much of a mess as you think you are," he said, his voice steady, sincere. "And even if you were, I'm not going anywhere." His words settled over me like a warmth I hadn't ever experienced. I didn't know who this man was or why it felt different with him but something inside me shifted that night. Maybe I wasn't so dead inside after all. Maybe, just maybe, I could let myself believe in something good. And for the first time I didn't feel the need to push him away.

From that moment on, our connection deepened. We talked every day, sometimes for hours. Ben was funny in a way that made Me laugh until my sides hurt. He was kind, especially with my children, charming and gentle with me. Ben gradually began to stay over with us more and more and the house began to feel empty if he ever wasn't there. He brought calm, sunshine, laughter and love into all of our lives. The idea of a future, a real happy future suddenly didn't feel as impossible as it once had. Slowly over time, without me even realizing it, as he stayed over with us, caring for us, I began to fall in love with him.

It wasn't about control or fear. It wasn't about walking on eggshells or losing myself. It was about partnership, kindness, and the gentle way Ben had filled my life with light after so many years of darkness. I had never expected to find love, but now that I had, I knew one thing for certain, I wasn't letting it go for anything no matter how afraid I felt.

Chapter 37

The day of my brother's wedding dawned bright and clear as though the sky itself had been arranged for such a perfect occasion. From the moment we arrived at the church, I could sense that this was going to be a day none of us would ever forget. The church, with its soaring ceilings and stained glass windows, was nothing short of breathtaking. Every inch of it bathed in golden sunlight streaming through those ancient panes of glass. It felt like we were walking into a dream.

I stood next to Scarlett, my heart swelling with happiness and pride as her bridesmaid. She was radiant, a vision in her wedding gown, every detail perfectly reflecting the joy of the day. Her smile was infectious, her cheeks flushed with excitement and I felt honoured to be by her side. Charlotte and Lily, adorable in their flower girl dresses, giggled quietly, waiting patiently with us in the back of the church ready to lead the way down the aisle for Scarlett. They added a touch of sweetness and innocence to the day that made everything feel just that little bit more magical.

Liam, was standing tall as one of Jack's ushers, he looked so grown up and handsome in his suit. His quiet confidence and pride were evident as he helped greet the guests, and I caught him glancing at Scarlett more than once, his face filled with that unmistakable love for his mum. And Mum, oh, Mum was a picture of beauty, glowing with happiness in her pale blue dress and fascinator as she watched her children come together for this celebration. She stood with David, her eyes sparkling, beaming with pride at how far we'd come as a family, all of us gathered here for this perfect moment.

Ben, who looked as handsome as ever in his suit was Jacks best man and would be waiting at the alter with him, calming his nerves. It filled my heart with even more love for him knowing how close he had become to my brother. It was clear how much this day meant to all of us, especially to him, being right there by Jack's side. We exchanged glances as I walked down the aisle with Scarlett, butterflies in my tummy at the pure sight of him waiting next to my brother and I knew deep down that this was everything I had ever wanted.

As the music began and the guests rose, there was a hush of anticipation. Scarlett began her walk from the end of the aisle, arm in arm with her father, looking more beautiful than ever. The whole world seemed to stop as she walked toward Jack, who stood waiting at the altar with a look on his face that was a mixture of awe and love. It was one of those moments you only see in films, but it was real, happening right before our eyes.

The way Jack's face lit up as Scarlett moved closer was enough to bring tears to every eye in the room.

There was something indescribable about standing there, all of us together in that church, united by love and family. It was as though every past hardship, every challenge we'd faced, had brought us here. That day, standing in that beautiful church, I realized just how strong our bond was. Nothing in the world could break it.

The ceremony was flawless, filled with laughter, a few happy tears, and moments that will forever be etched in my memory. When Jack and Scarlett exchanged their vows, it felt like time had slowed down, as if the universe itself was pausing to witness this incredible love story. When they were finally pronounced husband and wife, the entire church erupted in applause, and the look of pure joy on their faces was a sight to behold.

The reception that followed was everything they had dreamed of. The food was exquisite, each bite a testament to the care that had gone into planning the perfect day.

The dance floor was alive with balloons, disco lights and energy as we all joined in together - Mum and David, Scarlett and Jack, and Ben and me, spinning hand in hand, lost in the music. Liam had Charlotte and Lily one on either hand twirling them under his arms laughing with them. There was no sadness, no lingering shadows of the past. The toxic memories that once weighed us down felt distant, like they belonged to another lifetime.

I looked at Ben, our hands intertwined, our smiles never faltering. In that moment, spinning together under the warm lights to Save the last dance for me, I knew with absolute certainty that this was the man I wanted to dance all my dances with. Every step we had taken, every twist and turn in our separate journeys, had led us to be stronger individuals and to be together. The love and happiness I felt were unlike anything I had ever known possible. This was my future, him and laughter and dancing, surrounded by our happy, healthy family.

As the evening wore on the last dance was announced. Jack took Scarlets hand and they swayed together to the music, signalling us to join them. David led mum to the dancefloor, he put his arms around her, resting his chin on the side of her forehead as they glided around the dance floor. Happiness, calm and contentment radiating out of her smile. Ben took my hand and turned me towards him smiling that handsome smile of his, mouthing the words to me of the song that was playing 'All of me.' Charlotte and Lily were skipping around the dance floor as the couples all swayed together and Liam was batting balloons to them. Their laughter infectious as they danced with joy and batted the balloons around us all and skipping round in circles together.

The moment was the epitome of perfection. A night celebrating a journey of love and strength surrounded by all the people that mattered. Feeling like the world had finally aligned just for us. It was a day that reminded me of the power of love, family and unity. The kind of day that showed me just how strong we are when we stand together.

We danced that final dance under the twinkling lights and Ben pulled me close to him. His eyes locked on mine and that captivating smile that turned my insides to jelly "I love you" he said "Now and always." I smiled back at him "I love you too." There was nothing more to it. I loved him with all of my being. He was everything and more that I could ever have wished for.

At the end of the dance my brother came over with Scarlet and without warning threw his arms around me hugging me tightly. My tears appeared out of nowhere as we stood and cried together for the first time ever! Happy tears for all of us and an overwhelming relief that life was good. We cried together for the years lost, we cried for the emotions that ran deeper than anyone could imagine and we cried for the overwhelming contentment of our new found happy endings. Sensing the room and everyone staring at us the DJ decided to announce one last song. As the intro to Sweet Caroline began Jack and I broke our embrace laughing at how silly we must have looked and Ben appeared by my side with a tissue. We opened our arms for everyone on the dance floor to join us as we started singing. Ben and Scarlett, a teary eyed mum and David came over and linked arms with us. My two girls squeezed in and held onto our legs trying to dance along and giggling at the same time as they mirrored everybody's actions. Our circle grew wider by the second as more friends and family joined in singing and linking arms with us until we could barely fit on the dance floor. It was a perfect end to a perfect night. We were all swaying together in one big circle kicking our legs like a slow drunken cancan. Liam came out of nowhere and stepped between me and Jack wrapping one arm around my shoulder and the other around his. The smiles between my mum, Jack and I were audible, exchanging glances between the three of us that spoke a thousand words. We continued to dance, belted out the chorus and laughed for the duration giving a huge round of applause at the end.

If ever I could freeze time and pocket a moment in history it would have been then. Our faces ached from smiling and our hearts felt so full. I knew in that second, deep inside my heart, this was just the beginning for all of us.

About the Author

J odie lives in the beautiful county of Norfolk with her amazing husband Adam who has stood by her side with his unwavering source of love, strength and support along with their incredible children.

To Jodie family is everything, her brother continues to inspire her every day, her sister always a calm influence and her mum, a true pillar of strength and encouragement, always keeping her going when things felt the hardest.

Jodie and her family have faced many heartaches over the years, experiences that have only brought them closer together and made them stronger.

A lifelong lover of words, she has always found solace and joy in writing, using it as a way to explore the world, express herself, and spark imagination. Through life's challenges, writing has remained her creative sanctuary and powerful source of healing.